Touch of the Unknown Rider

a novel by Robert Wintner

Twice-Baked Books

Wintner, Robert
  Touch of the Unknown Rider / by Robert Wintner
ISBN: 978-1-7366222-9-2
1. Motorcycle—Fiction. 2. Life Crisis—Road trip—Fiction. I. Title
Printed in the United States of America

Twice-Baked Books

$11.00
ISBN 978-1-7366222-9-2
51100>

9 781736 622292

Also by Robert Wintner

Fiction:
    In a Sweet Magnolia Time
    Lizard Blue
    Whirlaway
    The Modern Outlaws
    Reefdog
    A California Closing
    Homunculus
    The Prophet Pasqual
    Hagan's Trial & Other Stories

Memoir:
    1969 and Then Some
    Brainstorm
    The Ice King

Reef Politic in narrative and photo/video:
    Dragon Walk
    Neptune Speaks
    Reef Libre, An In-Depth Look at Cuban Exceptionalism
                    & the Last, Best Reefs in the World
    Every Fish Tells a Story
    Some Fishes I Have Known

Memorium:

Rob Simonsen, road brother

Where is your heart?

—Geronimo

I

Mo Dowd

Time finds a rhythm from back then to up ahead. Might have been falls away. Treetops glimmer with nearly was, and maybe yet drifts in the clouds. Sunbeams warm with potential. Dust devils swirl like regrets.

Out of a curve and up to a crest, the valley view shimmers in iridescent blue. From the haze, God sings in basso profundo, and the wide world hones in on sixty-five along the ridge.

Mo Dowd's dream recurs until it comes true. Beyond smocks open in back, bedpans, traction, sympathy and have a nice day, this is no dream. She thinks and hopes this is real, on top. She tingles in soft pleasures: blue sky, sunshine and excellent bud. She first saw it on a morphine drip and made a promise. Now she rides it and thinks again: this is no dream. She'd get no throttle response in a dream. She'd feel no joy in a dream, unless….

Who cares? Keep dreaming. Maybe she'll meet a two-wheeler up ahead, one with a warm heart and normal hygiene, not too fat, one who might sense a woman's needs. It could happen. Or maybe she'll have a few beers and turn in early to get a jump on tomorrow.

Either way, a girl couldn't ask for a better route to middle age. Not that thirty-five is old, but it seems a milestone. Or is that forty-five that begins the end, or ends the wonder?

What a birthday surprise, Mama insisting tearfully that an adoptive mother can love a daughter like a birth mother or more. What kind of send-off is that?

"You were adopted, Mo."

"That explains the freckles and curly hair."

"I'm serious."

"I figured."

"Your birth mother was a gal named Tina. She got herself in trouble with a man named Jimmy Hatrick...."

"Jimmy Hatrick?"

"That wasn't his name, but they all had them funny names, carrying on like they did. Wore the god-awfulest clothes, Jimmy did. Colors and stripes to make you dizzy. Made me dizzy. I suppose Tina liked what she saw. She was my friend, came down to Puyallup for the birth, your birth. Then she left. Some might tell you she got paid off to leave, but it's the meanness makes them talk like that. Your gramma is ninety-three years old and every bit crazy for Jesus as fifty years ago, but neither she nor Jesus can stop the meanness. She's the one started the ugly talk. We didn't pay Tina to leave. Shoot. Helped her out is all. Tina couldn't hold on to money. Your Aunt Betty might tell you your Uncle Jack is your father, but he's not. Anyone could see Jack liked the ladies. But he ain't. I knew Tina, and Jack ain't. It was Jimmy. He was nineteen. She was eighteen. I heard a few years back, both of them were up there again, her hanging paper and him on the lam with them motorcycle boys. Boys, hell. Older'n me, some of them. Richer, too. But not Jimmy. I don't know but you'll want to go up there looking for him or her sometime like so many of the adopted kids do nowadays, when they find out. But you be careful if you do. Don't go using that name, Jimmy Hatrick. He's a hunted man. I can't tell you his real name, 'cause I don't know it. You be careful on them motorcycles too. They're so damn dangerous. I don't know why anybody'd have to ride one."

"You rode plenty, Mama. For all I know, so did Tina."

"It was different then."

"Oh, yeah. It was much nicer then, right?"

"It didn't seem so dangerous then."

"That's because it was you having the fun. Now it's me. Now you watch TV, day in, day out. Next thing you know, you're brain dead and don't know it, didn't even see it coming. You could have been out there having fun."

"I'm too old. We're all getting on. I can't say I would have told you this. I always thought I would, but then I always put it off. I figured you ought to know, nearly dying like you did. I don't want that to happen for a long time, Honey, not till way after I'm gone."

Amber waving plains fill in with honky-tonk as traffic thickens. The tube twists; shards tumble to sundown on Nanaimo, where a rider wants a warm, dry place to sit still. A lone rider coming off the road wants a break from solitude and sorting, so things can settle out for a while and make room for a little bit more of the social side.

Mo Dowd wants a beer. It's only seven, plenty of time to find a motel and get dinner. A bar this close to town might provide insight on tomorrow's event, the All-Harley drags. With the party boys down from the hills, the fun might start any time.

Buzz's Tail Dragger is neither memorable nor dynamic, but Canadian draught at sundown fairly flushes the tap free of the build-up and bitter taste accruing to taps of lesser flow. This brew can be a road hazard, smooth as it is with so much horsepower. Then again, why hold back, so close to the barn?

The cordial nod moves down the bar in a weak rendition of the rider's wave. It's mostly road-weary grunts looking wore out from seventy cents on the dollar and too much wrenching to keep the old rigs rolling. A few older guys smoke and jaw at the tables with a few holdover mamas from yesteryear. But the golden elixir puts a finish on the moment and a smile on twilight.

A second beer could slide down easy as the first, but Mo Dowd knows an easy pace can allow things to open naturally rather than jam gears on a power shift for no good reason. What's the hurry? So she carries the second draught to a far wall and a motorcycle video game. She laughs at the idea of another few miles, as if three-fifty won't do it for one day. She laughs alone, and nobody asks what's funny. That's okay. This isn't the first conversation between a road woman and herself and won't be the last.

And give the thing a chance. The video graphics are great, the action manageable. Radical curves and banks are easier after a day of the real thing, and shooting the gap with a semi coming on is more fun when it's only a cartoon. So a girl finds the groove, opens it up and careens fearlessly at a hundred-ten. What's to lose?

Well, you can smash yourself to cartoon smithereens and make those embarrassing lights and sirens go off and turn every head at the bar to see who crashed and burned.

"Oh, boy," Mo says to her friend, herself.

"You're not bad," says an old fart standing back in her blind spot, stepping up now as if ready to pass.

Oh, boy, Mo thinks again. *Spare me. Old fart thinks I'm game just because nobody else seems interested. Give me some time, Mister. And some space, if you don't mind.* She turns and smiles halfway to let the guy know she doesn't mind him watching, but this is no open house. Yet an eyeful of him bunches her brow like a crumple zone. What a number. *Yellow plaid pants and a blue poly shirt? Why?*

The old guy asks, "You like motorcycles?"

"Yes, I do," Mo says, as a chill pours over, head to toe. What a dumb question. *Here I am in blue jeans and a leather jacket and helmet hair, and the guy asks if I like motorcycles. What does he think, that I dress and blow-dry like this to look the part?*

"You ride?"

What do you think? "Yes. I ride." She takes him in, sees him past his loud clothing to his body language and facial features and past that to his mannerism. He fits in to the smoky light and stale funk of Buzz's Tail Dragger like a coordinated accessory.

"You know you look so much like a girl I used to know. I just can't believe it."

Lifting his outside hand he shows a fresh beer. It's for her, if she doesn't mind. Brimful and frothy, the offer makes her blush, but she doesn't miss her manners. "Hey, thanks," she says, covering her loss for words with a new game, if she can find three more coins.

"Here you go. I have them." As if palming them all along, he reaches with the inside hand, stepping past and turning to face her. "You're pretty good," he says, slipping the coins into the slot. He smiles like a man on a quick scan of life passing before him. They clang down to register credit. He hits the start button. Lights flash, engines rev. Pick your machine.

She picks an old, chopped Shovelhead this time, just for fun, a bare bones rat bike with cojones, and she plays on, going slower now because the old man in her blind spot is running his mouth over this girl he used to know. They rode together up and down the island and way east into the wilderness. Sometimes they logged more clicks than anyone cared to count.

Nobody counts clicks, Mister. That's why God invented odometers. She doesn't say this but gooses the throttle, maybe to leave the old guy and his wilderness nostalgia in the dust.

"We didn't have speedometers then," he says, and she smiles at his skill in reading her thoughts, not that such a read requires much skill. Who ever counted clicks? "Oh, we had 'em. We took 'em off. Front brakes, too." She passes on a curve doing a hundred thirty, but he doesn't even notice. "Suspension. All that chrome you see now. Jiminy Christmas, it was different then."

She hits the skids on the next curve and smashes into a telephone pole and steps back laughing at the cartoon carnage, scooter parts and body parts melting together as the cartoon ambulance and cartoon wrecker come on to clear the mess. She lifts her new, brimful beer to her lips, wishing this guy would stop staring, knowing the Canadian draughts sneak up on you with the velvet tire iron. But it tastes so good; too bad it'll bend your knees and lay you down quicker than a cartoon Shovelhead.

"Tina," he says, causing her recent gulp to go down the wrong pipe and threaten an unladylike spew.

He doesn't falter but gazes on Mo Dowd like her pint tumbler is a china cup and the brew inside is tea, and instead of an inadvertent "Fuck, man, wrong pipe," and a backhanded lip-wipe it's a *peu, peu, pardon me,* with a pinky in the air....

"It's like.... Well, her habits and the way she did things. Exactly. You got the same shape. Them freckles. You even got the same hair and all."

"My name's not Tina," she says, settling out and trying again with three more coins. She wipes her lips with the back of her hand again to be sure she didn't leave any flecks and says, "Boy, you'd think I didn't know how to drink one of these. Or three of these." She laughs at her own joke. He stares. She drinks again and sets the beer down to pick a more modern motorcycle for the next game. She holds the throttle wide open and roars down the cartoon road, but either the beer is taking a toll, or this new cartoon motorcycle is going faster. She could slow down a tad to work the curves and traffic better. But what's the diff anyway, if game three scores less than game one? So she holds it open into the head-on and pile up and all the lights and sirens. And then she's had enough.

"These games are stupid," she says. "Take your money. Make you feel like a fool. Give you a headache." She picks up the beer and says, "My mother's name is Tina." She turns and in the moment corrects herself, "I mean my birth mother." But she speaks to thin air again, seeing the old guy going out the door. "Jimmy!" But the old fart won't look back.

"Nice," she says to herself. "Nice family, the way we sit down at the table for dinner and catch up on each other."

II

A Life of Disappointment and Regret

A real rider sloughs the cold, even as another huff chills the garage and stings his face. A long miler reaches for distance and the feel of it, past the pain. Who would head out in forty degrees for a frosty mug but a macho idiot, or a man who misses the feeling?

This may need rethinking. Idling on a steady lament, not the smooth rumble of summer but a more tentative chug, the motorcycle also reaches for warmth that may not be found. Engine winterizing guidelines discourage cold-weather starts, because an engine is better undisturbed than slightly warmed. Better to hibernate until spring, when some real heat can cut the sludge. Winter starts will dislodge the crud, but a rider would freeze to death by the time he got to running temp. Nothing heats up in winter, much less does the crud burn off. The only option for progress is shutting the door and waiting to drop fucking dead.

Starting and sitting feels bad, but Buster Fetteroff wants to feel something. So he fired it up. He can't head out for a beer like it was August. An outing is delusional, best imagined from a freezing garage than suffered in the bitter breeze. In a while, he turns it off and dismounts to fire a fatty. Getting high might absolve the challenge. Mo Dowd calls his habit worrisome. She says greater frequency will numb pleasure centers to natural stimuli.

What does she know? Better to endure winter than die, and he's not addicted; he just doesn't like to run out. Besides, it's her bud. Besides, standing in a cold garage by a ticking motorcycle is nice, if he's high. Alive and well is better yet.

The little ember glares as proof of life. Slow as a critter caught out and far from nimble youth, he recalls livelier times with less mentality, when his fancy turned to love in the spring every time. Where'd that go?

Common interests fall away over thirty years. Married life isn't hostile or vindictive. Colors simply fade to grays. The pulse feels like a fish on deck, throbbing intermittently in base need. The man of the cloth called the physical part "an important bond" all those years ago, and the bell still tolls, more in nocturnal dirge than a tintinnabulation, more like a dream run than internal combustion, more in relief than rendering power to the rear wheel. Then it's over yet again. Like strangers in passing, they share stimuli as if by chance.

She's fashionable and conversant; he likes the blues and marijuana. He calls it marijuana reefer, but gets no laughs. She browses catalogues, seeing life as it might be lived. He's pushing sixty but doesn't look a day over fifty-three, or fifty-five. She's fifty-two and way doable on everyman's scale. She cringes when he says as much, and she asks, "Do you mind?" He regrets her regrets. Soon they'll part, to salvage the years remaining rather than sacrifice themselves to society's delusion.

The house sprawls, elaboration on a vague theme: saltbox simplicity gone wild. Four thousand square feet sounds big but is only practical, with so much stuff that needs a place to be. A man wonders why. At least it's paid for. Buster Fetteroff doesn't borrow, because debt free is home free.

Yet he longs for distance and ponders the layers of his need.

The house is easy too. If she wants it, she can have it. In the end each will pay what he owes and take what she needs. They vowed wedlock to the end, till the first one croaks. But things change. Why would a single man need a huge house? Less is more, and a settlement takes the place down to dollars that weigh nothing, leaving more room in the saddlebags.

Louise is more challenging, with her goodwill, her good nature, her sense of humor and her love. Middle age and itchy, the mutt's devotion is boundless, without rationale. Louise shines like high noon. You can hire a maid and a cook—and a hooker and a chauffeur. But true love night or day with no moods or catalogues takes a dog. She needs daily play, but who doesn't?

Besides leaving home and dog, Buster faces the end of work. That should also be easy. His office over the garage is apart from home and hearth, and money is a tortuous pursuit. Having money is lovely; getting it is nasty. Survival and prosperity are one and the same. The ultimate client is the United States of America, which doesn't blink at three hundred dollars for a blood test costing thirty cents. Additional billing accrues on enhanced saturation subsets and substrata analysis, leading to a hundred fifty grand gross in ninety days, which seemed good at the beginning, until returns compounded through a subsidiary subcontractor, because a low profile two steps removed seemed prudent and discreet. Gross revenues of two million last year with seventy-two percent guaranteed by Medicare and unpaid balances rotating on the monthly point and a half seemed best of all. Buster Fetteroff conformed to more and more. What could he do, live with less?

But two mil a year only seems adequate if you don't have it, so one more year of rubbing the turnip just right got another bit of blood. Three point five should make this year brighter still, even after taxes, stress, a carefully crafted paper trail and a hefty budget for legal fees, that won't likely be necessary. Fetteroff Associates Medical Services will make millions, unchallenged. So why would he stare into space as unhappily as his unhappy wife?

The answer is plain as the nose on his face: Progress in America demands more. Slowing down can be perilous, as overhead creeps up and exposure feels like aberrant cell growth. More may not be better but is necessary, and necessity is a mother.

Buster Fetteroff shares his angst when his accountant offers congratulations on a record year. Buster says he doesn't feel better than last year, only more tired. Gittelman, the CPA, asks: "Do you know the definition of a fierce competitor?" Fetteroff groans. "A guy who finishes first and third in a circle jerk." Ha. Ha ha.

On the bright side, the Spring Fling approaches, with the guys, the ride, the good times. Something warm up ahead softens a woeful winter day, bearing down.

Why not leave it at that, watching the machine tick, cooling at zero rpm? Why not embrace a thought of warmth? How joyful life will be, down to rain gear, long johns, sunscreen, spare plugs, rags, wrenches, odds and ends. Some bungies and Band-Aids. ChapStick. Reefer. Smokes. Water. Clothes for two days. The road gear litany plays sweetly to a sad and wealthy man slumped on a stool in a cold garage, a man who wants out of his days and into the light.

Call it a pilgrimage, seeking horizons beyond a house of moods, where Larraine waits, perplexed. The TV does not amuse her, though she gloms onto it as the studio audience cackles with glee. He drifts in to squat by the fire. Louise shuffles over for the evening tableau, two mutts rubbing muzzles. Louise licks his face and groans. Buster joins in. They shift and repeat. He feels no urgency, other than needing to find the world again, while he can.

He needs a destination. This horizon stuff is fine as fluff, but after so many stops for fuel, pissing, hotdogs, yesterday's fried chicken, tater wedges, frozen burritos and burned coffee, a rider wonders how much farther. Where is this road bound? When will he arrive?

Arrival is foregone, achieved on mounting up. Still, a physical destination can round things out, can bring this idyllic ride into the real world. A name or face can add promise to the miles, lest a journey deliver a wayward soul yonder, alone. Could this ride encapsulate another constraint, a still life in movement, a plastic bubble, with Band-Aids and lip grease and snowflakes?

These thoughts are squelched through the night, as questions drift in. Ghosts of youth and yearning ask why and wherefore, until birds chirp and the daze thins. A day shapes up like another slog around the block, but it won't be too many more laps.

Notable cash flow makes for heavy demands in a house of mirrors. Money is not love but is loved for what it might provide or relieve, so a man rises and steps into it—or steps in it. He can't veer in the stretch but will close things in tidy order, if he can stay calm. Wits regroup through morning movement, bowels, bladder, brushing, shower, two over easy, toast and coffee—ah, caffeine, on which prospects are enhanced. With few hurdles remaining, the path not yet taken beckons. It seems clearer on a morning: game on. He will leave the scene of the crime, make that murder one on his life…. No, scratch that. Involuntary manslaughter is more like it. He could call it the scene of the crimes, if the rap sheet included over-starched appropriateness and resentment of real life. But that feels like bitterness toward his one true love, or former love, and he doesn't want that.

Buster Fetteroff doesn't exactly defraud the federal government but waves the red flag for an audit. Things cannot stand for long. He's only a man with a yen and a motorcycle, seeking distance. The federal government yields to lobbyists for Big Pharma, Big Farma, Big Oil, Big guns, mercenary military and Pentagon contractors. Fetteroff is merely righteous, after all, if only the feds would see it that way.

Impregnating Moira Kunzler was neither intentional nor illegal. It merely happened, and he did the right thing, proceeding with plans for a divorce for himself and further plans for eighteen years of support for the impending person. He hopes his moral failures will also sort with distance. She was ripe. He was wrong.

A man ponders failures in context. What has he loved? He lived his days well enough, but truth underscores failure. The world is failing, and the future could be far worse than scooting down a road, if he let it. A mindset takes hold. Fetteroff's chronic inadequacy has led to irritable mood syndrome, until he matches the moody wife. Is he so guilty? Yes, Your Honor, but....

He is not mean spirited. He is a man of regrettable weakness that affects the lives of others, a man who is weak and strong, a man failing by rising to do what he doesn't want to do, as he squirms to be free. Today, he'll sort and wait.

Buster Fetteroff is a seasoned rider who's come to terms with essentials, except for weaponry. Not a hunter or gun owner or nutter, he sees many two-wheelers packing heat. Many also run chrome, loud pipes, fringe, conchos and gewgaws. He doesn't want that stuff, but he's not sure about weaponry. He doesn't want to be caught out. The world is armed and dangerous, so he seeks guidance.

"You ought to know that it's people with guns who are most likely to be fired on. Will your gun be an asset or a liability?" Rolly Snead is in Parts, a minimum-wager who gravitated to the motorcycle scene. He's not a grunt but a seasoned road dog, given what he knows.

"Here's how it plays: you will get fired on if you lose the move." Rolly is up from West Texas, where the move is second nature. "You can see your gun as half empty or half loaded, just like a glass o' water. Or you. It's your fuckin' call." Rolly is colorful and sometimes confused. He's seen things and wants to share. He hunches in with guidance. Buster is spending eight hundred dollars on fairing lowers and three hundred more on little glove boxes that fit inside the lowers for glasses or gloves or a handgun, or none of the above. Buster's boxes will house four-inch speakers for hundred-watt output on both sides.

Rolly never sold lowers for speakers. He pegs Buster as a rich guy, and the computer confirms. "Hell, you spent more on that motorcycle than I made last year. That's cool. I got job security."

"Some years are better than others."

Rolly nods, wondering when twelve bucks an hour will feel better. Many earrings, spikes, and tattoos show his commitment. Dragons circle his biceps among barbwire strands. Skulls peek out his T and spiders crawl across his shoulders. On his neck, a woman with terrific tits and a hairy crotch indicates traditional values in Horny Toad, Texas. Rolly gazes, perhaps seeking prospects for prosperity. "I gotta tell you, Buster. It's more than that. I see you tooling around all over the place, and I say to myself, 'Buster likes to ride.' That's good. You know the whole scene changed. It's a fucking embarrassment now, man, with your Harley fucking Davidson underwear and your Harley fucking Davidson pickup trucks. Next thing they'll have is your Harley Davidson dick warmer. Man. Wished I had a dollar for every pot-bellied couch spud comes in here with three hundred down and permission from the wife. You think they like to ride? Fuck no. Grocery store and home. ATM machine and the fern bar, maybe. But you, Buster. You like to ride. And now you're fixin' to pack some heat. That's what I mean. That's how it used to be. And it don't likely make a gnat's ass difference to you, but it makes me proud to know you. See you come up to snuff like that."

"Well, thanks, Rolly. I like to ride. I'm thinking of...."

"Show him the cable locks, Rolly!" Mo Dowd calls out from a pitch in progress to a squat fellow staring at a Softtail, feeling the emergence of the inner man. Mo sells motorcycles and knows how to close. She allows the mark to stare until the fat, fuzzy moth squeezes out of the pupa, until the new image and identity merge. She suggested Rolly as a gun counselor, because he's from Texas.

Rolly pulls a Kevlar cable and lock from a shelf in back. "Hunnerd eighty dollars, but this won't stop'em."

"I heard that," Buster agrees. "They say locks only discourage honest people." Rolly squints at the chickenshit way Buster sometimes talks. "But what else can you do?"

Rolly explains the open road. "Look at me: six-four in my boots, two hundred forty-four pounds. Now who's gonna fuck with me? I'll tell you who: any fuckin' one of 'um thinks he can get away with it is who. I'm coming all the way up here from Texas with fourteen yards of stuff crammed in a twelve-yard U-Haul. The dog and cat and snakes up front, man, I had a show going on. It's the same no matter what you're driving, and especially out alone on a motorcycle. I was in my truck, but I still carry a small frame .44 that'll blow a hole in whatever's in front of it. You want to get there in one piece, you better be ready for the guys who want to take your shit away from you." Buster squints at the thought of blown holes. "Hell, if you're not used to carrying concealed firearms, a .38'll do."

"I guess just showing it can calm things down."

"Fuck, no, brother! You clear leather, you gonna kill somebody! That's how you think. You don't pull that thing out for show'n tell. You gonna pack it loaded and ready. You gonna pull it out to use it, and you gonna aim to kill. You wanna go alone, you pack the heat. No matter what."

"I see your point."

"I like a Walther PPK. Gives you seventeen shots in a clip. Reloads in five seconds."

"So you get thirty-four shots on two clips? Or fifty-one if you want to carry three?"

"You get a fuckin' range war in your pocket if you want."

"So the cable and lock are worthless?"

"Negatory, brother. Nothing is worthless. You might want one of these alarms, but the fuckers go off every time you scratch your balls. Eight hundred motherfucking dollars for Harley fucking Davidson, excuse me. You just park outside the window. Get a ground floor room and sleep with your ears open. A cable and lock ought to give you a few more seconds to get the jump on 'em. You better be ready once you jump, though."

Buster takes the lowers, glove boxes, cable and lock and heads out, as Rolly calls out that he could just trade up to one o' them new fucking rigs with the tunes built in. "Only forty-five fuckin' grand!" He guffaws at the world his employer hath wrought, so Buster shakes his head in agreement.

The neighborhood gun store is a half-mile down, allowing time enough to see that a gun is to dominance what LSD is to insight, quick and certain. The gun store feels like LSD too, with its tingling air, robotic men and showcases, still as lizards, eyes orbiting as mouths chew on stopping power, weight and recoil for other men seeking balance.

Buster steps up to a counter and says ".38."

"What .38? You want to see a special? Or a snubnose? I got magnums and look at this: Glock 38 45 compact. Gives you eight rounds in a magazine." Buster shrugs. The small man says, "Tell me something. What do you want to shoot?"

"Self-defense," Buster says.

The clerk lifts a forefinger and stoops to pull a magnum Derringer from the showcase. "Look at this. Two shots o' turbo .22. This model is very popular for a little self-defense. Light. No bulk. Carries nicely on your shin. Two shots, light action, stopping power to get the job done."

Stopping power and light action sound efficient. Two shots sound safer, in the event that bad people take his gun. Then again, two shots could leave a guy caught out worse than no shots. It's a tricky call. The clerk sees the wheels turning. With service and sales motivation, he points out a few other choices. Buster points to an AR 15. The clerk grins, "Talk about stopping a gang o' sumbitches. It's light and concealable, considering size and firepower. You can't get the parts here to go fully automatic for ten rounds per second, but you can get the parts. This one's on sale for a thousand dollars. That's four hundred off. You want it?"

"It'd be fun to spray this fucker down in lawyer town, huh? Why is it on sale?"

The clerk takes the gun back on such ill-advised humor. "You don't make terrorist jokes at the airport, do you?"

"I don't know any terrorist jokes—wait; okay, Osama bin Laden gets to heaven...." The clerk smiles politely and puts his inventory back into the showcase. He drifts away but keeps an eye on Buster, who can take a hint and drifts to the children's department. He likes a pellet pump gun with a plastic stock molded like a vintage frontier rifle. He thinks it's for boys who want to shoot birds. It's a toy but seems less risky and might discourage a bad guy or two.

Back at the motorcycle shop, Mo Dowd laughs, "A pellet gun. Perfect."

"It seems like a toy, but it suits my comfort and does have some stopping power."

"Some slow-down power, maybe. Buster, you carry a gun or you don't. That's not a gun. It'll mess you up. You'll see."

"I won't carry it visibly."

"What'll you do, sleep with it?"

"No. I'll shoot it and see how it feels."

She leans in to whisper, "How do you think it'll feel?"

"I don't know."

She shakes her head. "You take the cake. Get rid of it. Listen: I been to Alaska and back by myself and Hollister and back and two years ago to Sturgis. I never packed anything but a smile and thoughts of having a good time. Guns are for people who think they need them. You're a cream puff like me. Get rid of it."

"You think so?" Creampuffery is difficult.

"You're a strange one."

Strangeness is a better note, not so weak and more ambivalent. He steps away and says, "Later," as a man of few words would do. He curses the heater for taking so long to warm up and wonders if Mo heard what Rolly said about him, Buster, liking to ride. She must know. He's not hardcore, doesn't want to be. He's married and vested in the machine—the machination of life with no abandon. Maybe she's right on the creampuff issue. Maybe Rolly was only blowing smoke up a creampuff's ass. Buster could feel puny. He gets no air, but he will, and soon, and he's not soft.

He's in between, like the Scarlet Pimpernel. The Pimpernel was a fop, but that was a front, and he could handle a sword with the best of them. Would a sword be better than a pellet gun? Hmm.... Maybe not.

Well, a man only has a cable-stitch sweater because his fashion-fixated wife gave it to him, and he hasn't worn it, and it'll look okay with some grease and soot. He doesn't rev at fern bars or trailer his scooter to bike events. He doesn't run stock pipes or travel packs, and he wears a peanut helmet. He smokes more dope than the average bear and steps to the line when it counts. Now he'll run fairing lowers to house his speakers and keep his boots dry. So what? Music and dry boots do not a pussy make. They make for comfort and longer miles in any weather.

He'll remount his passenger pad in case he meets a passenger. Larraine won't notice because she doesn't relate. She's polite and sad and sometimes whimpers when they go in-out like stick figures with no whispered nothing to the last gasp. The event is infrequent yet inevitable, ephemeral as life itself and over. It brings relief, like a death in the family after lengthy illness.

A blowjob in the truck seems long ago and worlds away. She lost at Scrabble, and the victor picked the spoil. She'd wanted a foot massage, but she lost. Not to worry; in the spirit of good sportsmanship he pulled over and walked around and ate her on the shotgun side, looking up to make her blush.

She touched his jaw this morning. "What's this thing?"

"What thing?"

"On your jaw. It wasn't there before."

"Is there one on the other side too?"

"Yes."

"They're not things." He pushed up the skin in front of his ear. The thing disappeared. "Jowls."

She moaned.

"It's only the beginning. They get worse."

On another milestone, she laughed.

He twists the rearview to see his jowl and touch it. It's been decades since he sold that truck, but he recalls her crisis as she met his eyes. In those days, he could pull her across the bench seat and put his arm around her shoulders. He can't imagine such affection today.

A road sign shows his exit, one mile up, and he can't remember the last ten. Cars pass on both sides, as he pokes along in the center lane. Tibetans assess the flesh as a stopover on a longer quest. The body is a brief interlude, and so is desire, for the vigilant spirit. He feels vigilant but not ready to die and hoping to get laid again. So why does he feel like a monk out of time?

It's the momentous change ahead and lack of clarity. He leans out the window till his face flaps in the breeze. A woman one lane over looks and laughs like Larraine, her poised mirth reserved, her tolerance strained for something droll, something removed. She should try a face flap of her own, because a life of no effacement is preserved like a specimen. She won't; it wouldn't look right.

He comes back in, more confident in his plan to depart sooner rather than later, so they don't beat this thing to death. They might stay friends with fond memories. He wants to eat the woman one lane over on the side of the road, but she steps on it, as if she knows. Well, any romance can end. Life should simplify in the stretch, should get easy on good times and stimulation, maybe.

Sitting in a cold garage is a symptom. Listening to the radio, smoking dope, installing new toys fills a few hours of winter. It passes slowly, like dormant seed, waiting to crack. Buster starts the engine for perspective on his new fairing lowers and throws a leg over for the feel. He eases in, going nowhere. The cold drops like a stone late in the day. Or is it evening?

He slides off and moves to the upturned bucket by the oscillating heater. The cat jumps onto the seat for the lingering warmth and purrs. A mouse nibbles crumbs on a shelf.

The phone rings. He answers as he would upstairs in the office, his toneless austerity meant to cover the dope. It's not a client but Moira Kunzler. "Dr. Schurz will be on the line in a moment."

"Moira."

"Yes."

"I...."

"Buster and Henry. You're connected."

"Buster!"

"Henry."

Henry Schurz became aware of blood testing profitability and then painfully aware of up-charge potential on microanalysis. Dr. Schurz is ready to mobilize on P.O. boxes and letterheads for four new labs. "If you could stop by tomorrow, we can formalize documents on a partnership."

"I don't want a partnership."

"I think you should. You will have capitalization requirements if you choose to expand, and, as you well know, medical credentials will be your greatest asset. Buster, I'm here for you."

"I don't want to expand, Henry. If I did, I have the means. This is not a medical practice, Henry. It's a business you might want to develop peripherally, based on your professional status. Capiche?" Buster wants Henry to buy his obscenely lucrative, risky business, not to come in as a partner. Who would ever want a doctor as a business partner? He wants Henry to come up with the idea of a purchase all by his lonesome, but Henry is either slow or devious.

"The means might be more than meets the eye," Henry says. "Wealth acquisition requires that a position be improved or lost. I don't have to tell you, my friend, that one man's expansion is but a spec of another man's empire." Buster hears a veiled threat or buffoonery; they're interchangeable with Henry Schurz. "Don't forget, Buster. I'm a doctor, a practicing physician licensed by the American Medical Association." Henry burbles credibility, credence and creativity, moving ineluctably to the healing process. "In the final analysis, my friend...."

"Wait a minute. You're a doctor with capitalization capacity?" Buster hangs up softly to finalize the analysis. Henry is not yet aware of anything more, but he'll chew on the last audible concept. He may be devious, but he's terribly greedy and does have borrowing power. What a...a...a doctor, as if his ragamuffin persona will suggest that he works too hard to worry about grooming. Buster understands comfort but tucks in his shirt for business calls. He sets his purchase price at three times earnings, around six mil, which sounds like some dough, and it would be in greenbacks, in a paper bag. But it's not enough, once risk and stress are factored, taxes and legal subtracted. Buster raised his price to seven point five.

Settling onto the upturned bucket, he savors the oscillating warmth and congealing stillness. The cat and mouse settle too. Eastward, behind budding limbs, a full moon rises, drawing oceans and stirring blood, clearing perspective on a clean getaway.

Henry Schurz is another symptom. No man comes away clean. Henry wants in for the money, and so he'll get his chance. Henry can come up with six mil. Henry has a solid future in medicine. He's a consummate pro, patting the collective thigh to clear a million a year, more or less. He's wanted more, and now he sees it. Medical curricula may not include greed and bluster, but they could. Henry could be easy with Moira's help, with her alignment and incentive. Buster warms, wishing Moira and Henry the best. She's so attentive to detail. He's slovenly and floppy as Raggedy Andy. She's full-bodied and sensual. He's rich. She's worried. They could fit.

Any two people can be different. Take Larraine and her former self. She went from crazy in love to despondent. It took years, and the adventurous young woman gave in to longing for the world of prestige. She craves imagery. She's disaffected at home and with he who shares her home. Kissing and hugging, as seen on TV, tapered. She calls him cold. She says libido is no substitute for love.

He sees their connubial life as a still shot.

Men she used to "know" show up on TV, in the news, but it wasn't romance with any of them, not really. Buster doesn't question but wonders why she eggs him on. Would he be more lovable as a news item, in a button down shirt, a Brooks Brothers suit and a fine how-do-you-do? She mentions professional help as a means to cure what ails him. He returns her sad smile. He thinks they've had a decent run, terminal from the outset. The man of cloth said "till death do you part," and it's dead. They veer apart, each to her own, as people do. Their time was good, however faintly at the end, and that should count for something.

Did they marry too young? The early days felt combustible, full of life on a head of steam, wheels turning and ramrod churning as they rounded the bend with a *whoo whooooo!* The future seemed certain, until it came to pass. The last need shared is for something new. She endures as a woman, martyr to marriage. Headaches are meant to discourage him. They do.

He thinks she'll suffer but not for long. She's cold, a looker with disingenuous charm. She used to reache and rub and ask, "Yes?" She pouted for a morning kiss, not too much to ask. But if she had to ask, never mind. Maybe he'll pay more attention one day. But a man confuses sex and love, until both default to civility. Happiness ebbs.

The bold moon rises.

The space heater warms its radius with communistic efficiency. He and the cat and mouse wait for spring, incarcerated. Waiting to break out, they exist.

Buster trembles at the thought of sunny, blue miles. Goose bumps rise when the heater comes his way. Do cats and mice sense a future as well? The cat purrs. The mouse sorts crumbs with an eye on the cat. The heater wheezes.

Buster stands, folds a shop rag twice and sets it near the mouse, who ducks back while fresh crumbs are sprinkled on the rag. The mouse emerges, a fuzzy form in moonlight settling on the rag to sort the new array. "You'll catch your death on cold metal," Buster says. The cat turns to remind that death has many forms. Buster reaches for his toy gun and walks to the house with the cat's meow close behind.

III

Hundreds of Thousands without Power

Larraine stares out the window as if sorting gray tones into a more sensible arrangement. With a sigh, she moves to dinner, because he cooked last night, grilled salmon to fend off the heart phantom, steamed broccoli to discourage the cancer phantom, salad with pumpkin seeds to defend against the prostate and sphincter phantoms. Oh, the Fetteroffs eat well, as informed people should.

Buster pours kibbles for the cat, as Larraine garnishes a plate with parsley. He idly asks if she remembers the old riddle: What's the difference between parsley and pussy?

She remembers the joke but not the point, except for gratuitous vulgarity. Does he really need to be an ill-mannered teenager at his age? He laughs, not giving a shit, for the youthful feeling of indifference. Could he feel this way all the time?

"Nobody eats parsley anymore. I guess we've come full circle." With pretzels and beer, he moves to the living room, to watch the weather woman review some fronts.

In hardly a shake, it's leftovers with a twist, admirably arranged, or would that be formatted? The paper-thin lemon slices are not squeezable but can be squished. The parsley is old and bitter. Buster fumbles a lemon slice while channel surfing to a teeming jungle, where a python engorges a rodent. He hates melted cheese, especially on reheated broccoli, so he slips it aside and watches the snake.

She says cheese helps slide things along.

It's pure fat, he says.

She ignores him. He concedes the point; all he had to do is shut up. But it's rained forty days and nights, and the strain is apparent. He nudges the cheese. Another snake hits a bird. Buster also unhinges and gulps, hating his compulsion but laughing.

"Must you?"

He nods, "Yoah netsht." He swallows in time and allows, "It's a beautiful thing when mates can communicate non-verbally." He surfs back to the weather woman, who chirps that the barometer is falling.

She turns to him. "I don't feel like we're mates."

He asks, "Why is she smiling? You think she's got a butt plug?"

"Get twenty-two," Larraine says.

On twenty-two, a tittering starlet wants to ask the Dalai Lama what turns him on, "I mean really turns him on." The starlet thinks her chance for meeting His Holiness is terrific; her latest movie made millions and proved her bankability and future. She's built and presented as doable but dumb.

Larraine nods and says the starlet is interesting and valid.

Buster slows on intake to fend off the bile phantom. It rises like fog on a moor. He says the starlet is a bimbo, and her last movie was shit. "Shit should not be bankable, but it is." He surfs, a unilateral decision dangerously precipitate. The next channel yields aftermath and sorrow on another mass murder, either an office shooting or another day at school.

The next channel brings flooding, mudslide, building collapse and aviation tragedy. Around the dial are continuing grief and game shows. We'll be back with the finalists and families of the victims after these important messages.

The second lap arrives at a student shooter on the mass murder channel. "Get twenty-two." Larraine says. "I can't watch TV like this." Twenty-two is still *Show Biz Today*. Larraine often disclaims Hollywood drivel; "It's not my cup of tea," She likes to say. "I just want see who's up to what. It's so stupid." Yet she follows like an addict to feed her habit for the painfully tasteless. He gets twenty-two, to keep the peace.

Show Biz Today caroms to a political woman who beams with luscious enhancements to make people cringe. But men watch. Her fixed smile could be set in clay, as she spews family values. The bosom heaves. Larraine calls her unspeakable. "What is it with her chest? I can't watch this. She looks like the evil queen with a bad reconstruction. Why get a facelift, if she can't cut back on the make up? Those tits could stand alone. Who'd want to have sex with her?"

Buster would, because he'd give a woman the benefit of the doubt in her need. He imagines the driver's seat. Would she beam optimistic for a better tomorrow? He looks up to see Larraine watching his private scenario. "You'd be surprised," he says.

"Would you?"

"I don't think so. Not my type."

"Not your type?" Meaning what? That a vaginal opening with reasonable surroundings would not qualify for his type? Her eyebrow scrunch conveys comprehension. So they surf. Back in the jungle, a sapphire tree viper hugs a red-breasted titmouse.

Larraine covers her eyes.

"It's only natural," he says, but she moves to the parlor to clarify deeper needs.

On the Nature Channel, a whale roils the surface, feeding on krill, so many billions of krill, their biomass is greater than that of humans. The comparison fails to factor the non-biomass of cars, appliances, sheetrock, shag carpet, drop ceilings and convenience to church, schools and shopping. The krill live without. So Buster returns to the jungle. Snakes swallowing rats and birds is part of the ingestion series. Next come spiders sucking flies juiceless. Cookies squirm, so he surfs to India's one point four billion humans and nearly as many rats. Eighty thousand babies are born daily in India and a few more than that in China, because the Chinese don't cull like they used to do. After India and China comes the USA. "And we're gaining," says the newsperson with a civic smile.

One click over, a woman is having eight babies, and one channel beyond is a him 'n her news team. "We have an amazing story. It's something that lurks in the darkest cellar of fear for every parent," the woman says.

The man says, "We'll learn what it means to fear the reaper."

"A seventeen-year-old boy in Smithville played a practical joke on his father, career farmer Deke Pluff. Deke Junior's arm was severed. We'll see how doctors responded," the woman says.

"And put it back on," the man says.

"So don't go away," the woman says.

Buster returns to the weather woman. Hefty and saucy in her Italian suit with elegant flounce and suggestive V, she says tomorrow will be flanked by a high-pressure ridge that should darn near deflect storm cells like billiard balls. We'll have to wait and see. Who knows how long it will last? Meanwhile, she's amazed. "High pressure at this time of year? Are you kidding?" Could she be so tacit in flounces and a deep V? Billiard balls deflecting off a high-pressure ridge? He would like to ask the impolite company he favors, if the weather woman is teasing. Larraine's chronic complaint is his reflexive opposition to social norm.

He thinks she's blind to a world gone wrong, and the truth is, most of the male viewing audience would share his view, given the courage to assess the weather woman's ways.

He read recently that weather women can turn a half mil annual, which seems more amazing than high pressure this time of year. Income demonstrates a niche in society, but where does she fit in nature? Rivers are swelling to the southeast. Authorities call for evacuation. Hundreds of thousands are without power.

The weatherwoman turns, profile right, to the weather map. She holds and turns to the camera with concern. She fades on full body and a promise to be right back, after these important messages. Thunderheads stack up. Is that also coincidental?

Buster Fetteroff does not fit easily in society but tries to make do. Indifferent to the home team, he cheers with the home crowd. He pays taxes and drives on the right side of the road. He stayed married thirty years. He makes few demands on his community. He makes solid money but doubts his sanity and stability. He worries, that this same society can frame a frilly, flounced woman as a weather authority and pay her so much. She doesn't know weather but takes a lead from the weather service, from people in khakis who gather data. She's no authority but commandeers ratings on personal concern in a lusty package. She would perish in the wild, even with a prompter.

Back with the news, a camera pans rubble for survivors, as a voice narrates devastation and grief. The landscape looks like LA on descent, Earth scabbed over. No deer or antelope at play. One station over, children are weeping at school....

The phone rings, perhaps with guidance: *Hey, Buster, it's me, God. I called to let you know you're right. I'm putting the world back in order. It might be noisy and rough for a bit....*

But it's a man wanting to know how great life is, with a terrific new car. They muddle through the facts, that Buster is married and white, which is his option to disclose. He's forty-nine to fifty-nine. Annual income is nobody's business, but he consents to over a hundred grand. He enjoys the car well enough, though it's not new but was purchased a year ago as a used car. And it's not his car but his wife's. "Weh-heh-hell," the man says, "a Mercedes Benz in the family certainly qualifies as an event of newness. I'm willing to bet the wife loves it,"

"What do you want?" Buster asks.

"We'd like you to rate your purchase experience from one to five, five being excellent, one being poor."

"Rate my purchase experience? It was a pain in the ass. Why don't I rate my experience crossing the street?"

"You don't buy a car nearly as often, and we want to ensure high standards in your Mercedes Benz experience."

"Would I get a call to rate my street crossing experience if there was money in it?"

"You may! When civic authorities want to improve that experience, they'll need your input."

"I think buying a car is more like sexual relations with my wife."

"Oh."

"But that's none of your business. What's your name? Who's your supervisor?"

"I hope you enjoy the rest of your evening."

"I hope you vaporize."

And that's that, except that hanging up can't settle the pond. Buster is emotionally suppressed and troubled. His social rut runs deeper. His reason to leave is justified. He suffers, as many do, the byproduct of meaningless life. He's known for a while that when he dies, nothing will change. It won't matter. Maybe a being here and there will recall him with love. Meanwhile, they won't leave him alone. They circle and nip. He's confused and disturbed. The world is dying at the hands of fools.

Raising his new toy gun, he aims at the TV. But it cost twenty-nine hundred. The same model is down to fourteen now, but still. He pumps twice as instructed and feels better with two more pumps. He aims at the weather woman and makes the guttural sounds of firing and the TV imploding. But he won't, repeat won't, do that, because he's still constrained on practicality. A man unhinged won't worry about a few hundred bucks, but Buster still feels the difference between scratching an itch until it bleeds and letting an evening be. And unhinged is a common component of the home viewing audience. He knows this.

Feeling better, he heads out for the soothing ions. Tad Pollack's anti-crime lights light the night like an urban street. Larraine calls, "Where are you going?"

"Outside, to the land of the free."

"What?"

"What?"

"Where are you going?"

"Where?"

"What?" Life transmutes to numbing volley, until exit fades like the rest, underfoot in crunching gravel. Turning from the blinding lights over Tad Pollack's yard, Buster shrugs off the cold and looks up. Stars sparkle in cloud fissures and swirling mists. Spotty wattage in the firmament should comfort those hundreds of thousands without power. Maybe they'll talk in candlelight with the TV off. When a star falls, he feels power restored, except for the amber dazzle next door.

The gun clerk advised respecting this toy as if it were a real gun, which anyone can see it's not. It's an air rifle, double pumped or otherwise, and a steel pellet charged by CO_2 isn't a bullet. Maybe respect is meant to protect the average lumpkin from himself.

Yet the toy at his shoulder lets Buster glimpse a consequential moment, in which a steel pellet connects three dots. One is above the little gun's chamber, the peep site. Two is the tiny exclamation mark at the end of the barrel. It fits neatly into the peep site V, and three is just yonder, on the bullseye. How rare and marvelous is dead certainty? How can anything happen, unless it is allowed to happen?

That is, Tad's anti-crime lights look big enough to survive the urban core, yet Buster suspects that a steel pellet can pierce the giant's armor. What's more, the little rifle trembles, which could be from the cold, but Buster likes to think it's from willingness.

Will shooting a light satisfy the night, or must he extinguish all of Satan's flares? The spirit prevails again, spinning the verdict on this one. So he raises the tool of redemption again and takes aim. Knowing he can't stay aimed for too long without impairing his night vision, he ponders two more pumps; the glass is so thick. Ah, well…exhale and squeeze…. *Thwack…. POP! Tinkle tinkle….*

God. That felt good. That felt better than….

He changes grips for another two pumps on his way to four—but wait! What's that? Something is rustling next door.

Tad Pollack often references values, presuming his values as the base. Overbearing and tedious, Tad wants to steal time from anyone who'll stand and listen. From *these kids today and their marijuana* to *the Eyetalian place up the road. They got your pizza and your spaghetti all the way to…you know…your garlic bread and them hot sprinkles right there on the table and your, you know, cheese powder…. Oh, it's good.*

A gentler assessment would be that he's a harmless bumpkin running his mouth. But Tad used to sell insurance and wants to tell you about it. He owned a boat and knows a few things about boats too. He doesn't have, you know, with the wife much any more, and when he does, *well, sir, it takes a might longer. Ha, ha. And in case you didn't know it, the neighbors two doors down are talking d-i-v-o-r-c-e. But you didn't hear it from me.*

Tad is a nosy man with a motor mouth and floodlights. He window-peeps through the hedge, but nobody cares. Buster joked once that he'd like to set up a periscope so Tad could watch him take a dump. Larraine said that was disgusting. And sick. Which sounded intolerant but played easier than Tad's wife Mildred. Mildred is proud of menstruating at her age. Buster can't imagine.

Tad is out to see what's up, and in his hands—could it be? Yes, it's a shotgun, twelve-gauge, loaded for bear. Tad is not complex. He calls softly over the hedge that he hates ravens. "They're so darn sneaky. They fly away when they see me come out here with my shotgun. Can you believe that?" He aims his voice up and whispers louder, at the ravens. "Can't see me now, can you?"

Tad must have heard the anticrime light breakage and concluded that the ravens broke it, as a man of values might reason. With his cover blown, Buster whispers back, over the hedge, that flight is a cornerstone of survival for birds, not sneaky but intelligent.

Tad says the crows ate the apples from his trees, every one. "Why have fruit trees, if the crows get all the fruit? Is that supposed to be smart too?"

Buster asks why the birds, who spend their days searching for food, should not feed on the fruit they find.

Tad scoffs: "Nah!" He's had enough and will execute the plan laid this afternoon, to end the oppression of the birds. "Why shouldn't I be able to grow fruit trees in my own damn yard?" Tad hunches low, raising the stock to his shoulder, as a man to be reckoned, by God.

The ravens brood high in the conifers between the Pollacks and the Fetteroffs. Tad takes aim at a perch the birds favor.

"Please don't shoot the birds, Tad," Buster says.

But Tad sighs deep, like a sportsman in kill protocol, exhaling for control, in the zone. He scans, holds again and....

Fortunately for the ravens but not for Tad, Buster's toy also rises. With more natural reflex and less ceremony, Buster surrenders to the inevitable end of a terribly long day, honing on Tad's head and squeezing. Tad's big bang is preempted by two tiny thwacks, hardly a moment apart. The first is the sudden burst of CO_2 propelling the steel pellet. The second announces the pellet's arrival. This second thwack is much louder to Tad than anyone else and grants insight to Buster, who is armed and dangerous, possibly insane, shooting a man in his own front yard, a man minding his own business.

Reverberation is merely imagined. It too fades, and silence reigns in both yards. By the time Tad's inner bang stops bouncing off the canyon walls, he stares skyward, a fallen warrior gripping his shotgun. A fine weapon should never hit the dirt, but Buster cuts him some slack on this one.

Tad lies still on the cold, wet ground, looking hit by a water balloon full of blood, or a blood balloon, as it were.

Ravens snicker overhead.

Buster knows these phrases and mimics them, concurring on the aftermath, or displaying further leave of senses. You can't get bird talk right off without some practice, but it's amazing how accurate these simple expressions seem to be. Is Tad dead?

Buster sees now what the salesman meant by respect. The effect of a single pellet is appalling. Well, it's lucky Buster didn't buy a real gun. Maybe.

Tad's anti-crime lights still light the night like an industrial wasteland, but in fairness, those lights facilitated accuracy and will show the way, so someone can help Tad up. Best not shoot out the rest just yet.

Buster ponders a scenario, whereby Tad shot out a street light in his yard, and a fragment must have ricocheted into his ear. Yeah, that's the ticket: a fragment. Ricochet.

Tad's not moving but doesn't seem dead, unless seemliness is another delusion, and what's dead stays pale pink and puffy on the first paces into afterlife. Buster would check his pulse if not for the hedge and fear of rousing Mildred, the wife who still menstruates, or did, into her fifty-fifth year, which was only a few years ago and seems like yesterday, if you're willing to listen to what it takes to be a woman, a real woman, and at her age. Mildred's mere presence could engender further chaos. Best preserve the peace and quiet.

Best take solace, that if not for Buster Fetteroff, entire families of birds might now be dead. But beware the road to Hell and all that.

So Buster retreats to call 911 to report a man next door lying in his yard with a shotgun, a man who may have shot himself. Larraine asks what's going on, so Buster tells her Tad Pollack fell down with a bloody ear. She pokes her head outside as Mildred rushes out whimpering then shrieking bloody murder.... But she stops! She harkens to the sirens growing louder and joins their refrain, which is bloody murder, second chorus.

Larraine ducks back in and hurries upstairs.

"Where are you going?" Buster asks.

She responds with the look, which really should tell anyone where she's going, if anyone ever paid attention. She's going to change into something more appropriate. Let's face it; we'll have doctors and police and firemen with their, you know, PMS thingies.

"How did we get here?" Buster asks the thin air in her wake. "You and me." The answer is more of the same, so he yells up that he's going for smokes.

The toy gun's demise occurs on the bridge over the river in a sad arc out the window and over the rail to the swift, frigid waters below. Alas, its brief life had purpose, and like so many martyrs dying young, it kerplunks with no complaint. Regretting the wanton violence, Buster further regrets the loss of his new toy. He loved that little gun and all they went through together.

At the Reservation Smoke Shop, Charlie Never Walks makes change as Buster browses the Slim Jims, vitamin packs and Kwik

Fix Energy Drinks. Buster makes small talk, that so much rain with no sun can make you feel a little twitchy around the rafters.

Charlie moves robotically, without emotion, without hope.

"Not so bad for you," Buster says. "You don't wear a necktie." It's a joke, but Buster doesn't laugh, good thing, because Charlie Never Walks never laughs too.

Charlie speaks to the snuff, chew and firecrackers on either side of Buster, as if consumers and products are the same, inanimate objects with predictable behaviors.

"Yes," he says. "This is winter."

IV

A Love Restored

Charlie Never Walks makes Buster laugh. "You know, Charlie, it wasn't so long ago, the world turned slower, with tethered telephones, paper and pens. All the news took thirty minutes. You knew what you wanted and couldn't always get it."

Charlie Never Walks says it was a long time ago when he was young, and the world was a good place to wander. Buster would like to be friends with Charlie, but no matter what he says, Charlie will find him deficient, without experience, without wisdom. Of course that's not true. But what could they talk about, he and Charlie Never Walks, except for everything that's ruined? They could go for a beer, but Charlie sells beer, and he may be alcoholic. They could talk about the rising cost of firecrackers, but neither one gives a shit. Besides, the Smoke Shop stays open till ten.

But he can't go home. Well, he could, but it seems unwise, and besides, short-termers like he and Larraine have no check-in or curfew.

Moira Kunzler might be home. The die seems cast on that one, but what harm in a little visit, for commiseration between friends? The damage is done. She's a few weeks in, likely lonely, maybe confused. Achingly luscious, she compels a man, in spite of the bind. She's sweet and merely practical, and any man can panic, until recalling her blessings.

Buster responded to nature, and nature responded back. He loves nature but decides against a visit, in spite of her charms, and he chuckles, recalling his fortitude in keeping his eyes on hers. She saw him peer into the windows of her soul, and she blinked. She moved, opening the gates of heaven.

He veers south, errant asteroid giving in. He calls.

She's home and up and no, it isn't too late. She titters that a visit would be great. She'd love to see him, and he'd love to see what she's wearing, though he'd really be seeing through it. And something else: "Buster. I'm not stupid. This was your idea. I went along. Now I want to be a good mother, and you can call Henry a greedy, overbearing slob, but I haven't known very many men, and he's the sweetest guy I ever met, and yeah, you're right. But you can't come over to make love with Henry's girlfriend, unless I break it off with Henry, because he loves me, and I love him too.... I love the idea of him and can't flip-flop back and forth like that, because it gets me depressed. So great, come on over, but you'll have to call your wife and tell her you're staying. Or I can call her. I think she'll understand. So? What'll it be, Buster?"

Buster regrets the melodrama. The evening could offer such rich rewards all around. He won't share his predicament with Moira. She's too demanding and really not up to counseling at that level.

"Or you could come out to the Lakehouse tomorrow. That might be nice. It's cozy out there, and we'll have the weekend. Henry says he'll make it out or not. It's up to him. Things might be different if he can't. I'm in it to win it. Isn't that what you guys say? See you."

That would be the Lakehouse Resort, where rich people get away to be away and watch the lake. Moira seems focused. Tomorrow seems distant. The road home is cold and wet.

On the sofa in firelight, Larraine snuggles under a blanket. He sits beside her. She covers him in spite of things or because of them. Free of poses, she stares at the tired tree, months ago adorned with ornaments, candy canes, popcorn and cranberries. "I love a tree," she says. "It brings joy to the house. Can you feel it?"

"I think I did. But that tree wants to live or die outside."

"Where it can run free and be happy?"

"Where it can breathe and freeze and warm again in spring like a tree should." Larraine draws near as if to confide. She says the ambulance took Tad Pollack away. He was so bloody.

Buster says the Ebola virus causes bleeding from the ears, and he certainly hopes it's not that. "It comes from eating monkey brains. Who'd a thunk? Tad and Mildred over there menstruating and eating monkey brains." He shakes his head over perversion where least expected. They dislike Tad Pollack and wish him quick passage to somewhere else, somewhere less annoying, less threatening.

Truth is: Tad is not dead. A blown eardrum can bleed profusely, and though a pellet gun might kill a person, this one did not. "He was going to shoot me. I stopped him, Your Honor."

She says she watched a movie about this guy who walked a thousand miles after breaking out of prison. She thought it was just okay, but Buster would have loved it.

"Why would I have loved it? Was it off color, in poor taste, grubby and roughshod?"

"All of that and a great adventure, as far from home as Uranus."

He laughs at the silly line she hates, because it makes him laugh.

"That's what you like, I think."

He shrugs. "Home isn't so bad." He doubts she watched the movie in interest. He thinks she waited up. They retire to bed where they touch again sweetly, perhaps recalling original guidance, that love would be theirs till one of them died.

In a rolling fog at sunrise, she says, "Isn't it odd, how you know it's daytime, because it just...lightens?"

"Odd?" He queries, nine inches deep and sensing a diametrical difference in aging mates, as each becomes somebody else once more. One offers trivial commentary on reality. Larraine isn't stupid but can spoil a beautiful silence on a beautiful task. Buster murmurs that the light is fogbound, and he digs. And there they are, posing and pontificating, huffing and puffing.

When he takes a breather, she says, "You couldn't tell without the light, really, when night stops and day starts." She peers off, as if for meaning.

He thinks delineation is a human need, that knowing requires no such line, that nature is a soft transition, if seen as presented, simply, in silence. But he says, "That's how it is in Alaska. And Sweden. And the North Pole, where Santa Claus lives."

"Hmm." She ponders days and nights above the Arctic Circle without transition.

He grunts again for depth, holding his tongue, leading by example.

"Yes, but.... I'm not talking about those places. I mean, sure, they have nights that last for weeks or months or something. That's not what I mean. I mean they still turn on the lights in the morning."

He wants to ask what the fuck she's talking about but chooses the golden response. She's thinking herself into a corner and would be cornered sooner if he says anything, leaving her no recourse but to strike back, to assert her grasp of the basics, despite her inanity. That would only pick the scab. He digs. The joyless tree will go into this hole. It stands by, anticipating a better spring.

"I wonder how Tad is doing," she says.

"I wonder if I'll have scrambled or two over easy."

"Why are you so mean?" Her question sharpens the point.

"I'm kind to animals and you. Are you so concerned about Tad?"

She's moist, her elegant rain hat sparkling with mist that forms droplets that roll into rivulets to the edge of the brim, where they drip, drip, drip. He's wet and flecked with mud. She steps back to avoid mud flecks on her gardening outfit.

He thinks her concern for mud is like her disgust with his sense of humor. He won't ponder the likeness, because this morning feels better with a pick ax, a shovel and a purpose.

She watches until her phone rings.

He would remind her of the benefits of no cell phone at certain times, like a tender morning, when a quiet planting might offer communion with nature and each other. They might share a beautiful feeling, if not preempted by that thing and its demands. But he holds back again, sparing himself a shushing. She waits, perking to a purer light, and on the third ring she chirps, "Good morning!"

He digs. Alvin the chipmunk prattles from the devilish device. It's a woman inviting Larraine's participation in a neighborhood food drive, in which housewives will compete to out-dress, out-jewel, out-Mercedes and out-gracious each other, pulling out the stops to feed the children. Not their children, heavens, no. Their children are fed. No, they'll feed the children of lesser families, politely called needy, from which, you never know, a future President of the United States of America may now grovel for a crust but could lead the country with dignity and turpitude. Such is the potential of our neighborhoods and the women on guard.

Larraine drifts from the fogbound planting to avoid muddy sounds that could soil the noble cause taking shape. Wending gingerly over mole holes and dog shit, she prattles in response. He hears the sugary fluff: "It's a fabulous idea," and "Oh, we can...."

"Not to worry," he calls. "Manuel will finish here." Vitamin B eases transplant shock. A mound at the base will drain standing water and avoid root rot.

She trills in wonder over prospects for a spot on *Live 5 News*. "Oh, God!" The girls may actually meet *Live 5 News* man Duayne Dudney, in person, to discuss the spirit of giving canned food! She walks with greater purpose back to the house.

In stillness at last, he joins the little tree in communion. They commiserate on dormancy and hope, redemption and growth, bye and bye. They part company, the tree to spread its limbs, Buster to slog back in his wife's tracks for the lectures on muddy feet, muddy clothing and the work required to keep the goddamn place clean.

Larraine in the pantry culls old pork 'n beans she bought for her sister's children. He doesn't believe they sharpen their teeth with a file, but they could have. Like little mongrels, they mangle any soft tissue set before them. He won't call them vicious but won't pet them during feeding. The canned goods rise with magnanimity, those without labels form the base, julienne green beans and vegetable broth go on top. The stuff doesn't go bad, really.

Heading out for coffee and the Lakehouse Resort, rationalizing nothing to lose, he's taken by a man in a trench coat staring from the Pollack side of the fence. Not a small man, really, and hardly disheveled, the man nonetheless looks tired, with poor posture and wrinkles. "Inspector Colombo? Is that you?"

The man smiles with practiced difficulty, then underscores the gravity of the situation with a slow nod, indicating authority and finality. "Are you Buster Fetteroff?"

"I am. And you are?"

"Inspector Mumphry. Do you know why I'm here?"

"I could speculate."

Mumphry begins to speak but checks himself on procedural dictates. Beginning again, he says, "Don't leave town."

Buster touches his chin as if pondering travel, and he shrugs. "I don't think I'm going anywhere."

Inspector Mumphry stares, as if at the crux of the situation. "Mm. Mumphry. You're not a morning person, are you?"

Mumphry bores in, as if anything you say can and will be used against you.

"Pardon me one moment, Mr. Mumphrey, won't you?" Buster ducks back into the house for an apple from the bowl on the counter just inside the door. He walks back out while pulling a knife from his pocket to slice the apple, and he tosses the slices for the ravens. "I hate to see them go hungry. We'll tide them over till Tad gets back. He grows their apples, you know."

Moira Kunzler's lava red hair matches her eyebrows in a presentation to stop a young man or an old man short. A case study in spherical elegance with essence of ellipsis and crevasse verging on precipitous abyss here and there, she defies appropriate observation much less comment and cannot quell the moans in her wake. She plumbs the depths of curiosity, even as she prattles over weather or sports, hoping it will be nice, or we'll win the game, though she can't tell cumulus from nimbus, the Ms from the Js or sort the sox teams. She looks like a woman, first thing in the a.m., and merely stays that way. Naturally alluring, she conquers the world of men and their vile wants, defying possession, even to a man who had the knowledge but knows he won't have it again. How could he?

She has drawn the line, and he can't help but recall her fluid grace in early innocence. They talked often for a year in simple discourse. Buster sensed fondness; she laughed so freely. He told her he'd never broken his marriage vows and wouldn't until he was single, or good as. He wanted to tell her more, so she could sense his substance. But alas, she found out: base and weak, like the rest.

But today is different. They'd resolved their problem for better or worse, improving prospects for all parties on a happily ever after or a little while longer. It's a fifty-fifty chance. What man wouldn't rendezvous with Moira at the Lakehouse on a chance? Henry Schurz wouldn't, given an opportunity to display his wares, enhance his reputation, garnish his myth, make money, see a game or any number of practical pursuits.

If Henry defaults, the catbird is home free, or could be. And premeditated love in the morning, before liquor or reefer, allows the benefit of sobriety.

Perfect as a curvy cartoon, she holds up as few women do. He twists the rearview to see what she'll see, which isn't so different from twenty years ago. She gravitates to affluence and security in an upscale rendition of what a woman needs. He needs another mirror overhead for the aerial view, but she'll close her eyes, so it won't matter. He feels good, on the road to recovery if not safe haven. Moreover, he feels lucky, pulling in to the Lakehouse for the comfort, courtesy and respect mature adults enjoy most.

But Henry Schurz is shuffling up the walk with an ice bucket and a Double Grab Bag o' Ruffles. Henry is Buster's client and would-be business associate, Moira's employer and boyfriend, kind of. Henry hails, "Buster! Glad you could make it!"

"Glad to be here, Henry. Make what?"

"Make the cut. Come in." Henry is a happy man, backing in.

"What cut is that, Henry?"

"The cut for the team, Buster. Come on. It's kick-off. The Dawgs get tested today!"

Henry Schurz is hungry, a unique if slovenly fellow who might solve a difficult problem. Slobbery is a challenge for Moira; she said as much. Buster wants the best for her and tries to keep an open mind, even as his heart goes squish, more like a road kill than what he'd hoped for. Henry is hugely successful, a doctor of effusive good cheer and bedside manner that anyone could love. He drives a German sedan. His house is big enough to compound his solitude, but not for long. He is revered and seventy-two percent guaranteed by Medicare on carte blanche access to the bowels of his patients, for rearrangement and commensurate billing, at his discretion. Any bank would covet his accounts. Henry Schurz is a maximum operator, abundant on all levels.

He's happy to serve and holds the door for his friend and surprise visitor. Buster enters, to where the morning will remain chatty and foggy. Moira in a lounging robe makes less sense than an unkempt man dispensing health care. Henry plops onto the couch with a grunt and tunes the dawgs, then grabs his Double Grab like a big kid on the first day of summer. With true team spirit he says, "I been waiting forever for this game."

"This seems fast." Buster says.

She giggles that it's been happening all along, but they only just realized it. Now they're celebrating. Buster says, "Gee, you and Henry. Who'd a thunk? I mean, that's terrific." Moira's shrug explains the obvious, her blush giving rise to difficult images. The deal appears to be consummate. How else could he focus on chips and football with Moira Kunzler nearby in a lounging robe? She could make a man repeat this life of desire. Buster realizes his need is personal and aberrant and allows the rueful smile. Who can blame her for subscribing to vast comfort?

"Hey, Buster!" Henry is happy and will provide the easy out. Practicality can benefit all parties. "Sit down," he urges, slapping the cushion beside him. "How about it; Moira and me? Hey, I think we're going all the way."

"It looks like you've been all the way."

"Not that. I mean all the way to the Championship for the Western University Purple Bulldogs."

"Fuckinay, Henry. It's about time." Buster cannot effuse. "I can't stay. I just stopped in to say…."

Henry eats a grab, backstopping the load with an open palm, herding stragglers into the chipper. It's a greasy mess, but Henry's happiness grows with fulfillment. He works like a surgeon on loose flecks. Buster feels her sense of loss, her adaptation and confinement. She looks this way and that like a bird trying to comprehend a cage. She looks indentured, free of material hardship, kind of. Buster goes to pee as Moira chirps that she's so glad he could make it. She orders Henry to make drinks. Henry rises.

Lingerie and skivvies hang on the towel racks. So soon? Hers are indeed translucent but apparently not edible. Henry's boxers are mottled gray with rows of bunnies munching carrots that can't camouflage the skid marks and kumquats.

Acceptance requires discipline. The truth will set him free, and Buster does not love Moira Kunzler. So why the ache? She was merely a fling as great as imagined. She declined an abortion.

Back in the living room, Henry garnishes one of his terrific Bloody Marys. "Here you go, Buster. Try this on for size." Henry uses white asparagus, not green, and not celery, and a pimento-stuffed olive. "Celery is boring. Asparagus with an olive is better," he says. "White asparagus is best."

Buster sips. "Mm. Henry. This is very good."

"Yes." Henry hits the sofa again. "Maybe the best thing I do." Moira reddens like a Bloody Mary.

"I doubt that, Henry."

"I'll tell you what's amazing," Henry says, nodding at pre-game analysis on Sportline Update. "Borden gets his money from Texas. Go figure. Joe quacks about deserve, not deserve. Who cares? The point is, if you're a Js fan, is that a team that leads the league in yards after the catch can't even make the playoffs on account of defense. *Leads the league*! So trading Borden is good management? Get out! Next thing you know, they'll trade Falamoso and call it genius." Henry stares grimly and then laughs. "Ha! Hey, Guillermo went to free agency. You knew that."

Moira moves down her perch, seeking comfort. Buster says, "Unbelievable. Shouldn't happen in a million years."

"Bingo," Henry says. "That's what makes sports so great. Used to be religion. Now it's sports. Works for me."

"If you men will excuse me, I'm going to get dressed."

They watch her shuffle down the hall to the bathroom, where she closes the door, and they imagine her disrobing and stepping into the shower. When they hear the shower running, Henry taps Buster on the arm. "You notice anything different about Moira?"

Now it's Buster's turn to blush. "No. What would I notice?"

"Maybe you wouldn't. I'm a doctor. I see these things." Henry aims the remote for a quick surf to the other game that could affect the standings, the Crimson Chow Hounds against the Pissy Mutts or whoever.

"What things?"

"Moira's a beautiful woman. You know that. She's gained weight. You must have noticed. I guess even if you did, you'd be too polite to say anything. Eight pounds up in a month, and that's some gain, especially from one twenty on a five seven frame. Granted, she's carrying fifteen, twenty pounds of knockers—Christ on a crutch, you want to talk beautiful, and they get bigger on a weight gain. Tell me you didn't notice."

Buster shrugs. "Okay. I didn't notice, Henry. What of it?"

"It's just a kick in the ass. It's like I always say: Have faith. Your day will come. So Moira comes to me and says I'm okay...as a man. She says I might have a chance with her, if she could know where we stood. You know I was all over that. We, you know, got together, and presto, she's crying all the time. You don't need to go to med school to figure that one out. We talked. She was in...trouble. She got jilted. Can you imagine?"

Buster shrugs, sincerely pained. "I can't."

"Yeah. Me neither. I'm gonna tell you something, Buster. Strictly doctor-patient confidential."

"Okay."

"Heaven on Earth is what she is."

Buster won't press for details.

"She's so fucking great; I wouldn't care if she came to me from a weekend with Les Schwab. You know what I mean?"

"I don't. You mean Les Schwab the old guy who sells tires on TV?"

"Yes! Les Schwab! You get my point. Here's the kicker, sorry for the long way around." Henry sets up the punch line but leaves it hanging for a casual quench on his Bloody Mary, a knowing smile, a casual pause and another sip.

"What's the kicker, Henry?"

"She's not pregnant. Call me sneaky or practical. I heard her taking a whiz, and right when she finished I barged in and said, 'Oh! Gotta go, gotta go, gotta go!' I got a urine sample, you know. Negative."

Buster squints as if to plumb the depths of Henry's nature. "You're a sleuth and a genius." Henry nods. Buster stares off. "Why the weight gain?"

"I feed her. Oh, we eat well. It makes her happy, and I'll tell you what else, Buster. She's gonna get bigger, if I can help it. Guy like you might have a hard time with that. Not me. I see it as more woman to love. Frankly, I see it as security. It goes both ways, you know."

The shower stops. The curtain slides. They imagine Moira drip drying, reaching for the towel, dabbing her lovely self.

"It happens," Henry says. "False pregnancy. It can be a ruse, but I doubt it. Why would she confess, if she didn't think it was real? It also indicates stress. And love. Like I say, I think she was jilted and really loved the guy."

Buster takes the lead, patting Henry's knee. "Don't sell yourself short, Henry. You're a catch. You represent happiness, comfort, security and love. I wish you all the best, and hey, maybe she will be preggers. Soon."

"Not with me. Not unless we bring in a ringer. I'm shooting blanks. Hey! Are you game? I think Moira might be, and I haven't told her yet that it's ixnay on the idskay, I mean, unless we get a stand-in or go to the jizz bank. What do you say, Buster?"

Is Henry Schurz beyond devious to diabolical? Buster seeks but cannot find. "Henry. I gotta go."

"What's the rush? Oh, look at this: Navy and Auburn. Who cares? Why do they do that? They treat Saturday like a poor cousin, and it's the best slot of the week. We're missing Nebraska Oklahoma! Jeezus Christ!"

"Unbelievable," Buster says, as Moira steps into view.

"Hey, stick around, Buster. I'll fix another pitcher. Could be worse, you know."

"I gotta run. Larraine is cooking. She's on waivers, you know. I told her to shop around."

"Ha! That's good. You two separated yet?"

"Good as."

"Well, that's tough. Hey. Thanks for coming out and sharing our happiness."

"My pleasure. I have to admit, I was curious. I'm happy for you."

"It's strange all right. I told Moi I had a crush on her. Who wouldn't? Can you believe she had one on me?"

"No."

"Yeah. Love is strange. Moira's going into management, heading up our new blood-testing division. Isn't it amazing how things work out? I'm sure she'll need your help. I'll tell you, Buster. She's hell on wheels, if you know what I mean. I can't keep up."

"They have drugs for that, Henry. Surely you could write yourself a prescription."

"They don't let us do that. But I'll play it *au natural* for a while. I'm not that old. Not with Moira's program, anyway. Ha!"

"Goodbye, Henry. Moira. See you."

Buster takes merciful leave. The door closes on a grin and a smile and Moira's complaint over that kind of talk, until Henry clarifies the situation. "Moira. Everything is working out, if we play like a team, because I don't need him, if I have you around. Get it? He'd be depressed if he won the lottery. We know why he came out, don't we? Just remember: you're better off than Fetteroff. I can make you happy. Twice a day is good, and let's face it; you make things easier just being you—Oh, God. Sooners-Huskers. They *are* listening!"

Sociable people, Henry and Moira, needy but not so different. Buster imagines them as types in the formative years and thinks Henry was plain and quirky, and Moira was plain and pretty, until she filled out. Who knows? They could be a match. Does she know she's not preggers? Does she know she's eating for two and the other one is Henry? She's a pussycat with needs transcendent. Again, no fault in the way of the world, and women who apply natural resources to advantage while they can. Did he get off easy? No. His heart hurts, good for him, and he's married, and nobody gets off easy, and perspective can take a while when a trailhead looks so alluring.

He sorts it out, sensing victory over circumstance. She's not preggers, and the whole charade cost him nothing but brief regrets. It feels like a day at the track on an inside tip and a loss on two bucks to show, or something. The loss is a small price for salvation.

Unless Moira would never grow tiresome. But who doesn't? He looks in the rearview again, one eye squeezed shut, the other bulging over a tongue thrust.

Also coming into focus is Moira, dangling innocently as bait. Henry thinks Buster cannot resist such a delectable morsel and will soon be hooked on a Medicare scheme Buster could only dream of. Could Henry love money more than Moira? More than college football? What a nut. Henry will fade quickly in romance. That should bring her out. Buster is out, or will be out. Meanwhile, she's looking up at a basset hound in a jiggle and a sweat, one eye on the TV, the other seeking his Big Grab Bag o' chips. Ah, well, nobody ever said romance was easy.

At home, Larraine seems more compassionate. She bought fifty-pounds of white rice with an eighth-ton yield, once cooked, for the children. Just add water, bring to a boil, cover and simmer until perfect. Maybe the other women can pitch in with some of that gravy in foil packets. The stuff doesn't go bad, really. He carries the rice bag in, as she debriefs: *Live 5 News* has not yet committed, but the dialogue is underway. "Do you realize how many people actually watch that show?"

"As opposed to theoretically watching? Yes, it's amazing."

She touches him.

"A policeman was here. He wants to see your gun."

"How presumptuous. I have no gun."

"Your toy gun. The one you just got."

"I have no gun. You didn't tell him I have gun, when I don't, did you?"

She shrugs, "Whatever you say, but say it to Lieutenant McCarthy or whoever he is."

"Mumphry. Was he here?"

"I told you that."

"Well, he can bark up any tree he wants. I have no gun."

"Yes, I know. You want to know what else? Duane Dudney's producer has had her eye on this house for ages. She said it would be perfect for a shoot like this."

"Did the cop say anything about Tad?"

"He's stable. Did you hear what I said? Duane Dudney's producer thinks our house is perfect for the shoot!"

"Yes, perfect," he agrees. She steps near. A life together requires communion, and they've fallen short. Yet she seems awakened to satisfaction of one thing or another. Sex is not a solution to life without love, but something is afoot. This is nearly noon instead of sleepy in the wee hours, the regimen that facilitates biofeedback. Most often dismayed with his behaviors, tastes and traits, she lives without spirit, in a bubble of her making, cluttered with stuff. Yet her eyes flutter on a certain current. With no future agreed upon beyond the transplanted tree, some canned goods, a bag of rice and a gray winter day, they grasp the old, frayed rope like thirty years ago on first discovering the swimming hole and swing out and let go, hoping for grace instead of a belly flop.

He wonders if a food drive is so stimulating, or does she imagine a life with no man? Does she doubt her attractiveness or see him anew, a man willing to shoot the fuckwad neighbor? Is a screw meant to loosen her up for the season ahead?. He doubts there's another and hopes not yet.

Fairly relaxed and prone with her hair mussed, she watches him who stole her heart and left it in the garage. She wants to ask why the story between them most often reads with his thoughts, while she is bound to dialogue. But she avoids contentious questions to spare this interlude, so it might play out peacefully, serenely, lovingly.

He thinks a woman who stares out the window is not a complex woman but a depressed woman, but he too stays mum. Salvation is down to the moment, which is all they ever had.

Years ago she told him, "You make love like an old man."

"You mean slow?"

"Yes."

"I make love like me."

This one is slow and reminiscent. So they sense what might survive them.

She cries. He won't intervene; it's the sweet agony that chokes her up. Caressing his face differently than decades ago, she watches him weaken. Soon he snoozes. She rises to dress, to fix her face and dinner. It's his turn, but she feels like giving.

They loll away the late afternoon and dine early with a movie in utter civility, and they retire. Drifting again, he senses a bond that was absent only this morning.

He wakens Sunday morning to hear her downstairs, consolidating flour bags, as the authoress of *Weep No More My Sisters* weeps over her pile driver of a book. When he enters the kitchen, Larraine says fire imagery would make for a stronger title.

"Something like, *Smolder No More My Kotex*?" She laughs, a certain rarity on tasteless humor. She'll meet Duayne Dudney tomorrow afternoon, she says, to see.

"To see what?"

"Oh, skin tone, height, compatibility, that sort of thing?"

"What? He can't go on with a short, vegetarian, non-smoking, lesbian transsexual? Compatibility?"

She responds with industry.

He thinks compatibility is a form of tolerance, the basis of the marital contract, until nullified. But he remains mute on marriage and media mind-control, and says, "You'll do fine."

She ignores him but rises to the morning kiss, a thank you, perhaps, for an excellent screw to validate her desirability and a lovely evening of no bickering, to pacify these trying times. She lingers, lips on his, like she did at the outset long ago, when an extra moment could carry the day. Mature couples don't do that. But something seems afoot. Ms Better Lawns & Living Rooms is remembering something. With his eyes easing shut, her hubby for all time to date remembers it too.

This is not sexual but marital. Is love so ironic that it must taunt a man to bring him home to his senses? She moans, whether for bygone times or love gone away or what might come to pass is conjectural on a simple embrace.

Buster stares out the window, as Larraine likes to do. Hardly a man to ponder vagaries, he says, "Where's Tad when we need him?" He wonders what Moira and Henry are up to this morning, by way of securing their future and a playoff spot for the Dawgs, and he laughs. So ends the tender interlude on Sunday. "What's funny?"

"Life is funny," he says.

"You are strange," she says, with a different kind of sigh.

"You knew that."

She smiles, warmly enough to light up the end of the tunnel. "Everything feels so...foolish," she says.

"And then you die."

"That's the problem," she says.

"I didn't invent life and death."

"But you did. I don't mean death. That's easy. It's your chronic...mood that's impossible to live with."

"*My* chronic mood?"

Sunday brunch at the table with polite conversation feels like a truce, and he asks what she fancies in the months ahead. She blushes and looks out the window. She verges on tears, and he rises to clear and wash and wish he'd thought of something else to ask.

So ends the spontaneous revival. Yet they loll another day, and after dinner move again to the sofa for another movie and to bed. This pattern is not restorative but affectionate. It doesn't alter the end of a life together, but at three days and running, it's easier to live.

V

Buck 'n Rumble

Buck Dibble and Lonny Snodgrass are not a club. How can only two guys make a club? It could be one of those lone-wolf clubs like the Dust Devils or the Phantom Wheels. Or the Ghost Spokers, whose members cannot get along, so they ride alone, logging solitary miles. The Ghost Spokers know that riding on two wheels is a singular pursuit with no conversation, but they're a club.

Buck and Lonny ride together but are not a club, because it's plain to see that both Buck and Lonny would rather belly up to happy hour in a half-lit bar littered with ashtrays and empties sooner than pissing on their jackets or riding alone.

These two do not form up as a club in any way, for reasons of self-preservation. Buck and Lonny know the Law of the Road, in which discretion can mean survival. A rider scans both ways, up and back before entering an intersection and by the same instinct throws an eye over his shoulder now and then to monitor peripherals. So the boys avoid the wrath of the clubs, especially the dreaded club. Why stand on your brakes if the road is all wet? No reason in the world.

No, a club can come down on you out of nowhere like life itself making a delivery, which could be your head banging the curb or a broomstick shoved up your ass, so you can sweep up the mess you made.

"Mess? What mess? I don't know about any mess."

Maybe you don't, but you're dead certain to get another inch up the blowhole.

So what? You want to call yourself a club?

No, a club they will not call theirself, for practical reasons. Avoiding complication is easy. They wear no club colors, and that's all there is to it. They can wear the sleeveless denim jacket over the leather jacket like the clubs do. They can piss on their jackets, if they want to, though they have no reason to piss on their jackets, if they're not in a club, and a stray whiff o' piss could well be deemed a frivolous taunt to the spirit of clubdom. Let's say they happened to walk into a place where a stink could be taken as affiliation, and there they'd be, on hostile turf. Then they'd wish they hadn't pissed on their jackets. That confusion is also easy to avoid. It's as easy as not pissing on their jackets, which is much easier than missing their boots.

Most importantly, they must not wear any of the three components of official clubdom: 1) the name followed by M.C., 2) the insignia and 3) the bottom rocker stating the home base. For example, they should not format their jackets or sleeveless denims on back in any way similar to *Dreaded Fellows M.C.* over a skull with barbwire in the eyeholes and dagger blades for teeth and flames out the ears and blasting-cap pimples and so on over Honkaby, BC at the bottom. Or, they should do that if they feel their balls swelling up bigger than their brains, because that's how it is with clubs, as it is in nature: dominance prevails.

But Buck Dibble and Lonny Snodgras don't need to assess cost/benefit of such risk more than once. They agree that between the two of them, they can muster some decent wrath. But let's say they were a club, and let's say they came up with some awesome colors, like, say, uh, let's see, uh, orange and black and this skull, but not just a regular skull, say, a Canadian skull with, uh, how about eyes shaped like maple leaves, all bloodshot with smoky numbers in them that say *76¢*, which is all a Canadian dollar converts to below the line, which really pisses them off. Beyond that they could have some barbwire and daggers and flames and stuff and feel pretty damn good in expressing themselves with proper piss and vinegar, officially sanctioning them as a club in accordance to the Law of the Road, sanctioning them as well to drink in the bar of their choice and demand first dibs on the leg of the their choice, as long as they can whip any challenger.

But then what? What they would get then are nonstop challenges from every outfit around: dominants, punks, transients, you name it. Until you tooth and nail to the top, the riffraff come at you so hard and heavy you'll need to leave town to get a drink in peace. In that melee, strange leg will seem like something you had time and energy for a long time ago, in your youth. It comes down to potshots from genuine bad guys and wannabe's on every turn. Who needs that, when the alternative is a belly-up for a couple cold ones and a few smokes and talk about how it used to be and how it was only a few nights ago, with the speed and the curves and beer and so on?

So Buck and Lonny are not a club. They simply ride together, because a rider likes another rider alongside for the intra-personal experience, to share the vibe and know that someone else is seeing and feeling the same thing and can back you up later, recounting your exploits and amazing feats with the other guy right there giving the nod to any outburst or doubt or accusation that you're full o' shit.

All else being equal, they're like a club, which likeness remains unspoken for discretionary reasons. If pressed, they can agree on calling themselves a faction, but not a club. Never a club.

Factions don't have names and don't need names, but just between themselves, Lonny Snodgrass and Buck Dibble tacitly agree by way of practice that they are known as *Us Two*. What the hell.

They agree that waving to oncoming riders is bogus, and they wave to no rider, no matter what. Club riders don't wave. What, would a Dreaded Fellow go through living hell, getting beat up every day, pissed on, starved out and thoroughly humiliated, so he can wave to every candy ass with stock pipes and tour packs coming at him? Any rider can feel the answer to that one in his bones: No.

Such restraint isn't always easy for Buck Dibble, who's no gadabout but often waves back if waved upon, especially in spring, when the pent-up juices and chronic twitching of winter get ventilated like no tomorrow. Hell, he'll wave to a roadkill chipmunk or a weekend warrior either one, once things warm up. Of course, enough is enough, so you stop waving by late morning, but then some silly-ass insurance agent and his wife come at you on a Goldwing Honda with pinstripes and a Teddy bear bungied on back and pulling a trailer, and they wave, like you and them are asshole buddies from way back. Who do they think they're kidding? But Buck has a hard time holding out on the half-nod. What the hell.

Not Lonny. "Those guys make me sick," he says. Besides that, what's painfully obvious to both Buck and Lonny is the difference between them and the weekenders. It frankly seems unfair that two real riders like them have to exercise caution to avoid the wrath of the clubs, especially since anyone can tell the difference between them and the white-collar crowd, whose values go south from nine to five, Monday through Friday, who put more clicks on an elevator than a motorcycle, whose shirts are starched and whose biggest fear is outliving their money. Fuck. Buck and Lonny would have been dead a hundred times over and a long time ago if they had to croak before every time they ran out o' dough. It's not right.

Buck and Lonny would cringe at the term *lifestyle* applied to them, because that word is for pussies who have no life, except for kissing ass all day long, trussed up in a monkey suit and a choke rag behind windows that won't open. Then they go home to their posh digs and pay with credit cards for adventures at retail outlets.

Another word comes closer to the bullseye, where Buck and Lonny are concerned: commitment. Go ahead and use it in the context of the contemporary romantic relationship, if you want to, because this is love. This is life, no style required. Come on: What's the point of ape hanger handlebars and forks stretched to the next county, if you're waving at Goldwingers? Hell, it's just as bad anymore with Harley Davidsons, all these shirts with their conchos flopping and massive chrome and five to seven grand on average in boutique accessories, like your official genuine leather Harley Davidson steamer trunk with chrome billet mounting brackets and chrome billet mounting bracket screws and chrome billet mounting bracket screw washers and bolts. What do they think; this is supposed to be sparkly? Or wholesome? Do they think getting trussed up like Clint Eastwood in *Silverado*, where he was this closet tough guy who wore a canvas raincoat, will make them just as tough? Or maybe this is the movie starring them that they imagined all along? Canvas raincoat? Fuck. Motherfucker hung down below his knees.

Fuck.

No, some behaviors are clearly wrong, and others are clearly right. For another example, it's not for nothing that club riders often have nicknames for so long nobody remembers their real names. A nickname lets people know a man for something and might just let him beat the machine that knows everything. In time, nobody knows his name, because he won't have one. Anyone can play the name game and doesn't need to ride with a club to ride outside the law, which is not to say to ride like an outlaw, because they're a club, the Outlaws, which this is not. But besides the easy cover against "legal" oppression, a nickname can feel better too. Hell, look at all the Blacks who'd rather be called Kunta Kinte than Harry Washington Green.

Lonny Snodgrass is not Black, but growing up with a name like Lonny Snodgrass can leave a man sensitive to smirks from others. In Lonny Snodgrass's case, his name has left him a might quick on the draw. "What the fuck'd you say, motherfucker?" His eyes have done the asking ever since he felt his balls swell up big enough to shut that noise down. Well, to shut it down most of the time, anyway. They smirk no more, most of them, and when they do, it's not because of the sound of Lonny Snodgrass, because he goes by Rumble now. He wants Buck to come up with a nickname, but Buck can't figure out what's wrong with Buck. "It's your real name!" Lonny whines to no avail. Or rather Rumble whines to no avail. "They got it on record! You want to play into that shit?"

No. Buck does not want to play in, but he does kind of like the easy roll of Buck 'n Rumble, and he can't think of a nickname, because Buck is a nickname. His real name is Abernathy, but no way will anyone pry that one loose. Abernathy Dibble? Oh, man. Can you imagine? Buck knows plenty of nicknames, but they've all been used, like Crash and Coyote and Hoot Owl and Hawk and Sprocket and all those good ones. When he finally breaks down and sees a doctor for his hemorrhoids and has to wear support briefs made out of that Ace Bandage stretchy stuff, Lonny says, "There you go. We'll call you Spandex."

Buck smiles. He likes the sound of it. Spandex suggests modern times, with agility and all that stuff, until Lonny vetoes his own motion. "Fuck, man. That's a pussy name. Spandex. You want a name with character, not some pussy ass homo shit. Spandex is terrible. You want to be, say, Rebar. There you go. Rebar is strong but pliable. You can bend it, but only with some muscle, and, hey, now we can be *Us Two Rs*. Rumble and Rebar. Hey, Rebar is what they use in concrete. Concrete, man!"

Buck thinks it over, beginning with the slow nod that usually indicates his mind opening. But then going to a shake faster than he could change his mind, he reaches back for a scratch. But he can't reach the itch with a stretch-diaper barring the path. So it's down with the chaps and pants to get to the Spandex briefs and down with them too just to reach the spot that's driving him mad. No, Spandex won't work, not for the rhoids or for a name, and frankly, one Lonny Snodgrass is none too sure about a big, dumb, fat fucker working out as a friend when he has to lunge back for an ass scratching every time you get anywhere near to making a point. What the hell is that?

"I hope you're planning to wash that hand before dinner," Lonny says, looking away to avoid undue hygienic concern.

Buck looks off in the same direction at a different objective on the oblique plane. Squinting as if to focus, he feels the soothing vindication of fingernails answering the call of the itch and then dominating the itch and then ending the itch and then trouncing the itch to oblivion for all time. He eases up with better sense, remembering when a chronic itch was more figurative than physical, and scratching it meant finding what waited over the horizon rather than reaching back and digging in.

Hardly over the hill, he's happy to ride the home turf in a two hundred-click radius to satisfy a fifteen-thousand-click annual habit. Your average tourist will ride three or four grand annual, and that's the difference between a rider and a tourist, along with no windows, no doors and no heater. That shit's different too. And no windshield wipers or roof. And don't forget no heater. Now drop down to two wheels instead of four and see who clocks fifteen grand in a ninety-day riding season. Sure, it goes to a hundred fifty days for the hard core. So? Take a hundred fifty days and see what you get.

Horizons still beckon, but Buck mostly stays within his radius. He reaches back idly to scratch another itch. Hell, you grow up;

you learn about simplicity. Buck Dibble can scratch till it hurts, but he eases off, because soon it'll itch again, no matter what. These and other mysteries solve themselves, if a man can give them a chance.

Moreover, total annihilation of the itch can rust the hinges in a big man's gate, inflaming the tender membrane to the point of painful swelling, providing temporary relief but worsening his condition in the long run or the short run. The revenge part turns on him every time, hardly a minute after the sting, when the little sumbitch'll itch like a fire breather yet again, making a grown man wonder if life itself is a series of vicious circles, and how such a pattern ever got started in the first place. The aging process is bad enough with its failures and demands. Worse yet is comprehension of the truth, that benign indifference to natural law can be most sorely felt close to home, practically in his back pocket. The cold hard fact is that nature doesn't give a shit what part of you shuts down or that you get stiff in the back more often than the front. And he laughs at himself. Who needs an itch up the ass with no sense of humor?

Such is the changing face of reality and the pain of hemorrhoids. Buck Dibble's dilemma is that his rhoids remain unsprung. Time and again he triumphs over the treacherous itch by ignoring it, only to learn the ephemeral nature of victory. His nemesis invariably returns, turning him in a quick twist. A man who thinks he doesn't care will soon be cured of indifference, even as he digs in with four fingers and a vengeance. That satisfaction is brief.

"These damn pants got to go," Buck says, checking his fingernails but not for what Lonny suspects. He checks for blood. Blood out the ass is bad and can kill you. Well, it can mean you're a big step closer to dying anyway. Not that Buck Dibble is afraid, but given his druthers, he'druther have a chance to show courage against, uh, say the worst rain storm ever, with hail and wind gusting like roundhouse lefts and rights and big old fucking trucks coming at you and up from behind, and it's night, pitch dark on a mountain pass that just won't quit, and sheer drop-offs and no place to pull over.

He'd face something like that much sooner than blood out the ass.

He burns for a while, readjusting for comfort until the flames subside. Then he itches. Then he scratches again, but more lightly this time, sitting back now to remove his chaps and boots and pants and those damn Spandex briefs that won't even let a man scratch his ass without damn near burning his butt hole worse than a blowtorch. Hell, no underpants are better than these.

Damn.

Lonny Snodgrass considers *Preparation H* as Buck's road name. But as easy going as Buck Dibble can be, his height and girth and raw poundage make him a man to respect, or least a man not to be fucked with. So for the time being, it looks like Buck 'n Rumble. What the hell.

VI

Hobarth Grimes

His friends most often call him Grimy, though they're more associates than friends, members of a loose-knit social circle. Grimy is not a flattering name, but then Hobarth Grimes is a man who fares best against the grain. That is, he's at home in a slight, at ease with the unseemly, flattered by the unflattering. Grimy is a name to fit his need and aptly puts him in the nitty gritty, where he lives and breathes. Hobarth Grimes knows about soap and water but defers to practicality, just as some men don't make their beds; sumbitch'll only get messed up again in a little while.

Hobarth Grimes washes up when more dirt seems days away, which makes for rare washing, because Grimy Grimes lives for the road on a scooter that chugs with original muscle, a shovelhead, on which the loving wrench is applied often as not. Keeping torque specs to minimal tolerance of optimum performance is second nature by now. Grimy gets it right by the sheer feel of the resistance. Second nature comes from years of intimacy with the machine. Where an observer might see a greasy mitt grasping a ratchet, Grimy would feel the frictional communion, gut to cosmos, and get it right, so that goosing the throttle can spring him out of the hole from fifty to eighty in one easy heartbeat and shoot the slot with room to spare. Grimy knows what he'll get from a simple give. Some people call his ride ratty, but it suits him. He knows in his calloused heart that if a steamroller could fuck a dragster with a twiddle of Hobo spunk in the mix, his scooter would be the blessed offspring.

Some call him Hobo, which rolls off easy as Grimy and makes no difference to HG, six o' one 'n half-doz o' the other. He's as much hobo as grimy and doesn't give a flat flying fuck what you or the rest of your crowd has to say, think or feel about one single motherfucking iota on planet Earth, if you catch his drift.

Then again, the Hobo handle can tweak the dark side of social innuendo, like when Matt Grub, which everyone knows isn't his real name, gets a full-blown head cold and yells over the crowd one early evening at The Fuzzy Glo Room, "Here cubs fuckid Hobo with a fuckid wretch id his pocket. Or baybe he's just glad to see us!" Everyone knows it's Matt Grub's head cold that makes him talk that way, and no one thinks twice about Matt's ebullient good cheer on account of the nasal sprays, beer and decongestants. But then everyone guffaws, except for one person, who would be Hobarth Grimes, himself, because that line about being glad to see the boys with something swollen in his pocket and then translating the line from nasal encryption could easily sound like *Here comes fucking Homo with a fucking wrench in his pocket*, and so on, which will not do under any circumstance whatsoever.

Some call HG a hothead who's way out of line when he pulls a pistol from his jacket and shoves the barrel up Matt Grub's nose and announces a surprise inspection for mud skids, which means Matt Grub has to pull his pants down right now to check for shit stains, which will show everyone the level of fearlessness on hand or otherwise prove the chickenshit nature of the accuser. Of course, neither Matt nor anyone wants to drop his drawers in front of friends, even if he's confident that a cold barrel up his nose didn't loosen any squirts, or even if the taint streaks in his skivvies are worn in from years of usage and not fresh. But the alternative is getting his brains blown out by Hobo Grimes, or whatever you want to call him.

Matt calmly replies that he doesn't know what hair is pulling on Hobo's ass, but his pants won't be coming down anytime soon, because he has a cold and can't stand the chill. This gets everyone laughing, until humor fades to a lingering chuckle. The situational murmurs and awkward silence underscore Grimy's point, that this ain't no joke; he's no homo, and no man can suggest said alternate sexual preference without facing his maker, up close and personal. So Grimy holds the barrel up flush to the nostril for a long half minute before he eases off the grimace that signals his name brand of rough mercy and so much as says, *I'll let you off this time, you mealy mouth grub fucking piece o' shit, but next time....*

He keeps the barrel jammed up Matt's nose, which doesn't affect Matt's labored breathing, but some nasal residue does roll down toward the chamber. Nobody peeps lest they cause poor Matt's demise.

Satisfactorily restored to proper perspective, Hobo eases the hammer down and sticks his pistol back in his jacket. Then he nods to the bartender and murmurs, "Whiskey." It's a scene often seen in those cheap guinea movies Clint Eastwood made about ugly guys and a few dollars, but this is no weekender posing as a wild west cowboy, because Hobarth Grimes is about as close as a man can come to the real item. He doesn't say what kind of whiskey or what brand, because understood is that the cheapest shit rotgut rye in the house will jump start your heart and grow hair on your palms, if you're man enough to take it. Let that song and dance play out for the consideration of who's glad to see whom.

And play out it does for the few seconds it takes Matt Grub to gob up a hefty loogie from way under his tonsils, then snort back the residual sinus sludge to go with it and ball it up over some decent compression and loft it in a lazy arc that misses Grimy by less than one red cunt hair and splats on the foot rail where it rolls down and swings like a skinny little monkey with orange and green fur.

A few onlookers gasp at the heart-stopping margins between the foot rail and a major shoot out. All eyes hit the loogie for the drama to play out there, but it won't. It plays at eye level, where Matt Grub has plucked his own piece and thrusts it in a line shot to Hobo's nose for a *quid pro quo* in cold, blue steel.

Matt sniffles and says, "Sue-praz, sue-praz, you piece o' shit fer braids. Dow let's see who's trackid the bud."

Well, it's a showdown. Nobody expects Hobo Grimes to drop his drawers any sooner than Matt Grubb did, but Hobo smiles big enough to show a fearsome display of failed teeth. He nods again to the bartender and again sideways to his old friend Matt Grubb. Then he turns to Matt with the barrel still pressing his nose and says, "You'll have a drick with be, woh't you Batt?" Another chuckle down the line and another easy click of the hammer lets the rotgut flow. Hallelujah, brother, they'll talk this one up for a while.

And so they do, until the rotgut burns in the center of the chest and sloshes hard near the top of the stomach, where the doctor told Hobo his reflux malfunction originates, or some shit like that. Ninety fucking dollars to find out his stomach burns? Fuck, man; *I* told *you* that. *You* give *me* ninety fuckin' bucks.

Well, it burns, but a man has to drink with another man after an exchange of wills powerful as cold, blue steel up nose holes, because nothing but a thorough display of mutual respect with a few drinks can soak the embers between them.

Hobarth Grimes feels that three drinks ought to seal a truce if not renew the friendship. The evening is now adequately removed from guns and threats to suffice for a lasting peace, until next time. Then again, ducking out short can send a wrong signal and leave some embers too near the kindling or, worse yet, the fuel jug. But another round o' rotgut feels equally incendiary.

The old fool in the loud shirt walks in and takes the stool next to Hobo Grimes like it's just another empty seat and not the hottest seat in the house. Hobo lets it pass, because the geezer might facilitate a graceful exit too. He's not a regular but looks familiar, or maybe it's the smell on him that hits you worse than plaids going cross diagonal to stripes. Well, it takes all kinds, and a man smelling like last year's hash pipe draws all eyes in a fair radius. He orders a root beer.

"Root beer?"

The old fucker looks up to Hobo Grimes and takes in Matt Grubb too with a goofy grin and says, "I can get some now. I got some if you want it."

Matt Grubb bends way under the bar to snuk a fresh load out the nose hole that works. He tests the other side on a wishful thought, but no, the other side stays plugged. He rises, dragging a sleeve under his nose with his own goofy grin, asking how much and if a man might try a sample. Easing back a half step in polite accommodation to emerging discourse, Hobo Grimes scans the tables, as the old guy rambles about hundred proof, the finest money can buy, all or none "'Cause I can't be fucking around. Ten pounds, five kilos, whatever you want to call it, don't make a pinch o' shit's difference to me." Reaching into his shirt pocket he flips a chunk of dirt onto the bar and says, "Go on ahead and try her out, if you want to, if you ain't some durn tire kicker but know how to spend money like a man who's got some money to spend."

Matt Grubb picks up the sample for a look and feel if not a smell, as Hobo Grimes steps back. Respecting the privacy of two associates with business to conduct, he retreats. "'Scuse me, Matthew. I got my own business just yonder."

"Yeah. Could be a dight for biddess."

So Hobarth Grimes takes his leave from the bar and walks to the table of Rumble Snodgrass and Buck Dibble. He orders another round for these boys, because he knows they're drinking Bud

Light, because Buck Dibble watches his weight and the skinny fucker'll drink anything. "And bring one for me too," Hobo tells the waitress, pausing to check her ass as she walks away.

She doesn't walk away but asks if he'd rather have a pitcher.

"Just bring me what I ordered," he says, waiting resolutely to check her ass on departure.

Hobo hesitates and indicates with a half nod to Lonny and Buck that he's about to pull out a chair and sit. When the other two half nod back, he pulls out the chair and sits, making the evening productive, first in dispelling any similarity between hobo and homo; go fuck yourself in the ass with that head-cold bullshit. Second, in burning damn near indelible on every memory here what happens to those who dare to suggest said similarity. And third, in removing himself from the epicenter, so things can play out. Who knows what the evening might hold? "That Missy has a nice ass," he says, settling in. "You know, I go two, three days without some pussy, I need a piece real bad." Hobo keeps his eyes down, until he lifts them for commiseration. "You know what I mean?"

Buck and Lonny nod. "No argument here," Buck says.

"I'd like a piece o' that," Lonny concurs.

"You got to get rid of the pressure," Buck elaborates.

"That shit'll back up into your pores," Lonny says, "make the pimples pop out all over your face; you don't get rid of it."

"Fuckin' piece o' shit," Hobo barks, taking it the other way for no reason; or maybe he's on a new subject. He's staring at where his beer should be by now, if anyone in this flea-bit dump gave a rat's fucking ass about decent service, so maybe that's the subject for now: service. Buck and Lonny stare at Hobo's drink vacancy. They nod in agreement on woeful service and the woefully low odds on Missy the waitress letting any of them sample the wares so blatantly promoted. They further grumble over the woeful cold and wet outside and Matt Grub's terrible manners, pulling a fucking gun like that, and for what?

Grimy Grimes summarizes consensus among the three compatriots: "If that Matt Grub ain't one lucky motherfucker, then I don't know what. I swear. I mean, a man defending his honor is one thing, but impulsive gun pulling is another. Somebody's bound to get hurt, sooner or later."

The woeful nod comes easy to Buck Dibble, who knows how to get along by going along. So why not go along, if it's no sweat off his balls?

Lonny Snodgrass isn't so agreeable by nature, but this circumstance favors t-h-e Hobo, the Grimy one, paragon to those enamored of cross-grain attitude and behavior. So Lonny's noggin pumps too, as Hobo elaborates. "I mean, when you think about it, a loaded gun is a serious fucking weapon. I mean, serious. You know what I'm trying to say?"

"Fuckin' serious," Buck says.

"Fuckinay," Lonny concurs.

Buck and Lonny read each other across the table. Each wonders who in their right fucking mind would splatter doodle fucking tattoos all over himself like the guys in jail do? Those guys can't very well take a two-hour leave down to the tattoo parlor, so they wrap needles and paper clips and shit in thread and dip the works in ink and come up with these squiggly pictures like Hobo's got ass to elbow all over his body, which fairly tells you out fucking loud he's packing heat and doesn't give jack shit what anyone has to say? What's his excuse? Was he locked up for a while? He's tattooed like a NASCAR racer, or maybe more like a Demolition Derby rig, hand painted. You might find *STP The Racer's Edge* under his third shirt along with *Winston, Mobile, Krispy Kreme, MCI, Is This A Great Time Or What?* If Hobo sees it on TV and likes it, he'll find a spot. Hell if he won't.

Hobarth Grimes is a man of reckoning, which makes the nod feel natural on whatever he calls a fuckin' piece o' shit. It most likely is a piece o' shit, whatever it is, because the proof's in the puddin' and the boys have eaten their fair share and then some. Them little scorpions on his knuckles, hiding under the grease and scabs, and all that barbwire wrapped around his neck and running into his beard, and more thorns on his ears than Jesus ought to prove a thing or two. Jesus had those on his ears, didn't He? And them little spiders crawling right out of his eyebrows...wait a minute....

"What the fuck you staring at, motherfucker?"

"Your spiders."

Hobo slaps himself in the face with both hands like Curly Joe. He stands up to fight, if not a knockdown drag out then at least a solid hook back at the motherfucker who threw the Sunday punch. "What spiders? I don't have no spiders!" Hobo flushes red through his residue, but understood is that the red hue is from the impact of his own motherfucking bitch slap and not from fear of spiders.

Lonny shrugs respectfully. "Thought I saw some spiders."

"Don't fuck with me, boy."

"I ain't fuckin' with you, Grimy." Lonny shrugs again and leans back, making way so the pitiful waitress can finally serve the fucking beer. She stretches across the table to serve Buck, which makes Hobo and Lonny lean sideways for the cleavage shot. She leans the other way to serve Lonny, who rises for the superior view at altitude. Buck and Hobo lean over, but she reaches over Hobo's head, nestling his cranium into the vortex. She holds for enhanced service and tips, till Hobo seeks greater contact through said cranium but gets only a playful swat. She straightens with a smile for tip time, and sure enough gets a dollar.

The threesome sit in afterglow, each imagining how such cleavage and that ass might round out an evening.

Hobo Grimes sees her splayed on a workbench, legs hanging over the edge. She can hardly speak, she's so full of gratitude and remorse, but then she hardly needs to.

Lonny Snodgrass sees the top of her head, because she's down at the cleaning station, taking her protein.

Buck Dibble thinks she's the prettiest thing he's seen since sundown, and that's a powerful recollection after three months since the last sundown visible to man or beast this side of the North Cascades. She shows up clear and dazzling, and he wonders if such a woman has ever kissed a big, fat, hairy sonofabitch with a chronic itch up his ass on the lips, a soft, gentle kiss of real love.

They drink soulfully into the evening. Hobo picks up where he left off, and the boys nod again at his claim: fuckin' piece o' shit. Well, if it ain't one thing, it's another, and he soon finds the groove. "Three hundred fuckin' dollars Conlon wants for new paint, but I got a mind not to pay it."

"Is it done? Have you seen it?" Buck asks, since a paint job can't be fairly assessed, until it's done.

"Yeah, I seen it. It ain't right. It ain't what I asked for. It ain't what I ordered, and it ain't what we talked about. Hell, he admitted it come out different than what he thought it would. He says everyone in the shop liked it. Kiss my candy apple fuckin' ass, brother. I don't give a shit what those lacquer-head motherfuckers like. They'd like shit on a stick, if it was dipped in paint thinner."

"Fuckinay," Lonny agrees.

"What's it look like, Grimy?"

"Oh, it ain't bad. I'll ride with it for now. Hell, I have to! Motherfucker tied me up three weeks, so what am I supposed to do, go another three? Fuck, man, that'd shrivel my nuts quicker'n sideways sleet at Gumption Pass."

The boys drink to the conjured scene on the table, sideways sleet at Gumption Pass, colder'n the balls on a brass monkey in January and slicker'n snot to boot and ready to kill you quick with the cliffs and hairpins, the black ice and no shoulder. They've been there. They drink. Buck shakes it off. He hates that shit.

"It's this…. Oh, it's these fucking lines is all, sideways along my tank. They're kind of white and squiggly like lightning, you know. It's not bad, but it's not what we talked about. It's not 3-D enough for one thing. And that's not right for another. I'll ride with it for now, but I got a mind not to pay for it. Or pay less anyway."

"Why didn't you get some flames?" Lonny asks.

"I shoulda. Shoulda just got the fucking flames. You can't fuck up flames."

"Or some skulls," Buck commiserates. "I like those skulls they do." He nods to affirm his preference.

"Three hundred smackeroos. That's some fuckin' money for some squiggly lines," Lonny agrees.

"Not for a paint job," Buck says. "Hell, three hundred's cheap."

"Well."

They drink and ponder, until Missy returns with her pert smile and audacious tits that remind them of what she's packing in front of her taunting backside and renews hope for a personal inspection fore and aft. "You want another round?" She chirps like it's hardly a half-inch between any man here and the Promised Land, if he can come up with the right answer or a big enough tip.

Hobo leans back for a better angle. "You know what I want. What time you get off?"

She throttles down on the bright and cheery and says, "Far as you're concerned, I don't." Fuck you and fuck your dollar is what she appears to be saying, but then she reaches for the empty tumblers with a real eye popper, twisting sideways and half-backward like they do, balancing the tray way outside while clearing to the inside, practically mashing her tits right into the front of her blouse, stretching the buttons so bad that the ache gallops across three chests at once. Smiling sweetly to show she bears no grudge against any man stating what he craves, she leaves for the refill.

"Now that's service," Buck says.

"Some things you just can't figure," Lonny says.

"You know, it's not fuckin' right," Hobo says, watching the inscrutable ass like it's the goddess of truth and beauty.

"Looks right to me," Lonny says.

"Not that. I mean guys like us having to worry over three hundred dollars."

Buck shrugs and laughs, "No offense, Grimy, but I ain't worried."

Hobo hunkers low for what could be the point of the evening or, hell, of the entire season or of this particular phase of life, once you factor your long-term perspective and consequence. "It's like I'm trying to tell you, if you'd just get some Q-tips and clean the shit outa your ears for once, you might learn something instead of being the same old dumb pieces o' shit you always were. You know what I mean?" Hobo pulls his gun and lays it on the table like the hard ass in Maverick used to do before calling the bluff on that shoeshine faggot sonofabitch. "I'm trying to teach you something here. What it is, is that a gun is a serious fucking weapon, like I told you. A serious fucking weapon is a serious fucking tool. Look at yourself. You ever have any money the way you're going?"

Buck looks down for internal scrutiny. He knows he'll have some money, if Lonny ever pays him the two hundred owed since way before Christmas.

Lonny looks yonder and says he's flush with nearly a half case of real Bud and a ham in the fridge and next month's rent *already paid*, leaving what? Bread and mustard? Hell, he's got that in his back pocket, so he'd like to fucking know how much a reasonable man can want past what he needs and maybe a little bit more. Because it's reason that marks a happy man, a man who goes where he wants and does what he wants and gives no quarter nor takes no shit from any motherfucker. "Fuck, man; you want to talk money, I could go home and go to fucking bed and not get up for two fucking weeks fucking straight and the damn phone won't ring once with some fucker looking for his money. Not once!" And a man set up for two-weeks has got it dicked in anyone's book. Lonny verges on overconfidence with a smug grin Hobo Grimes could slap clean to the corner, if he was in any other mood but thoughtful.

"Fuck," Hobo says. "I ain't talking about fucking mustard sandwiches you shitferbrains idiot. I'm talking real money." Hobo hunkers a dramatic inch for the big question, which is not a trick question but one in painful need of a run up the flagpole to see who's paying attention. "You boys want to make some money? I mean some real money?"

"Doing what?" Buck asks.

"How much?" Lonny asks.

"First time I ever broke a sweat working for money, I was nine years old. Hauling sod. Can you believe that shit? I figure right around five thousand pounds of it in eight hours. I worked that job three months, all summer long. Five thousand pounds. Eight hours. Ninety days. Nine years old. Made eight dollars in eight hours. Eight fucking dollars. Trouble is, that was thirty-two years ago, and I ain't got but about a hundred dollars left."

"You worked Sundays too?" Buck asks, getting the quick answer in another cold, hard glare. So he looks down and agrees, "Life'll keep you broke. That's for damn sure."

"Piece o' shit is right," Lonny adds.

Hobo leans back on the hind legs and cranes for the tardy-ass waitress, who seems cruelly indifferent at this point. He eases down and comes back in close. "I'm talking twenty grand apiece, maybe a day's ride, eight, twelve pounds dead weight. Just us three."

"Hey," Lonny says with a grin aimed at Buck. "*Us Three*."

"Aw, no," Buck says, seeing the destination of the dialogue, ignoring the expanded camaraderie, sensing the striped pajamas.

"Twelve pounds apiece or all told?" Lonny asks. "'Cause I can carry a damn sight more'n twelve pounds, so I might want to carry some extra for myself, as long as we're making the trip."

"Naw, no," Buck says.

"I don't know about extra weight," Hobo says. "I can look into it. I got to, you know, find out. You got a point, long as we're making the trip." Hobo nods, savoring the developmental process.

"*Us Three*," Lonny repeats, grinning at the sound of it.

"That's what I said," Hobo says.

"Say, Grimy," Lonny asks, "You ever think about a, you know, a road name?"

Grimy Grimes lets his head sink between his shoulders for the privacy most available there. "I got a name. Got two names. Some of 'em call me Hobo, some Grimy. Listen what else I got...."

"No, I mean a, not a club name but a name, you know, like a road name. A name nobody can trace you to."

Hobarth Grimes stretches to watch the approaching waitress. "You know, she looks as good coming at you. I might work her sunny side up for a while before I turn her over for the basting." He runs his tongue across the fronts of his top teeth to clear the debris, though he hasn't chewed a plug since four and only ate a couple Slim Jims since then, and he'd know if any gristle or cardboard got hung up there. Either one will gross a woman out sure as not.

Lonny gives up on names, so Buck laughs and says, "He ain't even paying attention to you, Lonny. Call him Ozone, you know, 'cause he's spaced out."

"Here's your pitcher," the waitress says, spilling an ounce or two, setting it on the table but compensating with an even more difficult sideways reach that snugs her blouse nicely and this time surpasses the threat to spring a few buttons and actually pops one because it can't hold on any more than a horsefly could hang on to two melons, oh Lord. It's a sight to behold and every bit dramatic as her ass. "That's eight dollars," she says, sure enough scoring nine yet again, even with apparent deficiency in punctuality and respect, which more or less proves the open-mindedness of some men.

These men strike silence at the crux of a delicate transaction. They wait for the wipe-up, the change and a curt thank you. They stare in her wake and agree again speechlessly on the quality combo: nice tits *and* nice ass.

"Ozone." Hobo tries it on for size, sliding his chair back so the legs screech, as he stands with an uncharacteristically pleasant smile. "I like it. 'N'at way nobody'll know it's me."

Buck and Rumble look up with expectation if not awe. Hobo nods approval and says, "'Scuse me, boys. I got business here. Save my place."

VII

Opportunity Knocks

Hobo Grimes has had an epiphany. He couldn't have seen it this morning, because it wasn't staring him in the face like it is tonight. It's actually staring Matt Grubb in the face, rambling over a young trout's weakness for maggots, and what gives whiskey its punch, and how they'll steal your scooter if you don't watch out and sometimes even if you do.

Hobo eases in and says, "Hey, Matt, you buying a load of hash?"

"Doe. I ca't eved fuckid breathe! What'd I do with hash? Fuckid Dyquil's got be looped tighter'd a dud's cut to begid with. Or baybe it's to ed with for all I doe. I feel shot at add bissed add shit at add hit, if you doe what I bead."

"How much you want, old timer?"

"Well, it's like I told this fella, it's all or none, don't make a pinch o' shit's...."

"I asked you a question, old man."

"Ten, twelve pounds."

"I asked you how much you want."

"I reckon, say, a thousand."

"A thousand what?"

"A pound. What the fuck you think, Junior? Didn't you go to school? Goddamn, they grow'em dumb around here."

Matt Grubb laughs through a nose blow and a wipe, offering his unsolicited opinion that the geezer is about to get the best of the nitty gritty man. Every person in the place and few more besides has seen Hobo Grimes cold cock a bigger sonofabitch for hardly as much lip. But what can Hobo do, punch an old man? Besides, this geezer's got class. Well, maybe not class, but style. Style might not be right either; maybe it's just balls. Old fucker doesn't give a shit about the roundhouse radius. He dishes it out.

But Hobo has more important time to keep than an easy clock cleaning might provide, and besides, the crusty fart stinks like a skunk turd. "I want to try some. You got a sample?"

"I do," the old guy says, plucking the dirt from Matt's shirt pocket and dropping it into Hobo's. Hobo picks it out and smells it. "It ain't been through a rabbit, if that's what you're thinking."

"I'll check it out and see if I can, you know, line things up."

"Stick your head up your ass and check that out. Fuck, yeah, I know what you want to do! You want to see if you can sell it before you buy it. That's what I shoulda done. But I wasn't smart as you. That's okay. But don't go trying to sell it to the wrong people or you'll fuck us both up."

Hobo Grimes is sorely tested not to strangle this ugly fucker. Who the fuck does this ass wipe think he's talking to, some kind of fucking dumbass chickenshit motherfucker? "I know that, dumb shit. Who the fuck you think you're talking to?"

"Who you calling dumb shit?"

"You, dumb shit. I'll see you in a day or two."

The old man looks puzzled and asks, "Tell me one thing, professor. Is it a day. Or is it two?"

"Hard to say," Hobo says. "How long does it take a old fart to go get his load? Now if you'll excuse me, I got other business here."

"Yeah, you got business. Monkey business. Might be the only way a fella like you's gonna come up with twelve grand."

Hobo steps up, toe to toe. "It's ten grand, old man. You ought to be careful with your numbers, leastways till you're done with me."

"Oh, I'll be careful. You be careful too. Don't want to read about you in the newspaper; halfwit sells hash to mounted police."

Grimy Grimes holds a snarl to establish dominance—and consequence, should the slack-jawed fool utter one more peep. Then he turns with equal deliberation to his associates back at the table. He moves with the same dramatic flourish of James what's-his-name in that one with the woman with the big old floppy tits who had that saloon but wouldn't put out for any of them but him, because he had balls enough to walk away slow, like he didn't give a rat's fucking ass about anyone shooting him in the back, because they wouldn't, because he was just that bad that he'd get up from dead on the floor to beat shit out of anyone in need of it.

Hobo returns to the business confab ready to change three lives from suffering the loose slag and potholes of poverty. It just don't seem right for a man to scrabble hand to mouth ever since when and on into the future with no account whatever for who he is or what he's done. The alternate route now opening is the high road, which a man needs to see and sooner or later take, if he wants to part company with the rest of the knuckle busters. "You need the balls, but it won't get you shit without the brains. Anyone can plug theirself in to what they got, but they won't. Look around; you think these bozos'll change? Hell, no. But we will. Why shouldn't we?"

Neither Buck nor Lonny feel the need to ask Hobo what the fuck he's talking about, because he's fairly wound up and should reach the meat and potatoes any time now. Or the bran and the raisins—no, that was the brains and reasons. Both Buck and Lonny also feel that no matter what, the evening might be shaping up historical. When's the last time anybody heard Hobo Grimy Grimes wax philosophical on the path not yet taken and success? Standing on its throat and taking by God your rightful share?

A walk out back with a makeshift, beer-can pipe secures the near future. The hash is the real item and then some, not too paralytic but fuzzy like a sweater, fluffing the boys to high cozy with coherence hardly hampered. With a crackle here and a stray spark there, this hash is so good, it lets you keep talking and wouldn't make you worse for wear no matter how much you smoked. Hell, you could smoke this stuff all night if you wanted to. But they run out, which is how it goes and just as well, what with important business and the future on the table.

"You got any money," Grimy Grimes asks the general company, who stare into the night as if nobody spoke. "Well. We need ten grand. Ain't shit, when you think of it."

Back at the table, the long term fills in. One pitcher leads to another and so on and so forth, and hardly a shake, three friends have smoked and soaked happy hour to witching hour. A half dozen relief breaks ease the pressure and a Jumbo Supreme with Everyfuckingthing and double chovies quells the hunger.

Missy the waitress hardly minds when Lonny asks, "What's the hardest part of a sex change operation?"

She learns that it's sewing in the anchovies and laughs and asks back, "Are the only anchovies you ever get to taste on a greasy fucking pizza in a dump like this?"

The question drops a jaw or three, and the boys have to respect a woman with grit like that, and they do, except for Lonny's concern that she might doubt his record on the pussy-eating issue. It's impressive, and people shouldn't think otherwise, but he lets it go, because, hell, everyone is laughing, even Hobo.

Missy warms a notch in a few more rounds, realizing that a dollar a go adds up better than three bucks at the end, which is what some cheap bastards try to pull. She gets off at midnight and moreover shares so much personal info, like the general vicinity of her home and her acquaintance with a guy who Buck went to trade school with, that she seems likely to offer the contents of her underwear as well. Lonny thinks three dollars a round would do it and pledges to lay it down, if he can be sure she'll reciprocate. But neither Buck nor Hobo can make such assurance, because it's not up to them. So she only gets a dollar a round.

But then it seems like a fair chance with the bigger smile and saucier swagger in response to the most suggestive innuendo. She seems natural as a heavyweight soaking up punches in the later rounds. Oh, she's a looker at the peak of womanhood, when an extra thirty pounds is nothing but beautiful and gives a man some handles to grab while the wild rooster rides.

Besides that, three dollars shrinks proportionately as success in business gains momentum, once the conceptual horseshoe clangs the imaginary steel post. Discovering the plain blind luck before them, they move to detailed planning and fine-tuning to perfection. The plan is simple: buy low, sell high. Make that very low and very high. Why the fuck not? And why didn't anybody think of this sooner? Then again, reality doesn't get easy until you stumble through an opening like this one.

Hobo explains that most motherfuckers take for granted what they do best. Call it low self-esteem or the curse of the working class, because you get some shirt who can't do shit but yammer on the phone all day, saying ignorant shit like absolutely and win-win situation. Motherfucker'll talk about moving forward on the ground, and the lame-ass piece o' dog fuck calls himself a technician of modern times. He'll ride high in unscuffed leathers, like a dude for all seasons and worse yet, he'll call himself a biker once he drops a few grand on the lined chaps with the chrome studs, the eight-hundred dollar jacket, the heated vests and gloves, the hand and ass heaters and the hot chocolate jug with the chrome mounting bracket and boutique emblem. Fucking dipshit'll make no bones about knocking down fifty, sixty grand a year. And for what?

Yet a man who busts his chops to get a damn thing fixed—that's fixed right and fixed to stay fixed, which often as not means fixing it twice and three times, well, the shirts look down their nose at his sorry ass. As if value should accrue only to he who shuffles some fucking paper, as if a bunch of fucking shirts could keep the world turning. They can't.

And once you see what's holding you down and how you can merely pick up what's yours off the table, why, three bucks is laughable. It's shit! And what's a fulsome gal like Missy Malone supposed to do, lay back and spread 'em for a dollar a round?

Lonny Snodgrass has seen it before and plenty: the flirtatious lilt and blossoming beauty of a waitress who goes from a solid four to an iffy six by nine. She'll break eight by eleven and clang the fucking bell, a ten by twelve. It's only been a few hours and a few gallons of beer, but it approaches the long, cold night ahead.

Every man accounted for hopes she won't drop back down to a point or two under where she started, once the sun comes up. She'll be three inches shorter then, barefoot and with no denim to smooth her ass over, so all those beautiful extra pounds will feel the gravity of a brand new day. Dimples sprung like eddies over catfish tell you there's some heft lurking below the surface. With her hair mussed and the make-up smudged, she'll look worse'n a windshield after two hundred clicks of mayflies. You can't see where you're going with this, and she's breathing on you worse than the landfill access road, and you can't wait any longer so you let one rip that's been cooking all night, and she sits up on that note, exposing you to the stink and cold, and she wants to know, "Where's my bra?" She groans like an old door, bazoombas bouncing off her belly and her coming in close for a morning smooch....

Get the fuck away, will you? I'm sleeping here.

But worse than all the negative potential above is the solitary reality that she'll vanish into thin air or out the back door once her shift is done. *Fuck us, is what she's thinking*, Lonny thinks when she beams blissfully and stuffs another three bills into her apron.

Yet he thinks again, not five minutes after midnight, *Well I'll be damned*, when she comes out of the kitchen in a new blouse without the apron and looks every bit delectable as she did ten minutes ago, savory as a hot buffet, freshened for the late shift with clean linen. She's standing up straighter, accentuating her high points, which stay accentuated when she sits down like she's been saying she would do all night, once she had a minute, which she didn't till now.

Hobo Grimes is a cool breeze, full of shit as the next road dog and hardly able to hide his surprise, but he tries. "Hey," he welcomes his presumptive date to the table. "*Now* how we gonna get some service?"

"I can get us one more. What do you guys want? Is it time for shots?" Six eyeballs bounce off the bumpers asking who'll pay for this one, and what the hell is she driving at now?

But Hobo takes the lead, because he's obviously the man with a stake in the situation, and everyone knows that a woman drinking is a woman priming the pump. Setting an example of confidence for all the success and prosperity waiting round the bend, he calls, "Hell yes, make 'um doubles!"

To which she says, "I'm ready," and marches off for the drinks, real drinks. She returns quickly with six doubles, one each for the boys and three for herself in a most impressive line up. This is not the rotgut rye that opened the evening but tequila, house brand maybe, but still a leg up. "I won't drink them all at once," she says. "But it's last call, and that's the same as now or never with Harry behind the bar. It's not really now or never, but it's now or tomorrow. He's an asshole. Mud in your eye." She toasts all around, growing more beautiful on each sweet syllable. The three men stare, imagining her naked as she drinks, each in his way. She slams the first and then drops back to a dainty, delicate pace, sipping the second as if for the taste. No one asks for lemon or salt, because.

The boys are reeling and rocking, not rocking and rolling but fore and aft and side to side. Missy fills her first empty glass with beer from the last pitcher to refresh her palate. Then out of the blue, which is apparently where she comes from, she says, "I'm so sick of these tattooed toothless wonders thinking that all a woman wants is to get up next to their hairy ass."

"Well," Buck ventures, unable to look directly into her beauty and feeling singled out for the obvious condition of his ass and perhaps fearing further indictment as a man with chronic itching too. "What's a woman want?"

"Plenty!" she says, easing up with a playful smirk. "But not so much, really. Okay, here's a trick question. Who knows a love sonnet?"

"What?" Hobo asks, since questions on love are his to field, since it'll be him and Missy pumping the jam here in a bit, after all. "How do you know if love's on it?"

"That's not it," Buck says.

"It's a fuckin'... a fuckin' poem," Lonny says. "I knew that."

"Whoop de do," Missy says. "I didn't ask if you knew what it was. I asked if you knew one. And it's not a fucking poem. It's a love sonnet." She turns to Buck. "Do you know one?"

Buck blushes deeply in proximity to such power and the numbing knowledge that she'll never in a million years take the fat ass of the litter. Hell, she could have her pick of the place, which may not be much better, but hell, she could head down the road to any place she wanted and walk through the door and point her finger and say *You*, and get herself horsefucked till sunrise. Hell. Then again, Buck Dibble's deep hue could well be an embarrassment of a different color. The question on the table tempts another revelation.

"Does he know a love sonnet?" Lonny too wants to know, "So? Do you?"

Raising an eyebrow and looking away, Buck lets his tablemates deduce what he knows, as he mellifluously intones, "How lovely are thine thighs."

Neurons surge in Hobo's eyes, like he's locked the back wheel on his brain and nothing else but holding it tight in the skids will avoid a high side flip to the ditch. "What the fuck," he mutters.

Lonny laughs at his apparently worldly friend, big Buck Dibble, the Buckmobile.

Missy brightens, like Buck got it right. She lays a hand on his and asks, "What is it really, Buck?" She speaks his name softly as sunrise in July, which sweetness and light raises goose bumps fine as blow-by mist off scorched rings.

Looking down and breathing hard as a blown manifold, Buck grumbles, "How lovely are thine eyes."

Hobo laughs with scorn and then laughs again, in case anybody didn't get it the first time.

Lonny follows.

But Missy brightens to high noon and says, "Yes. That's it. You win. I'm going home with you."

Buck stops breathing to look up and see what snakes wriggle between her ears. He can't birddog Hobo Grimes, nor can he let a piece of tail poison the future so affably developed these last few hours. Then again, this isn't any piece but a rarity *in extremis*, and though no man should view any female as once-in-a-lifetime, Buck knows down deep that this frequency projection may well prove accurate. But then, how can Missy the waitress, who every rider in a hundred clicks wants to bag, get down with him? He's so overweight, and his rhoids are real as Harvey the giant bunny. He could get some rubbers in the men's room, but hell; home is a mess with the dishes and stuff and no sheets. He could keep the lights low or maybe off, but every woman wants sheets. Peering tentatively sideways, he knows she's real, unless she's another cruel dream....

"Gotcha," she says, pouncing on the mournful lull. "But you see what can happen if you ditch the bullshit and get real."

"How lovely are thine eyes?" Lonny asks.

"Too late," she says.

"So?" Hobo asks. "What the hell can happen?"

"You know what can happen. Come on, boys. We're only human." The boys trade glances. Only human? What the fuck's that supposed to mean? "I gotta go," she says, sensing the impasse. She slams what's left of the second shot and all of the third, gasping admonition, "Don't try this at home." She laughs at her own labored breathing and allows, "No, really, I only live five minutes from here and this stuff won't come on for ten."

And that's that. She rises, turns and exits, looking back at the boys who gaze at what the wee hours hath wrought: perfection in her ass and a perfect sense of loss. Add a dash of agony, and it's a good time for any gal. With a last sweet smile thrown casually over a naked shoulder, she says, "Drinks are on me, boys."

A half minute later the stunning silence will not be broken. Reality is easy to figure, because this one is an old familiar: drunk, stoned, late and alone again. None of these three have fished since realizing the cost/benefit shortfall on the worms, the sniffles, the constipation, stiff neck, frozen fingers and waiting on the one hand, and a piece of fucking fish on the other. Yet all three feel the loss of a lunker at the boat, a beauty played lightly with a soft touch. No muscle here. They'd let her run. She nearly jumped into the boat. Truth be told, all aboard thought she would. They bet on it, three bucks a round.

Hobo finally rises. "Don't forget," he groans.

What should not be forgotten is *not* the fillet that vanished into the depths before their eyes but the greater potential still in reach. Forget the fucking fish is what Hobo means. He goes to attitude, which is all you need, really, to bring home the big 'uns. "You got to *see* what's out there." His eyes go wide and he breathes short, like full throttle in first gear, grabbing for traction on loose gravel. "We saw it a while ago. We need to see it again tomorrow. That's the trick. Keeping your fucking.... Your fucking.... Whatchacallit...your fucking eyes on the fucking thing."

He means the deal on the table may be less tangible than the battered salt and pepper shakers and empty napkin holder, but unlike those items, the deal evolves. The deal shines in a stellar orbit and may sustain life, given attitude and fortitude. It shimmers and lingers and just might germinate with life.

They must see a new sunrise, leading to a golden day, when they'll stuff some knapsacks with dirt like it was hash and ride south across the border to confirm the ease by which raw wealth might be plucked from thin air. "It's called a dry run," Hobo instructs. They won't take the main highway under the Peace Arch because every fucking camel jockey who ever wanted to blow up Seattle takes that route, and three bikers would get a flashlight jammed up their asshole quicker than a border guard can ask business or pleasure. No, they'll take the Ho Chi Minh trail, which is Highway 42 or 91 or one of those go-kart tracks nobody uses.

Below the line they'll find a buyer, maybe some Goldwingers, except that they don't smoke it. Might do better with some Twinkies for those guys. No, best for a hash sale would be some yuppie biker scum with the chrome and doodads and plenty of money to round out their accessories with some real hash, just like the big bad bikers like to smoke. Those guys love anything that makes them look tough, especially if they can buy it. "Too bad we can't take American Express."

They'll set the price at two grand a pound—that would be dollars, U.S., which ought to clear twenty fucking grand with the discount on the front end and the premium on the back.

Buck shrugs. "How do we make twenty grand if it cost ten grand to buy? We only make ten grand."

"The day HG Grimes can't steal candy from a old man is the day I hang up my spurs."

Spurs? What spurs? But Big Buck Dibble only looks aside with a humble nod, accepting the brave, new reality of success. But Buck can't help pressing another issue on account of because it seems bound for pressing sooner or later. "It ain't like I don't want to think about this opportunity, but what do you need us for?"

Lonny swats his arm. "What the fuck, man?"

"I don't," Hobo says. "If I want to fuck the little bitty dog's been nipping my heels all these years, I'd go by my lonesome. If I wanted to shag ten, twenty grand off a scumbag, I'd go alone. But it's like Lonny here says...."

"Rumble," Lonny says.

Hobo nods. "Like he says, any one of us can carry more 'n ten, twelve pounds. Hell, we could run fifty, sixty, seventy. Hell, we could run ninety pounds each, if we wanted to!" HG Grimes is up, and so are the wrinkles on his forehead. Throttling down to sensible speed, he eases back in his chair. "But we won't. Two hundred pounds. All told. I like the sound of it, and that makes the math more easier. We carry the hash on top, you know. Get the money and get the fuck out. And get the fuck in, don't you know. You'll see a few waitresses follow you home then, Buckaroo."

Flashing the biggest and maybe the only grin ever seen on his bristly, smudged face, Hobo Grimes ruffles Buck Dibble's hair. Buck smiles. Hobo assures him it's all within reach. "It won't be your sorry ass reciting homo poetry then. It'll be all them women that's begging for mercy."

So Us Three savor prosperity and social ease, easy as that and bingo, it's the big time. You can retire on two hundred grand. Hell, it wouldn't be but a third of that, but hell, you divide the dollars by the years; you still got plenty. Or the years by the dollars; whatever the fuck. Don't make a pinch of shit either way if you never had more than twelve hundred on any given day of your whole entire goddamn life and called it flush. Fuck.

Bringing the mood back around to serious if not sober assessment on planning and implementation, Hobo Grimes assures his colleagues that nothing is easy. But they see a chance, so this here is a damn site more than the knuckle-busting grunt and grumble of the last ten hours of daylight seen by anyone of these three.

Buck shrugs. "Hell, Hobo. Today wasn't all that bad."

Lonny Snodgrass and Hobo Grimes turn the synchronized stink eye on Buck from north and south. Nobody says will you just shut the fuck up, because they don't need to, because the eyes have it down and dirty, set to go, because it's about motherfucking time.

VIII

On Reviewing the Situation

Most riders think fringe is for girls, or women, except for minor exceptions like handlebar-grip ends and brake-lever and clutch-lever ends. Much more of that stringy, floppy shit makes a rig look like a basket case stuck in a car wash, or an overgrown treble-hook snagged on seaweed, or the bride of Frankenstein during PMS, or one of those pickled dog hearts in a jar with worms crawling out the aortas and ventricles and shit.

A long-miler, with the dings and crud to show for it, won't run fringe down his chaps or sleeves or across his jacket, unless he's a woman or a pussy, which is paradoxical. For one thing, a long-road woman is as rare as a beautiful waitress getting off work and giving the nod for a night of it and then following through with what shouldn't be any big deal. And long-road pussies make about as much sense as road dogs with exquisite good taste, except maybe for the Goldwingers, whose taste is for shit, with their pinstripes, teddy bears and reverse gear, but they do go long distance, some of them. Hell, it's just as bad with the boutique boys on their brand-new Harley Davidsons anymore.

Then again, on the extreme exception, comes the rider who knows his road, his wind and crosscurrents, his buffeting factors and variable-radii curves, knows the exact number of tread grooves pressing lips to asphalt on any given angle. Such a rider knows the physics of rubber and steel from experience, not from school, which was a waste of time anyway. He's a graduate of Highway U with 10W/50 coursing his veins and twelve-volts charging his battery.

It takes a rider like Hobarth Grimes to run the load of fringe he now installs on his scooter and still demand respect. He knows that so many leather strips this thick and long look limp as a mule dick at midnight. Yet he envisions the mule waking up like a rogue stallion, given speed and wind to generate some decent floggage. Stepping back for perspective, he sees his new invention, himself, landed and fringed.

It's too cold for a long ride, especially with some miles coming up in a few hours, but a short ride in any conditions is right for a real rider. A ride lets the action unfold.

The goose bumps freeze in place at forty-five. At sixty they molt to a size up, but Hobarth Grimes warms by the fire in his heart with the beating on his forearms. These dual matched cats o' nine tails hanging a foot and a half from his grips and levers jump to a leather jig. Leather strips flail and thrash him numb, till he murmurs nose to nose at the onrushing cold, "Come on, motherfucker." Like a thoroughbred craving a proper flogging, his lips curl, and he whinnies through gnashed teeth, loping for the stretch at seventy-five as his new whips beat him silly.

Pulling back in through the front door—what the hell; it's only three steps—and into the living room, he considers more fringe, because he can take this beating and then some, daring any man to call him a pussy or even think it and then come on in and join the fun. Then we'll see who's man enough to run fringe.

Turning his five-gallon plastic bucket over quick enough to keep the trash inside, he sits. He sees more fringe here and there, erasing it here and adding it there. This exercise is common to a rider with an eye for extras, a rider who sees a thing in his mind before wasting money on what could be wrong. The new paint job sets a theme, which isn't 3-D enough but isn't bad, considering the discount.

As Hobo Grimy Grimes ponders fringe, Buck Dibble also sits and watches his motorcycle, hardly fifteen clicks away. Buck stares past the machine at the oblique plane of potential. He ponders motivation; why does a rough-and-tumble rider like Hobarth Grimes need partners on a twelve-pound load or two hundred for that matter? It's more fun to have some road brothers along, and long distance can turn tricky, requiring a road brother's help. And two hundred pounds is more than one man wants to carry on back. But certain phrases stick like dog shit to his boots, no matter how he tries to rub it off: *the discount on the front end*, or *steal candy from a old man*. If Hobo is willing to fuck the old guy without a blink, he may well plan to fuck anyone, as necessary, road brothers included. Oh, Hobo'd rant and rave and call the old guy a crooked old coot and hardly the same as a road brother, but then Hobo can twist things around. Buck ponders a test on Hobarth's loyalty.

But what's to test? Hobo Grimes serves nobody but himself.

Preempting this uncertainty is another tricky scenario. *Yes, that's it*, she says again on a playback Buck wishes would stop. *I'm going home with you.* Like a pop tune that won't quit, Missy's little joke pricks his heart. She's a burr in his shorts all right, just having some fun maybe, but it hurts. Buck takes a woman at face value and wonders how much of any joke is based on truth. Sure, he knows what she sees, Which is mostly his age and poundage. Every year sets a man farther out from the Promised Land, up to two-forty already, which would be okay if he'd grow taller and shed wrinkles at the same rate, but he won't. He only hauls the heavier load at five-eleven, well, nearly five-twelve in his boots.

That's not exactly fat, and a seasoned man can still romance a younger woman in her prime. You see it on TV, maybe not so often, because most of them fancy pants fuckers on TV are thin, unless you count the comedians. Buck isn't so quick with a joke, and the fatties who get the beauties are rich or smart or both; and they don't lunge for their itchy assholes any time of night or day. Unless they do and don't show it on TV, which seems unlikely. They probably get the best medical treatment too, because they're rich. Then again, what could a asshole job cost?

Sometimes it plain pays off to sit and sort stuff through, like now, when Buck Dibble pledges to shed a few pounds starting right after breakfast, since the toast is already buttered, the bacon's damn near done, and it's hardly a half shake to throw the over easies on there and call it the best hangover helper on God's green earth. Or gray, which is what it looks like out there. He pledges as well to see about a asshole job. How much could it be?

In the meantime, it might be a gray day, but it's a brand new motherfucker, so what the hey? It'll warm up to decent riding temperature in a while, or bearable temperature anyway, so he could swing by her place. Stopping by might be awkward but would clear the air on who wants what and doesn't mind waiting till tonight or next week or three months, if this is the genuine article. He knows women on TV complain most about it not being the genuine article, but Missy Malone is not your average TV personality. The l-word could spook her in a blink. Why should she give up the ultimate power for the likes of Buck Dibble? Not that she'd need to give it up, or that a romance would lead to happily ever after, but still. It's a mystery of nature, how beautiful women hate to tie up like that.

Maybe going by with flowers would be good. Most women are weak for flowers, but then flowers might be too much too soon. Flowers might spook her. Making intentions too clear would only set things up for rejection and despair. He knows where she lives and knows she wouldn't shoot him down like some of them would. She'd let him down easy, but down could still be all she'd let him, and you don't outgrow the bang at the bottom. Motherfucker hurts. No, he'll wait till he sees her and can take a read on her warmth and level of loneliness. Maybe he'll ask how she's doing, and that's all it'll take.

Or maybe he'll ask if she'd like to, you know, go for a ride or something, except that a ride might have to wait a few months for things to thaw out so she won't freeze her fucking ass off.

He ponders her frozen ass and imagines himself blowing warmth on it or pressing his cheek to it to make it feel better. He considers the long odds that she also suffers hemorrhoidal inflammation. He wouldn't wish that on anyone, except maybe a few of them, but not on her, but then a common problem could provide common ground to make a match.

She's old enough for rhoids, but he feels in his heart that her asshole is further from the itch than he is from handsome. How could she be so tantalizing with hemorrhoids? Then again, too much time on your feet is a primary cause, so maybe she does. He contemplates a personal inspection and laughs at the idea of spreading her cheeks for a little peek, which is funny, but the rest of the image damn near sends him to the dirty socks pile.

He sits, wondering if another hour of solitude will shape up like the rest of the day, week, month, year and life, with knowing that her asshole, like the rest of her, is fucking perfect. But enough depressing stuff, because this day won't be like the rest. This is the first day of the rest of some shit, whatever Hobo said that sounded like the billboard for the old folk's resort up near Whistler....

Aw fuck. The motherfucking eggs is hard already and not even over. Fuck.

Four more clicks away at Hobarth Grimes' place, another dazed rider sits on his can, sipping yesterday's coffee, or maybe it's the day before's. Lonny Snodgrass doesn't give a shit how old it is, as long as none of that fuzzy stuff is growing on top. He'll nuke it. *Little motherfucker; I'll teach you not to cool off.* He sips quickly so the magic can start working on the pain. Tastes like burned shit, but it won't mean shit with seventy grand coming on like a semi drifting over the double yellow on a blind curve. Maybe it's more like sixty-five grand, but that goes to more and more in no time, not that Rumble Snodgrass would ever become a shirt, but he aims to make scads 'o dough like they do, picking up the phone and softly ordering some punk on the other end to buy this or sell that, motherfucker. Hell, the dough'll have to go up to more and more. A new scooter runs twenty grand, make it thirty after tax, tags and dealer tribute. And don't forget the replacement parts and gewgaws.

He laughs at the idea of Rumble Snodgrass, scooter dude. Hell, it wasn't so long ago, a new scoot was hardly ten, and now they want twenty because of the fucking suits throwing money at them like no tomorrow. Well, he'll show 'em some money.

But he can guarangoddamntee that first money will not go for a new motorcycle. Fuck that, and fuck every last one of those boutique motherfuckers who think riding and wrenching are separate pursuits. A man rises in society with seventy grand in his pocket, and he might get a paint job like Hobarth did and maybe save a few bucks when it comes out wrong. He might get his engine re-blacked and re-chrome his derby cover and get some dings banged out. Or he might leave the rat tracks alone and get one of those guinea carbs that don't choke so bad on the high passes and stick out like a steel kneecap, because wrenching heads, valves, cams, tranny cases and bottom ends down to the damn crank case is one thing. But fucking with an old carburetor with the sticky floats and gummy jets and needle valves floppy as wife one's tits and gaskets looser than wife one's romantical inclination is a motherfucker nobody gets right. That means nobody, and that means ever. Can't be done.

Carb rebuild my ass.

Maybe he'll stop in at the dealer this afternoon for one of those newspapers with all the ads for guinea carbs.

He lights another smoke off the nub of the last and wonders why in hell he forgot to tell the bitch to wrap up the last few slices of Jumbo Supreme, even if it meant getting up and going out and stashing the box in his bags. He had to get up to piss every ten minutes, anyway. So? What the hell? Nuke a couple three slices of Jumbo Supreme, and you'll see a fucking hangover take a fucking hike, clear a head so a man can think about numbers.

Hell, you can't just say twenty grand on twelve pounds goes to two hundred grand on two hundred pounds. You got your volume discounts and market absorption and variables like that. But then two hundred pounds won't be a drop in the pond down there, and two hundred would be easy as four pounds each. You don't do shit but pack it up and strap it on. They sniff at the border, or they don't. So what's the diff, four pounds or a hundred, if you're making the run?

You have to wonder what people are thinking, when ringing the bell is no more effort and no more risk than a half-ass try. You come out a half-ass winner or a big fucking loser. So why not ante up to ring the fucking bell and leave that loser shit *buried* in the dust? Why not set yourself up for life instead of a year or two? Why not belly up to the fa fa fa with your nose in the air and pick out the fanciest motorcycle on the floor, one that hadn't even been sat on, and say, "I'll take that one, motherfucker. Now fuck you!"

Well? Why not? The women would come around then, clawing and scratching to see who gets to be first on delivering the goods, just to get up next to a new scoot and scads o' dough.

And what was that little bitch up to last night, jerking everybody's chain like she couldn't wait to get down and dirty and then telling Buck to learn some poetry and then leaving like the little prick tease she's always been? Rumble Snodgrass thinks her tune might change, once he gets his money. She'll beg for it then....

With thoughts drifting beautifully on the big why not, Lonny asks the thin air, "Who the fuck?"

He checks his watch. Hell, after ten already. Still, motherfucker doesn't need to bang like that, practically ruining a vision.

It's Buck at the door wrapped up like Nanook of the North and looking more alert than a hungover man ought to look. "I'm going for something to eat. You want to go?" Lonny stares, measuring the cold, then shaking it off. "Why didn't you call? Coulda saved yourself a stop and been that much quicker at the biscuits and gravy."

"I'm going anyway. Besides, I'm having oatmeal. Come on. It's not that cold."

"Oatmeal?"

"Yeah, for my asshole and.... I'm gonna lose some weight."

"Yeah? How much? Two hundred pounds?"

"Nah. Maybe forty."

"You think you're gonna lose forty pounds eating oatmeal?"

"No. I told you; that's for my asshole. I'll have to do some other stuff too." Lonny nods with a shiver and heads back in. Buck follows for another nuke on the coffee, which finishes the pot, good riddance, and Lonny dresses for cold weather, asking if they maybe ought to swing by Hobo Grimes' place to, you know, see what they need to see. Buck doesn't care where they swing. He looks down and looks away and says he wants to first swing around by that waitress, what's-her-name, Missy's place.

"What the fuck you want to do that for? You think she's gonna wet your willie before you have your oatmeal? You think she's hanging around waiting on a few more lines of poetry? Besides, what do you need me for?"

Buck shrugs. He doesn't need Lonny to swing around and see a woman, except that going with someone else makes it easier, unless you count the potential for Lonny to mess it all up. Or you can go ahead and scratch the potential and call it a certainty, because there never was a romance Lonny Snodgrass couldn't mangle like a train wreck, given half a chance. Besides, this first visit won't get easy, no matter who or what. "Well. Yeah. Maybe I'll just...."

"Yeah, we can swing by there," Lonny says. "She's probably in there with some rich fucker honking his horn since last night because he knew the rest of the poem, and you didn't. She's probably horse fucking some muscle-bound fucker much better looking than you, fucking piece o' shit."

Buck looks up to ascertain Lonny's sincerity on this theory regarding his new love interest and the suggestion that she might be sharing intimacies with a rich guy.

But Lonny addresses his right boot, which won't go on without pulling his sock so tight it squeezes his toes, like to cut off the circulation, so he has to pull it off and pull out some slack and try again. Buck checks himself on asking if Lonny really thinks she's, you know, doing it with a rich guy, and instead says, "You're right. I'll go by myself. You swing around and see if Hobo wants to get something to eat. I'll see you at the Grotto in half an hour."

"Half an hour? You gonna make a love call in half an hour? Where's your respect for a woman's needs?" Lonny pulls slack from his sock and glares at it as a warning: Don't do that again. He looks up more reasonably. "Take your time, Buckless. You ain't at the Grotto in forty-five minutes, we'll know you're eating out at the Y."

Buck blushes and grins, since Missy is way too pretty and nice for anything like that. But then someone, somehow, sooner or later is going to have to get down there and, you know, because a woman doesn't want to go through life without trying out that sort of thing at least once. No matter how pretty and nice they are, they still have their needs. That's what she said. Well, he won't speculate on what might happen, though he knows she wouldn't dream of getting next to a galoot like him. He'll shed the pounds, if he has to use his knife. But some things won't change. "That won't happen," Buck says.

"You know, you sometimes have a attitude problem, Buckaroo. If it was me, I'd march in there, tongue first. I'll guarantee you, you won't get much in this life you don't ask for it first, and you might be surprised what a plain old question can come to."

"You mean like, 'Mind if I eat your pussy, Ma'm?'"

"Yeah. Something like that. You got to have your manners and a direct approach. That way you won't be kept waiting."

"Yeah. I might try that. You're right. I'll go alone. There's no reason I can't swing by and visit a girl. A woman."

"No, it ain't. I'll go with you."

"Well. Don't talk dirty."

Lonny grins and pulls the boot on again and works his toes. "I'll try. How about we swing by Hobo's first and we'll all three of us go by what's-her-name's?"

"You mean so Hobo can ask her if she wants to pull a train?"

"Him and me think alike on that score. You might be surprised there too."

"Yeah, and maybe I won't be."

And maybe he would be.

At the front end of that same hour and hardly eight clicks down the road, Missy Malone transcended speculation by pressing her lips to those of another, this other set also nestled under a full beard. She flicked her tongue to raise a whimper at will and moved in to set free the birds, a fulsome flock at that.

Trouble was, somebody left the cage door open. That's how it is with these young'uns, always in a hurry to be somewhere else. It reflects poorly on the parents, teaching them nothing of gratitude or the needs of others.

Hardly into squealing freedom, this teen wonder was up and squawking about her morning stuff, with hardly a care for anyone else's birds, like maybe things were even, which they weren't.

Missy Malone won't forget, but she won't complain either, because she cuts the young'uns some slack; they're so fresh and firm. Next time one flutters up and lights on a branch for a little scratch, she'll lay down the law on who scratches first. Then she'll take her own sweet time with her birds and the cage door and all that. Let the teen wonder work it a while, then see what she thinks about gratitude.

That's how it goes. Some people are plain more considerate than others. At least she's up and getting the pets fed, until she stops on intrusion, which is Buck Dibble and Rumble Snodgrass coming up her driveway. She's not surprised. These aren't the first biker boys to come around after a night of foolish flirtation, which was nothing but a working gal earning tips. Fools focus on sportfucking, except for the big one. Boy, oh, boy, he'd be a ride, like to crush a woman, unless she called dibs on top. But she doesn't think so; ten to one says a fat guy's gonna have a little dick. Who needs that? "Come in! It's open!"

The boys hoof in, mumbling that she must be out back in that glass shed, and they shuffle on back. Missy, in her makeshift greenhouse, supplements her southern exposure with heaters and humidifiers. Buck and Lonny are impressed with the fancy flowers growing there and Missy with her blouse half open and *no bra, no shit,* and fucking woolly worms crawling all over her. "I guess they got names and get to breast feed," Lonny says.

"Yes, they do," Missy answers.

"Can we watch?" Lonny asks, generating profuse blushing and regret in his shy compatriot.

Missy sees and thinks the big one's sensitivity is the most touching display of manhood she's seen all week. "They just finished. You poor boys, always late. Maybe another time."

"Do they usually feed about this time?" Buck asks.

He's not on the same track as his friend but merely stumbles down the rocky road of conversation, showing his crush and discomfort. "No, Buck. They eat all the time, any time they want. And I don't breast feed them. They're insects in the larval stage. They couldn't ingest the milk of a mammal. Besides, female mammals don't have milk in their breasts all the time. They only lactate before and after giving birth. Do you have children?"

Buck looks down and says, "No."

She ignores Lonny, which pisses him off and worries Buck that Lonny will up the rudeness, till she sees it his way. She won't. Buck wished he'd come alone, now that it's underway and could go damn near anywhere. "Did you ever want to have children?"

"He's not sure he can," Lonny says. "He needs to practice. How about you? You want to practice?"

"No. He doesn't need to practice, and neither do I. You should know that. Making love is as natural as falling down or getting up. I thought about having children, but I don't know if I'll ever meet anyone who's up to my standards. Men are so deficient in so many ways, no offense, but I'm sure you know what I mean."

"You mean like not knowing poetry?" Buck asks.

"Yes," she says. "I guess I could find a prospect and teach him his lines." She moves her woolly worms gently from her torso back to their habitat. "I'm deficient too. Can I offer you some coffee?"

"No. We had a shitload," Lonny says. "Besides, we're headed out for breakfast. Then we're riding into the future."

"How perfect," she says. "Don't get turned around."

Buck smiles at her subtlety and delivery, and she didn't even say fuck.

"Ha, ha." Lonny says.

"I'll have some," Buck says, to which Lonny takes his cue and says they'll hook up down at the Grotto. Buck nods and Lonny nods back, raising his eyebrows and shrugging, unseen by Missy, who tends her woolly worm habitat, and damn if she's *not* breast feeding *someone* down there.

Which she's not. She's dawdling, so these road dogs can sort their gross needs and leave. Or stay, which she fears the big one will do, along with his crush, and that means the hammer's gonna fall. What else can she do? Let him down easy? Does a carnivore comprehend table manners?

Or celery?

Go on. Get out.

IX

A Warm Up

A black bagger blossoms with two small speakers behind the windshield on either side of a leather pouch with the mini-amp. Two more speakers in the fairing lowers harmonize to a hundred ten decibels with tremulous highs, unwarped lows over a bassline syncopated with power. Buster anticipates the desert on a horse with no name, a noble steed with a heralded approach.

"Stuey's on his way." Larraine is pert, nearly cheery on her way to the car. Dressed to kill and glistening for camera contact, she moves with intention, muttering disdain for a Mercedes sedan washed yesterday and already showing dirt. "Dirty," she says, troubled with the ways of nature. George Harrison said all things must pass, but Larraine still suffers. "That's so annoying."

Buster recalls the lighter times, when dirt was organic and merely dirt. Never mind: blue skies make the day official, a season opener, over fifty degrees by noon.

She pauses at the garage door for a pirouette and a wistful smile. "What?" She asks, brightening, knowing well what.

"You look great."

"I don't. Not like I used to."

"You have some good miles left. You know that."

"You and your mechanical talk."

"What do you see in the mirror?" He asks, knowing she spends time enough in the mirror to see the worst of it.

"What am I seeing now?" She stares at a middle-age man with greasy hands and gets into her car. The cat meows. It's like that, up and in and out, clean as a stiletto, briefly bloodless, till the wound begins to leak.

Stuey arrives in spastic syncopation, his headset wired to a cell phone dangling from his neck. Squeezing past Larraine at the top of the drive, he stops till she lowers a window, and he leans in for a smooch. She hates his gratuities and smarmy manner but often can't help laughing, as perhaps intended, like now. He's so…goofy, puckered up and waiting. She grants a tiny peck to preserve her lip-gloss. He doesn't press but eases on by, as she throws rocks from her back wheels on her way out.

Rolling to the garage, he twitches like a man in a shower holding a toaster. Buster drowns him out, no headset required. Stuey grins. "That's insane."

Buster nods, underscoring the best antidote to domestic strife. They smoke the hash Stuey brought home last year from Canada. "Last of the Mohicans," he says.

Buster inhales. The ember flares and shrinks. "You mean us or this stuff?"

"Man, if I didn't know you, I'd think Larraine was the hottest piece of ass on the wet side of the mountains."

"Yes. But then you'd get some. Then you'd take the time to know her. Then you'd need a friend. Me. So? What's the diff?"

Stuey squints to see the point and resolves to sort things later, as Buster pulls on gloves and tucks his scarf, and they head out.

They ride.

Buster wonders if the hash is very strong, or does the cold make it seem more potent? Do his hands know when to squeeze or twist on their own? Do they need him at all? He thinks he's good for the timing part, if they can remember the physical part. Numb with cold and drug, he bumps the volume for KZZK's non-stop Beatles hour and sings along. The lyric feels profound, or, as they say, appropriate:

Aaaaaah shoulda know-own better with a girl like you, that I would luuv everything that you do. And I do. Hey hey hey! And I do….

A first sunny day this festive surely leads to better miles ahead. Why else ride, if not for better miles? The road rolls under, till it feels like the bridge in Tacoma that rolled until it collapsed, and the poor dog drowned. Sadness is brief, as another pup takes over:

Yellow matter custard! Bleeding from a dead dog's eye-e-eye. I am the spaceman! I am the walrus! Coo coo catchou….

Sweetly banking hill and dale, Stuey kerchunks to third behind Ma and Pa Kettle. Their one-owner truck putters and smokes, but Pa won't pull over. Stuey accelerates to pass between the Kettles and a semi at the crest, and Buster cues up to follow. But Pa gooses it for the squeeze play, glaring at the motorcycle punks, the old truck billowing smoke. Stuey and Buster ease off, till the semi rumbles by.

Buster pulls through the black cloud and up alongside Pa, confident he can out-asshole this asshole. He did not come for petty hostility on the open road, but it seems therapeutic, less demanding and more fun than most days. *Ba da da da da daaa da da! Bom bom bom. Ba da da da da da da da. They say it's your birthday! Bom, bom, bom. You gonna have a good time!*

He pulls ahead and flips a loogie that Pa drives under after ducking and cringing. Stuey pulls up and splats his loogie right on Pa's windshield. Pa's wipers spread it out, and it's funny but no longer fun. Pa could have a handgun or a road rage relapse. Pedal down, Pa veers sharply to hit Stuey but throws a rod instead, clanging and slowing with contrails, as the boys accelerate over the hill and out of range.

Fuck. Some people.

Soon it's the Bearded Oyster for Irish coffee. Peeling off the layers, Stuey laughs at Pa and says everything is more fun with hash.

Buster says, "Yeah, that would have been ugly without the hash. Lucky we had some. Fuck."

"I might bring in a few pounds."

"Great idea," Buster replies. "Tape it to your chest. They'll never suspect it. I saw it in a movie. It would have worked, but the kid got the shakes and sweats, so he got busted. But you won't do that. You're too cool. And smart. You want Irish?"

Stuey nods. The bartender mixes whiskey and coffee. Stuey feels his chest, where the taped hash would go. "I got a better idea." Fuck a bunch of tape. Stuey plans to pack the load home in his T-bag, the one that straps neatly onto his sissy bar. He's made arrangements, he says, ten or twelve pounds.

"You couldn't smoke twelve pounds in twelve years."

"I know that."

"And you don't need the money."

Stuey shrugs.

"You do?"

Stuey nods, sipping his Irish and burned coffee.

"You're in a jam?"

Stuey's smile is sheepish. "The divorce. Sixty-forty, her favor, plus six grand a month doesn't leave much. The alimony part is deductible for me and taxable for the witch, but that's only half the damage, and child support is after-tax dollars." He sulks. The witch is the woman he vowed to love, honor and obey. "You don't have to go," he allows. "I need fifty grand to buy my new house."

Buster sips, cheap whiskey and bad coffee balancing the discomfort beside him. "Why would you buy a house with an asset split coming up? You knew she hated you eight years ago. You want to go deeper under water? Why?"

"I need a place, and we're separated. It doesn't cost any more than rent, well, after the down payment. But I've lost enough, and I'll be on my feet in a year or so."

They drink.

Stuey bemoans the divorce settlement coming right after Christmas, so she gets half the annual bonus too. "Hash is a one-shot deal. It's a great ride up. You know that."

"What if you get the hash at a good price and sell it for a better price without a hitch?"

"What's wrong with that?"

"You'll go again."

"Won't need to."

Buster ponders need. "Need, hell. What about the fun? You wouldn't pick fifty grand up off the sidewalk?"

Stuey shrugs. "You don't have to come if you don't want to."

"You want to bring it back and sell it?"

"It'll sell quick. You'd buy some."

"At a discount, I hope. My house is paid for and the divorce looks amicable. We might share a lawyer. We get along better than we have in a long time."

"So don't get a divorce." Stuey shrugs. "See if it gets better."

Buster wonders one more time if it might get better. "It's good as it's going to get. It's us. I'm grateful we're still friends. I don't think of Larraine as a witch."

"Yeah? How do you think of her?"

"We're two people who can't relate to each other. We developed in different directions. It happens. Thank God we can still be polite."

"You still banging her?"

"What difference would it make?"

"Sorry. Hey. We're going up in two days, right? We don't have to do anything. I want to see what's to see." Stuey's summary of a drug smuggling outing is meant to ease the challenge.

But Buster crunches numbers on a napkin, where twelve pounds times sixteen ounces make a hundred forty-four ounces plus forty-eight for a hundred ninety two ounces total, making a hundred eighty ounces after road smoke and private reserve. Stuey nods. Buster asks, "What's an ounce worth?"

"Four hundred."

"Four hundred, at twenty-eight grams to the ounce. You're only getting fifteen bucks a gram."

"Closer to fourteen, but who wants to gram it out? I don't. You got to leave room for the gram seller. He'll get thirty. Who cares? You leave a little money on the table and things move quicker. Less exposure that way. Right? Hell, you taught me that. We'd buy some thirty-dollar grammage right now if we could. Wouldn't we?"

"So the payout is…."

"Seventy, seventy-five grand on an investment of fifteen to twenty. This project can get me straight."

"It's not an investment or a project. It's drug smuggling. It might get you out of hock, but it won't get you straight."

Stuey shrugs again, an apparent motif at this juncture. "You don't have to help me. I just thought you might want to…you know, get paid back quicker."

"Why should I share the risk and you get the money?"

"I'm carrying it. That's the real risk. If things don't work out, you're innocent. Besides, that's why they call it helping a friend out. I'll owe you a big one."

"An accessory isn't innocent. Even if he was, he'd need a lawyer, so he could stay innocent. I'll lend you the money for your house."

"I don't want to do that."

"Why not?"

He looks away and murmurs, "I want to clear up the debt. Besides, business and friendship don't mix."

"But a smuggling loan is okay?"

"Like I said, you don't have to help me. But I need to know."

"If I'm risking the money and making the trip, who needs you?"

"I already told you that. I'm carrying the stuff."

"So if the border guards catch you, they'll just wave me through? Have a nice day?"

"You never helped anyone before?"

Buster sips his whiskey, scanning the files for good deeds.

"The witch says I'm stealing her money and spending it on whores. She means Sue."

Sue is the new girlfriend, soon to be the former girlfriend; she's so clingy and nervous and can't finish a sentence without referencing commitment or appropriateness or good parenting. Her teen daughter comes over with Sue to watch TV. The daughter brings Willard. Willard is twenty. The daughter and Willard lay on the sofa against the wall under a blanket, so nobody gets too embarrassed when Willard and the daughter exchange crotch massage during movies. Sue giggles that it's good parenting, having them there on the sofa instead of out, getting into who knows what kind of trouble. Stuey hasn't been able to follow a movie in weeks. The kids moan until Willard gasps and goes quiet. "I got to end that one pretty soon."

"Does she put her head under the blanket?"

"She'd like to. It's a scene. I need to end it before it ends me."

"You'll be so horny without Sue."

"Yeah, that's the main thing."

"Besides, she just spent four bills on her new leather jacket."

Stuey shrugs, "Good for her. More for the next guy." They drink, pondering Sue, leather jackets and next guys. Stuey says she's a good girl, game and dependable, clean and cheerful. "The witch found a restaurant receipt for a party of two. I could have claimed clientele but admitted it was Sue. I don't care anymore. Fuck. The witch can't figure out why I'd play around when I can get it once a month at home any time I want." Indentured celibacy is the wife's revenge for motherhood, carpooling, child psychiatry, Zoloft for her and the kids and oh, what's the use? "Fuck. Compared to her, Sue's a dynamic woman."

"Was the witch dynamic when you vowed to obey her till you croak?"

Stuey squirms. "No. That was a long time ago. I fell in love during a blowjob. She's gifted. Or was."

"Was it your first?" Buster asks. Stuey laughs short. Buster downs the balance. "You're a sentimental fool after all." Stuey's bitterness seems sincere as his love once was. "She blew you, and now she hates you." Stuey looks pitiful, depressed and broke, part of the loan application process. "I might help you," Buster says.

"Thanks, man. I knew you would." Stuey raises a toast to another great trip, peeking over the rim.

"What?" Buster asks. "You think you just closed the deal?"

Stuey nods, looking smarter.

Larraine is distraught. Has she seen a lawyer? Buster braces, but it's not yet crying time, except that it is.

For starters: "Inspector Murphy called twice to say you can come in on your own, or they'll come out to get you. They have a few questions, so don't call your lawyer yet. I told him that was stupid. What a jerk."

Worse yet, the *Live Five News* man interviewed that snooty bitch, Vicki Smelling, with her ridiculous shoulder pads and pasty foundation. "She's sooo...*kitsch*! She's passé. She makes a mockery of grace and artistry." Larraine is suffering. "Look at this!" She laments *Live Five News,* featuring Vicki Smelling, the cow. It's true: Vicki S is not a fox but a shlump. "He's five-four, a shrimp. They shoot him from below. That's why I didn't get the part. He's half a head shorter than me."

The part? Truth emerges, or rather strikes: Larraine's ass would make Vicki Smelling a good Sunday face. Not only, but Larraine dolled to the nines, with results that only Larraine can get, and she got *nada.* Or did she?

"Did Duayne Dudney come on to you?" Old friends can talk. Buster and Larraine will survive the short term because they sustain the love. She's overly groomed, polite and efficient as a high-rise with fixed windows. He gravitates downward, tastefully speaking. But core differences do not weaken lasting bonds.

Buster thinks Duayne did not come on to her, which may explain the bitterness. Buster thinks Duayne had a choice and chose the unlovely one. Wrong again. Her lips tighten on the correct answer as she retreats to the parlor.

Buster hits the wobbles. The best response is not a firmer grip, because high-speed wobbles are like life; no matter who you be, you can't control them. You must let go—not all way, not like an idiot flapping hands in surrender, but with a loose grip to let the wobbles dissipate and rediscover the harmonic groove.

The sorting process breaks down. Just as pistons stop and start again in the other direction with equal vigor, so a mind changes on what is known. Imbalance or variable pressure causes vibration, and the wobbles can set in. Buster feels a worsening.

He won't front Stuey's hash. Why should he? If Stuey goes to jail, Buster would go too. Best stay ignorant and detached, so if Stuey weasels the money elsewhere, Buster can bail him out.

Moira Kunzler is perfect and gone. Good riddance; she's such a tease and so shallow, like him but with no ideas to share.

Inspector Humphries has nothing! And now, with warming weather, bones can loosen, eyes can open, and life can change.

A man best avoids the foibles of the silliest species by living free. Buster knows balance and will begin his rebalance with a new tranny, a real 6-Speed overdrive for the beautiful stretch, so ninety will feel serene as seventy. Three grand seems nominal, and back-cut gear dogs sound soothing as a sedative.

Larraine is despondent through dinner. Did Duayne Dudney spurn her? Well, rejection is no sleigh ride. They're both attractive, Larraine and Buster. They yodel together after all these years, when romance seems far gone, and the footpath feels like hardpan. Maybe Duayne fumbled or pressed a move. But who would favor Vicki Smelling, the cow, unless Vicki Smelling offered sweetmeats more discretely? What would make Duayne Dudney attractive? "Clear skies and fifty-five tomorrow," Buster offers, smooth as a weatherman. "Should hold into next week."

"I'm happy for you. You'll have a wonderful trip."

"Go for a ride?"

"Tomorrow?"

"Next week. Maybe run up with Stuey."

"That's a guy thing. What would I do?"

"Don't do anything. Might be nice to get out. It should be beautiful. We haven't had much of that."

She stares at *Show Biz Tonight* with a crooked smile and says, "It's okay. I'm over it. Really."

What?

In the next few hours she will surrender, confessing that Duayne Dudney did press a move. Larraine felt wronged but went ahead and, well, relieved him. But it was silly and sort of, you know, seedy and played hell on her emotions with things as they are. But you live and learn. "He was overbearing."

"He assaulted you? You relieved him because he insisted?" Buster won't ask the form of relief for sheer, cold fear, and interrogation would prompt a whitewash. But love pangs pierce his heart. She finally volunteers the hand job, which he doubts, which makes her cry, but come on; what man these days is happy with a hand job? These doubts and follow-ups bring on the heaving sobs. As her emotions resolve, he recalls Pa Kettle and realizes that he flipped a loogie as a loogie was flipped, so to speak. She sobs that it was nothing, nothing, nothing, and she made him wear a rubber.

Well, you don't need a rubber for a hand job, but silence is best served here too, and in no time she swears on her mother's needlepoint that she did not give Duayne Dudney a blowjob. Oh, he wanted one. They all do. But she did not, would not, could not; well, she could, but this subject is also best unpressed. Isn't it enough to see this man in the evening surf?

She swears regret; it won't happen again, and with a shudder, she's amazed it happened in the first place, except that it *was* Duayne Dudney; he's such a… such a charmer is what.

"A shrimpy charmer," Buster corrects.

"Yes. He's small. Much smaller than you."

Does she mean standing up? Maybe he should feel relieved, but now she sobs that after sex, Duayne Dudney took a call and dismissed her, holding a hand over the mouthpiece, telling her he'd be in touch.

"In his office?"

"Yeh-heh-hess," she sobs. In simple terms, Larraine had sex with a local news dog, and it hurts. She was shallow and weak. Her behavior justifies Moira Kunzler, who is luscious and not shrimpy, not arrogant or dismissive. Was Moira fucking that lump Henry Schurz while Larraine did Duayne Dudney? Does that hurt too? Not so much. Henry was likely taking a nap anyway. But the maestro mangled the movement. What a laugh, except for feeling old and alone, on the ropes, taking truths on the chin. The pummeling and aftermath take hours, until Duayne Dudney calls about nine-fifty-five, before the late news, which is "live, you know, so I only have a minute or two…."

Taking her dismissive turn, she says, "My husband knows you raped me. Don't call here again."

Hanging up, she slumps, tearfully vulnerable and carrying a load of regret. He sits beside her and puts an arm around her. She cries again, so he comforts, as if to absolve the misfortune upon them. She whimpers in disbelief that a man could be so mean.

"Let it go."

"Will you do something for me?"

"Okay." He anticipates a request for a hostile phone call.

But she sighs, "I want to kill that fucker." It seems like only yesterday, when she had such elegant good taste.

A man moves on, if not to happier times then to distractions that may lead to better feelings. The new tranny is a special order and hard to come by and then unavailable…but what's this? A guy ordered and paid and died, which just goes to show you. So it's back on the shelf and marked down by half. It's been there a year, because who can afford these things, and they haven't changed much at all, really. So it's onto the bench along with racing calipers of variable piston sizes to reduce heating when braking. New brakes in black continue a motif of dark into light. That is, the scooter is largely blacked out, gloss black, but still giving an impression of emergence or some such.

Mo Dowd says there is no way to finish today. But she'll try to squeeze him in, considering the tab, which is big. She also defers to friendship, though she needs this rush like a hole in the head.

"Thank you. I'll wait."

"Wait? You want to wait for hours?"

He won't say that he can't go home but reminds her that floating rotors won't warp like a marriage and should significantly reduce chafing. He adds, as if to change the subject, "Stock rotors are junk. You know that." Besides, these rotors have black centers that fit. He would share darkness into light as a concept by which....

But she calls bullshit. Warpage is only a problem for the crotch rocket maniacs who heat up faster than the cruisers.

"I'm heating up here, Mo, like on a ten percent grade, big rigs jamming the slow lane and everybody else doing ninety? I want to ditch a few degrees. Okay?" Fuck. Retail therapy ought to feel good, not like another domestic abuse.

"The calipers and rotors are twelve hundred clams...."

"Who gives a fuck? I mean, sorry. Thanks. I'm in a bind."

"No shit."

"Look. I might head out for a while. So let's flow the heads and ditch the sleeves and stick those other jugs in—those over in the showcase. I been thinking about it, and now's the time. Okay? Scooters back on the bench anyway."

Mo looks concerned, like a shrink on indications of psychosis. "You want the stroker kit too?"

"No. Strokers are stupid."

"Just checking. You will want the big cams."

"Yeah and...the hydraulic lifters. Fuck it." Bigger pistons and flowed heads will grace radical cams and hydraulic lifters for more punch than your average haymaker. It might feel stupid in the future but in the moment feels perfect.

Mo nods severely as a surgeon, approving a multiple organ transplant.

Hours later, a gunmetal day fades to dark. Fluorescent lighting will not displace depression as advertised, but a rider glows with hope, on a visit to the O.R, where his rig is splayed open for a radical hop-up to make it hump like a jackrabbit.

Out front Mo rings the biggest service ticket of her career and calls it false happiness, for now, because spending is no substitute for riding. Buster says the ride is nigh. "What do you think of bringing some hash down from Vancouver?"

She rolls her eyes. "It's a terrible idea. What do you have to lose? Or gain?" He looks down at the display case between them, as if browsing the chrome rotor caddies, braided-steel and billet bolt covers, high-amp ignition modules and chrome bolt covers. "I need a billet chrome wife warmer."

"I got 'em in back. Three speeds and heat."

He smiles sadly at his own pathetic joke as his cell quacks. "Larraine is warm...in her way, not like she was. But nobody is...." Mo drifts back for a service update and privacy. "Hello, dear."

"Inspector Murphy is here."

"What does he want?"

"Tad Pollack is in a coma. They want to talk to you."

"Gee, that's terrible. Tell them to leave."

"Did you shoot Tad Pollack? He says you did."

"Must be a low grade coma if he's talking."

"Not him. What's-his-name said you did."

"I'm God-fearing and law-abiding. We all know Tad's been shaky for a while."

"I hope you didn't shoot Tad Pollack."

"Whose side are you on?"

"Are you coming home soon?"

"Who wants to know?

"Goodbye."

Mo approaches, swearing at that idiot from Texas. "Why would he work in parts with dyslexia? You don't look so good."

"My wife is leaving. My girlfriend is banging a bum. Can you blame her?"

"Which one?"

"Thanks for understanding."

"The wife is leaving?"

"It's a work in progress."

"So you got a girlfriend. That should teach her."

"She doesn't know. And it's not a girlfriend, really. We flirted. Larraine's mood is chronic. You've seen it."

"She's making a point, so you go chasing strange leg?"

"I don't get the leg, and the only point she gets is that life should be appropriately accessorized."

"You get that from her?"

"No. My accessories have practical value."

"Then why the mood? You're perfectly matched. Believe me, Buster. You're no slouch when it comes to style statements."

"We're different. She's nice."

Mo lights another smoke. "You slap her around?"

"Please."

"Look at these." She lifts the latest with her pinkie: skimpy satin panties with appliqué pistons slipping into heart-shaped cylinders embroidered on the crotch. Thirty dollars.

"I guess you pay a premium for this kind of wit."

"They might bring her around."

"Would you wear these?"

"I am."

He looks away. "We're adrift."

"Who isn't? You got money and stuff. You got a soft life. That's not enough? So you want to risk everything?"

"Can I stay over tonight?"

She looks up. "She's my friend too, I mean, kind of. She's weird, but I like her."

"The police think I shot the neighbor."

"What, with your pellet gun?" She laughs.

"Don't tell anyone about that gun. It was in the ear. He was about to kill the ravens."

"So you shot him in the ear?"

"It sounds bad, if you say it like that. But he's bad, much worse than the birds. Hell, what did they do?"

"Two wrongs don't make a right."

"It wasn't two wrongs; it was only one. I stopped it with minimal damage and didn't kill him."

"You are sensitive."

"Can be. He's in a coma."

"Oh, man. So you want to hide out?"

"I'll buy dinner."

"Yeah, sure. But maybe we should get take out."

Thunder rolls like ninepins from the service bay around the corner. Buster perks. Mo shuffles papers; she's heard it all before. He laughs short and scans the retail area to see who else may have heard it, so he might explain that this jackhammer bassline defines his new self. He seeks someone to share his excitement. But it's only himself and the wrench, who comes out wiping his hands and nodding, telling Buster to break it in by the old rules. Buster tosses his credit card onto the counter and walks back to see what he hears. Money can't buy happiness, except for when it can. Look what fistfuls of dough have wrought. The machine at idle rumble brings an odd smile. It announces a new incarnation of love for a new season. He reaches in to press a button, *et voila*: funky blues on a downbeat make the blessed event complete.

"Sounds good," Mo says, standing behind him. "But it looks like a Goldwing."

"You don't like it."

"I know it's not a Goldwing."

"So you do like it?"

"Jesus. You have other worries besides how it looks."

"Not really. I'm repressing. This helps."

"I like it."

"See you here at six. I'll bring the car."

"Either or." She flicks her butt and turns to take a call.

Then he's homeward bound to see if the coast is clear, to pack his bag for a weekend getaway. Leaving a night early shouldn't make any difference.

He keeps it under sixty-five and varies rpm by the old rules, which fit with his age and habits. It's easy in the cold and dark. He takes the scenic route like old times because new times might rush a detective. On a pass-by he sees the homestead clear and hurries in like he did forty years ago to tell Mom he wouldn't be home for dinner. Or was it fifty? A kid has adventures out front and nothing but, and he might again. High times change with seasoning, mostly cayenne on the lam.

Larraine leans on a doorjamb, as if waiting for an explanation. She gets a nod in confidence. He tells here he'll call tomorrow. "Stay cool. Okay?" Urgency and brevity feel like relief, and in minutes, he's gone.

"Stay cool?" Larraine asks the chill night air, her voice lilting in a vapor cloud that fades like all else.

Soon he sits across from Mo Dowd, a checkered cloth between them. Mo is not masculine or feminine. Her figure-8 has driven a road dog or two the extra hours for a saddle change at her place. She gives good ear and is easy with her two cents. "You're heading north to avoid the situation?"

"Yeah. It's the spring ride anyway."

"Why would you bring in hash, with the cops already on you?"

"I won't. Stuey's in a jam. It's his deal."

"Yeah, right. You can tell customs it's his deal when they bust you. Why don't you lend him the money?"

"It's a long story. I am lending him the money, but don't worry about it. I don't step in shit every day."

"Except for the last few days? Hey, your friends wouldn't like women going along, would they?"

"You? On the Spring Fling?"

"It's kind of a long story myself. I'm getting a message."

"From me?"

"No. Do you ever see things? Are you sensitive to...." Mo seeks proper wording in the hazardous realm of sensitivity.

"Ah, a message."

She nods warily. This jargon is out of bounds for the macho elite. "It's my father. I never knew him, but.... I met him once, by chance. We weren't introduced or anything but we talked. It was only for a few minutes and not about anything but this stupid video game, but I knew it was him, Nanaimo and all. He walks up, this guy about sixty, in this loud yellow shirt and blue pants, and he says, 'I gotta tell you, you look so much like Tina, I can't believe it.' My birth mother was Tina. She's up there too." Mo looks down, thinking it through.

"What happened?"

"Nothing happened. We talked, and he split, and I knew it was him. But I didn't do anything. He knew too, but he left. It didn't seem like a big deal. We let it go, like it was bound to happen and shouldn't cause any hoopla or anything. He knew. I wasn't sure, but I am now."

"So?"

"So I'm going up. I was thinking of going for the All Harley Drags again, but that's not for another month, and the shop gets too busy then, and I want to find him. It's time. Jimmy Hatrick."

"Jimmy Hatrick?"

"Don't say that name up there. He's a dodgy guy, or he was."

"It's going around."

She lights another smoke and swears them off. "Mama knows I want to find him. I told her. I'm curious. She understands. I want to talk to him. He's on the run too. Or he was."

"What for?"

"He fucks with people."

Buster thinks it over. The guys would grouse, but who cares? He wouldn't mind sharing a room with Mo. "It's okay with me, if you want to put up with the silly shit."

She laughs. "You don't know silly shit. And if I don't go now, I can't go till August. Besides, the drags are too crowded and a real scene. I got grief last time. Some punk inductee and his little girlfriend start quacking at me on the ferry, that I can't ride in Nanaimo without a permit from the Dreaded Fellows. I told him to stand up straight and be his own man. Can you believe those guys? Call themselves outlaws, outside the law, and they want to permit everything, just like the fuckers they want to be different from." She smokes. "I go with you guys, I got protection, right?"

"What protection? We got no guns."

"I told you I don't like guns. Didn't I?"

"What if…somebody comes back with hash?"

"That's your business. I won't cross the border with that. Besides, we'll want to strangle each other by then. Won't matter."

"Day after tomorrow."

"Day after tomorrow?"

"Everyone's ready."

"Yeah, ready to get outa town. For all I know you embezzled a bunch of money too."

He orders wine in a carafe, size large, wondering how she reads him so clearly. "Yeah, well, it wasn't embezzlement, really."

She whispers, "I love that shit you rich guys do."

It's midnight when the couch is made up with two sheets, pillow and blanket. Asking what else he needs as he exits the bathroom, she plops onto the sofa, hiking her nightie for a backrub, just a short one because the sciatica is killing her and just bit of pressure makes it much better.

Buster doesn't mind, with his share of backache, so he straddles her legs because she's not a guy. "Do you sleep in your skivvies?"

"The liniment's on the coffee table. Do not get it in my crack."

"What, you'll catch fire?"

"Yeah. Mama always warned about the hell to pay if it gets in your butthole."

"That's so quaint," he says, rubbing briskly to reach the sciatica, asking who'll rub what's killing him. She moans. He says, "I guess a girl can't come out and ask for an ass rub."

"I didn't ask for an ass rub."

"That's what I said. It's cool." He rubs the pelvic ridge to the center of the cheek, stretching her out.

"Don't look at my asshole, okay?"

"Hey, no dingles."

"Go higher, will you?"

X

Jimmy Hatrick

Unless the good Lord calls me home, I got wood. I got customers. They know I got wood and give a fair count, and I got the money to show for it. I got plenty better to do with my money than spend it on elbow bending on what goes right through you anyway. Some of them now'll grub a cord and take their money on down to Buzz's or the Glo Room till it's gone and then go grub another. Not me. I buy myself all the toys I never could if I was still living on my wits. I'm sixty-two. You better believe I'm fit. I got a five-foot satellite dish and a snowmobile and two cars ready to race in the Demolition Derby, which ain't what it was, since all they want now is the mud. Nothin's like it was.

And a big fuckin' TV. Oh, I'm ready for the fun now. I done my time. Eighteen years in Seattle, I worked the steel, and that's for dollars, U.S. Thirty-eight stories up. I never once came close to going in the hole, not like some of them, until one day, this foreman's got about eight inches too far to reach a lead. He's all wired up with the safety line, but he hollers over to me, 'Hey, Jimmy, step on out there and give her a try, you can reach her better 'n me.'

Well, 'Fuuuck you!' I told him. He says, okay, sir, just get on down and pick up your check. I says, 'Fuck you, and don't let the door bang your ass on my way out.' That's why.

Don't mean shit. You work for the union anyway. Go on down to the hall and get on the next day. Eighteen years of it was enough, and I thank myself and the good Lord for every day of it, because I put away close to thirty cents on the dollar, same as if I was living here. You can head up in the cold and dark 'n fuckin' wet a hundred days in a row and know you might be coming down fast on any given one of them. You don't get warm and cozy knowing what you're building for yourself, but you go because of the logic involved. But you can't tell when the sense of it'll turn on you.

I watch these fellows on the TV news, day in, day out, do the same damn thing for years, and I think, now how in hell is it they manage to hang on to the same thing like that? Twenty years now, since I threw a leg over a motorcycle, and I swore I'd ride till my dying day, because that's where I wanted to be. Didn't make a difference to me if it was all alone or with the boys. The boys didn't like to get caught out on the road all alone. Get caught is what I said. Why, you'd think it was the devil himself out there waiting to get them. It's only their own fear and guilt because of what they did. They knew it was bad. Not me. I just loved to ride and never set out to cheat man nor beast but just wanted to have a little fun with those dice I picked up from a fellow owed me some money. He said I'd thank him plenty for those dice. Yeah.

Who can't see that a set a bones ain't set up for sevens? You'd think these rough and tough road boys could stand up man enough to what a damn child could see plain as first grade arithmetic. Hell, a shooter stays alive for twenty-five, thirty rolls and cleans up eighteen hundred dollars and then shifts his wad from one hand to the other and craps out three rolls later ought to raise a eyebrow or two if there was half a wit behind the lot of them. Who rolls fours, fives, sixes, eights and nines all night long but a shooter with funny bones, got twos on top and bottom and the same with three and one on the sides?

I like to call those boys plain damn dumb with some stupid to boot. But then you get in there and nobody says squat, and next thing you know, you're feeling like a man who might pull it together here and now, clean up for all time and then call it quits. Oh, those boys had some money, maybe not at one time, but they could go get more and wouldn't think twice of making me come too, on account of I was the reason they needed more. Any night of the week was good for two, three grand for them, easy as you please, stealing motorcycles. That was their best way to quick cash. Maybe still is. I mean any motorcycles anywhere. They'd steal from their so-called friends, just pull up, four guys jump out with the two steel bars, run them motherfuckers through the spokes and lift them onto the truck and there you go. Nice bikes, some of them good for forty cents on the dollar, which was damn near full value once you discount for the custom paint, which cost an arm and two legs, but the fancy paint had to go for purposes of identification.

Hell, they'd put me under one of those bars, little as I am, and threaten to kill me if I let her drop. I felt worse about that than any heavy bones I rolled. Some poor fucker works years to get his ride, and these boys come and steal it like it's a found dollar, which it was to them. I can tell you some of those poor fuckers got ripped off, thought they was all friends. They'd come on down to the clubhouse looking for help finding their scooters. Why, those sorry sonsabitches who stole them would get all pissed off, you know, at the bastards who would do such a thing. Then they'd put out the word and guarantee it'd be a hot time at the clubhouse once they caught the thieving bastards.

Don't get me wrong; I was one of them but not by choice. I mean I hung around with them by choice but never stole a motorcycle by choice. I think I'd rather sneak a piece o' pussy off a man's wife than steal his motorcycle. You can't get that back. And I won't make excuses, except to say that evil deeds begat evil deeds. That thieving made me feel no compunction whatever on going to funny bones and heavy loads.

You can't get goofy dice in standard sizes. Don't ask me why, but they're always a pinch too little or too big, so if you're the dumb fuck switching the goofy bones for the real bones from one hand to the other with your greenbacks, trying to look cool as a cucumber, you know that one of them little fuckers falls out, you're deader'n a Christmas goose.

Leastwise you drop a regulation size bone you can say, 'Hey, it's a spare.' Might not fool anybody for long, but then you might pick up a couple minutes, which might be all you need to stay this side of the daisies, if you know what I mean.

I drilled my own, right down through the dots to just past halfway. Two bones, one on the one and six on the other, which is easy enough if you go real slow and just plain damn start over if you leave one little burr or fuck up the dimple. Dropping in the mercury is easy enough too, but you can't be careless because that shit'll turn on you, stain anything it touches.

The hard part is recapping the holes so they don't leak, because it might as well be your fucking brains leaking all over the place, if they do. Painting the dots is easy, as long as you don't fuck it up, and all in all, the heavy bones are a much safer way to play it than rolling goofy cubes for twenty-five winners in a row.

With the loaded bones you wait for a loser to come up natural for the shooter before you, which is only a matter of time and might win a few bucks. But then you switch to the heavy bones and put on some happy horseshit about luck picking up, you can feel it, and you lay down a bet to make your evening worthwhile, if you know what I mean. You practice at home and see little things, like laying down that much cash making it easier to switch hands and bones. So now you're rolling left handed, but the boys don't see shit, and for luck and all, you turn up your one and your six right there on the floor before you roll, but you got to get them right, which is the scary part, because you need a sign, like a rolled corner or a black fleck or some shit on each one to make sure you got the right one and the right six. Otherwise you're still screwing the pooch.

But I got good. I'd find my one and six real slow and deliberate like a dumb shit would and then tamp both of them down on the floor to set the load. Oh, hell you blow on them and say your little prayer for show 'n tell and let 'em roll. You best stay under five hundred on a come out. Leastways I always did, because what the fuck, you got all night.

Hell, I got cocky, had in mind to load myself up for little Joe, which is four the hard way, just to make it look, you know, out of the blue. I was gonna load up for boxcars and acey deucey too, which is craps, which you sometimes need to roll right now no matter what it cost, once you see the stink-eye rippling round the table. 'Course it wasn't a table. We played on the floor.

I can't tell you how many nights I won or how much, but it was going on nine or ten nights around a grand apiece. I stretched it out over two or three weeks and mixed it up so I'd come out with maybe six, eight hundred or eleven or twelve. I swear I'd have given it back, every last dime, anybody said anything, and you can believe that or not, but you ought to, because I didn't swear it out of moral compunction but out of plain damn sense.

But they didn't, so I drove on out to Spider Lake by way of Grovener Canyon Road, which is a hundred clicks round about for a thirty-click trip, but that's the way I am, careful on the details. I parked it and walked the last click too, out to the end of the dock there and threw them damn dice as far as I could. Ten grand then was like fifty or sixty now, and it hit me like a rivet forge off the twenty-third floor, what they'd do to me.

It's funny how a single picture sticks so many years after so many times on Spider Lake with a spinning rig, thinking how blessed that place was, just me and God and a mess o' pan trout.

We'd go out there, one or two of the boys and me. We could troll all day long and get nothing, but I didn't care, which is what makes a true fisherman. It's having a line wet that makes you happy. But I always took a couple maggots along in case. They milk. The white stuff comes out your maggots, but not all at once. It trails like smoke and drives the little trout crazy. You see it once you cut a little trout open and find the flies and skeeters and gnats inside. They have to feed out in the middle, see. You catch your big trout close to the bank, shallow, and they're full of snails and salamanders, mud minnows and all manner of bigger baits. But if the big ones won't hit, you still don't want to go home and eat sardines, so I'd carry a few maggots just in case. Don't ask me how the little ones know a maggot'll grow up to be a fly, because I can't tell you. But they know and go crazy for the white stuff coming out. The little ones eat good. Takes more of them, but they fit in the pan better, and not one of those sorry-ass excuses for a fisherman had to go home empty-handed. They'd whine and huff, like the fucking fish gave a good goddamn how tough they were. I'd set them up for a dinner fit for a king. But I'm like that; I'll lend a guy some maggots.

And don't think they won't turn, each and every one of them, into a little trout, pretty as a picture.

Don't ask me how they found out, because I can't tell you. But they did. Wanted to kill me, which was reason enough to leave the country, even if it was only down to Seattle and up to the thirty-eighth floor in the dark and cold, fucking rain. There's nothing like fear to warm your heart for the future, when folks ought to forget. Hell, they tell you don't look down. Them fellows looking for me made down a whole heap easier than back.

I went up eighteen years and never once got scared but knew when to tell 'em ain't no fuckin' way. That's why I got three trophies for first place in the Derby, because I'm not afraid, and that's different than saying I don't give a shit, which I don't. But if you don't give a shit, you fuck yourself up, and I never aimed to do that. I only wanted some fun, you know. Like to get out there and mix it up with the boys. The Derby made me less homesick and maybe filled in for the other riding too.

Hell, you can't get hurt in a Derby doing thirty-five, forty, unless you get stuck and set up for a head-on. It happens, but if you keep an eye out, it won't. They ain't cars, really, just about a four by eight ball of sheet metal fairly crushed up already with no glass left and handles near the openings to help you in and out because the doors are welded shut.

Three years in a row I won. The fellow manages the track asks me to come on down for the figure-8 races. You get the most roll-outs; you win. He wants me to give it a try, says I got what it takes. Fuck no, I told him. He says that's good, because he'd really think I was crazy if I did that.

I am crazy, but I'm lazy. I didn't want to take my sign off my car, but you can't roll out with a sign tacked on, without fucking up your sign. Besides that, I might have polished off my car, and I couldn't afford that. But I wasn't afraid. I'm still not afraid, and anyone tells you they're not afraid, you just ask if they'd move back up to B.C. like I did with those boys still looking, after all those years. They don't forget like they ought to.

I don't give a shit anymore. Most of the old ones are older'n me. Let 'em come on. I'll introduce 'em to my fireman's friend. I got a couple mean-looking axes, but the blunt edge on a fireman's friend won't stick in the cut so bad, so you can get it out with a decent pull. You know you're a old man when you can't swing your fireman's friend without farting out loud. It's not incontinence, and I'm not that. You can't be that and have sex, and

I can. Get laid anytime I want, just call her up and go over. Tina's a fucking mess, and I can't forget how she treated me, and it's plain to see she never grew a brain in her head, still hanging paper. I don't regret that I loved her with all my heart, and I'd bet she did too. You have relations of a sexual nature every day for fourteen years, it better be some love in it. I don't miss her, but I miss something. I don't go over there but to see if I can. I can.

You can tell what's going away. A man walks in dog shit and doesn't even wipe it off; he's old. I don't mean that old is bad. It's only the lucky ones get there and only a handful winds up all alone. I got the dogs and Pearl, that little fucker. She drags one more mole in here, I'll teach her a lesson. But that's what they do. I don't hunt no more myself. I only killed two things. That mountain goat's the second. I had his ass mounted instead of his head. That's a joke. That's all most guys ever see is the ass end headed over the hill. Not that anyone comes in here and sees it. It's just me and the dogs and Pearl. I got my fancy guppies and my rats and the ant farm. Fuckin' ants don't know when to take a rest.

I got what I need, and when the good Lord calls me, I'll be ready. I been ready a while now. A man shouldn't talk to a freeze-dried rattler more than once or twice a day, but I think he's listening. I think he forgives me for what I did to him. We're all God's creatures, even him. Maybe it's killing that poor snake that put me up to what I've a mind to do. It's not sinful or dishonest, no more than he was, not like cheating with dice and sure as hell cleaner than stealing motorcycles.

I got a new line. I should have thought of it sooner, but that's how it goes sometimes; a thing has to smack you on the head so you can see it. What I got now is fun, and nobody gets hurt, except for losing a few dollars, which is a bargain once you figure how much they charge on TV for them fuckin' lectures that teach you how to be a better person and have a better life. That big, horse-faced sonofabitch never gets depressed or can't tell his ass from his elbow. Hell, I'd sign up, go take his lecture series and be a better person, but the sonofabitch wants three thousand, U.S.!

This is better and makes you a better person much quicker for much less money. It's the Lord's work in a way.

It's simple. I got a leather strip about four inches across, eight inches long. I soaked it down till it puffed up, and put it in a vice so it'd dry flat and stiff with the water squeezed out. I got a shop vice, not a rinky-dink piece o' shit for the home hobbyist. Thirty-five fuckin' dollars I paid. I don't give a shit. You want to be in business, you got to break some eggs.

It didn't look right, but I went ahead, because you can't know, half done. I trimmed the edges and got some of that hash they smoke now and rubbed it all over that leather. I planned to do that about fifty more times and get a stack of these leather strips and on top I'd put a strip of the real stuff.

I'm down at the fuckin' Fuzzy Glo Room trying to fit in, you know, with the kids, because a man might still be able to get some of that, maybe some plain girl who might appreciate the attentions of a man of vintage. Hell, I don't want but a little head job anyway, and I treat 'em good, let 'em use the hot tub and have anything they want to eat. Never lay a finger on 'em in the abusive sense of the word. I'm not so bad. But I'll tell you what; even the plain girls think they got it made these days. I swear; any one of 'em could get some action any time she wants. They know it too. It's from the overpopulation, has to be. Didn't used to be that way.

But some things don't change. You got to have a sample of your wares to give out. That's where my fishing instincts come into play. I took a piece of hash and softened it on the fire and rubbed it on my jacket and pants and all. Smelled like skunk. I told the boys at the bar they could take it or not, didn't make a pinch o' shit's difference to me. They wanted some. Tough sonofabitch looks me up and down and says maybe two or three days. I give him a chunk to try. Dumb fucker just walks away.

You don't sample with a chunk but only a smidgen. I give a chunk to get the word out. I told 'em it's the load or the road, so if a man could step up and be counted, I'd leave it to him to make the money. A thousand a pound, ten pound minimum. That hushed 'em up. I got to soak and squeeze and trim and rub a hundred sixty strips now, but I think I got that tough punk on the hook.

I figure a man's in for a minute, he's in for keeps. Money might be another story, but you can't make a bet without taking a risk. This dumb fuck thinks he's a cool breeze, shrugs it off and says he'll be back, but he won't say when. Says I'll be there too or I won't, no sweat off his ass if he keeps his ten grand in his pocket.

What ten grand? Hell, I let him huff and puff, 'nuff said.

I'll need two more strips of hash to rub all that leather and have one left to lay on top. Then again, a smart operator doesn't take a sample off the top, not to say these boys is any too smart, but you see a weak spot in your presentation, and you fix it or lose your money. This real hash ain't like corned beef 'n hominy. It's spendy, right around three hundred a strip, counting gas and wear and tear on the tires. That shit ads up. Throw in your opportunity cost, which is the money you could make more of elsewhere, times three strips plus that fuckin' vice, and there you go.

You count on a fellow taking a piece off the top, and you're shit outa luck when he don't, but I got Pepe Lepieux out back working overtime. He hadn't made a stink since he first come around for handouts. He's out there sniffin' the bushes up next to Brittany and Miley, most likely thinking rabbit pussy is pretty damn close to skunk pussy, and a man has his needs. He ain't getting some, because the hutch is closed. But you know how they are.

I planned to feed this hash to Pepe and the girls and get it blended natural with the grass and pellets and stretch it out. But you can't measure your stretch, so I got one of them Championship Blenders with the twelve speeds, like to chew up your fuckin' hat.

I mix in about a quarter strip of hash and a half cup 'o rabbit turds and another half 'o skunk turds and then throw in some pepper to make it smoky and give it some texture. I don't know shit from shinola what this stuff is supposed to do, but it's a man's fuckin' money to say get the fuck outa here or hell, yes, I'll take the load.

I'm into it over a thousand dollars counting the Championship Blender, but your modern merchandising calls for your regular, your deluxe and your ultra-deluxe. I got Pepe and the girls on triple rations and the turds raked out for even drying. So a man wants some ultra, I throw some carrots in the hopper, or beets and asparagus if he wants the ultra-deluxe. Hell, I'll throw in some rhubarb and sardines and call it Double Whammy Mammy. They love a fancy handle.

I'm on a roll, and you can't get squirrelly over a few bucks, if you want a roll to stay hot. I figure five to one on the turd/hash mix, and where I come from, that's convincing.

I can roll it and get the job done. I don't give a shit, except to fix a few things. A man knows when it's time.

"Come on, boys. Pearl! Get in here!"

XI

Touch by Intention

Thinking the situation over, Stuey figures his best strategy: low profile. He'll blend in like the guy who sold him cocaine years ago, because the guy never got caught, and some things don't change. He looked like middle management in gray slacks and a button-down shirt and drove a Buick with room for the whole family. Any fool can fit the smuggler profile, but a smart cookie stays low. Two bales of marijuana and a pound of toot fit perfect in a Buick trunk, and the guy breezed through customs on interstates or at airports, you name it. No gold, no Rolex and no Porsche, only a briefcase, wingtips, a Timex and a dull, "Good morning."

"You want to get a suit and a cheap watch and some clunky shoes and rent a Buick?"

"I think we should rent Goldwings."

"For the Spring Fling? Why not get the Buick and put the windows down?"

"It's different now. I make that drive all the time. They're suspicious of big trunks because of the bombs. Goldwings, full-face helmets, some microphones, Larraine and Sue. It'll be a cakewalk."

"Tie some teddy bears on back?"

"Yeah. A teddy bear and a purple dinosaur. We'll mix it up."

"You thought it through. You want me to pay for this too?"

"No. It'll come off the top."

"Does not compute. I been looking forward to this trip, working on my scooter and my plans."

"Yeah, fine, if that's how you want it."

"That's how I want it. Besides, you can't rent a Goldwing that quick. You got to set it up. Besides, I want to slip out. The cops think I shot the neighbor."

"Did you kill him?"

"No."

"That's cool. I'm calling Wade tonight, get things set up."

"You said it was set up."

"I'll get it set up."

"You said it *was* set up."

"What's to set up? You don't call the liquor store and tell them you're coming in for a six pack, do you?"

"You want to go shopping?"

"That's what you do. Hash is all over the place." He reloads and lights the pipe.

"This stuff gets you too stoned."

"Don't smoke some."

"I thought we finished it."

"Yeah. We did. This is just a little extra."

"How much cash will we need?"

"Might as well pack what we can."

"How much is a pound?"

"I don't know."

"What do you know?"

"Twenty-eight ounces to the pound.... No! Sixteen ounces to the pound. Twenty-eight grams to the ounce. Okay, it's two hundred an ounce, but less by the pound. We ought to get it fucking way cheap for twenty pounds."

"You said ten pounds. Or twelve."

"Wait a minute. Let's say it's three grand a pound. Get forty grand."

"You're a numbers wiz."

"This shit's simple."

"I'll get ten grand, so if you lose it, I won't have to shoot you."

"Three pounds won't bale me out. Besides, you don't have a gun." He smiles abjectly as a pup who can't tell the difference between the rug and the paper.

"Mo wants to go."

"The one with the body?"

"That's Moira. This is Mo. She sells motorcycles."

"Oh, yeah. What for?"

"She knows her way around. Good rider. Wants to find her old man."

"Is her boyfriend lost?"

"Not her boyfriend, her father."

"Why would we go looking for her father?"

"It'll give us purpose."

"We have purpose."

"A woman is good at the border. Looks more like a family trip."

Stuey fires the ashes and calls to secure his future but gets no answer. "As I remember, she doesn't look like June Cleaver."

Buster calls Mo with approval from the boys. She says it's a heat wave forecast for tomorrow, up to fifty-eight. Buster says he'll bring sunscreen. They agree on nine a.m. at the coffee place by the motorcycle shop.

Larraine in repose on the sofa the next morning looks ready for the wax museum. He sits beside her and props a leg on the coffee table with his jacket on. She rubs his leg, wishing him well on the trail now taken. Louise shuffles over for a family gathering, and Larraine smiles wistfully.

So he offers a road trip one more time. It's a routine of sorts, but this time she rises and leaves. He and Louise move to the fire where she licks his face. She senses action and wants in, and he wonders why dogs can't go on road trips. She'd fit in socially, her tastes fairly matching those of the boys, along with her general attitude, but practicality is a bitch.

Then, like a randomly changing atmosphere, Larraine reappears in her jacket and boots. And leather pants and another air of resignation, what a woman of fortitude wears to a challenge or a last chance. Kissing the dog, she calls the sitter, who can be there in a jiff, and just that quick, it's a family outing to reckon.

Louise whines but recovers nicely when the sitter arrives.

In no time, two up, Buster and Larraine Fetteroff seem well matched, on the mend and down the road like it used to be. They arrive to good cheer, Mo and Larraine calling each other girlfriend and catching up. Larraine in leathers does fit in, kind of, briefly.

Stuey shows up at nine twenty because he had to clean his motorcycle, because crossing the border is easier if you don't look like a ragamuffin. And because it's a shame to show mud and bugs on so much chrome. His spray 'n wash detail only took twenty minutes. So what's the fucking rush? He carries a towel and Q-tips in an outside pocket of his T-bag for easy access, to clear the smudge and bugs when he fuels up. Why shouldn't he look his best?

Mo and Buster are on second lattes. Larraine sips herb tea, a special blend to counterbalance her morning mist. Crisp air is the best antidote to lingering doubt and a late start. Mo thinks she won't find her father easily, but it won't take long to check a few bars and chop shops.

Larraine says something about mates of differing tastes and growing demands. Mo says her recent divorce was foregone; he was so young and such a jerk, and four years of marriage seemed forever, especially the last three. But surely thirty years with Buster is different.

"Seven times four plus two," Larraine demurs. "Not so different, long way around."

Staring at his motorcycle like a random admirer, Stuey sidesteps to the window and orders a double tall 2% mocha with half foam; hold the cinnamon but heavy on the sprinkles. "Chocolate sprinkles. You do have chocolate sprinkles? Dark chocolate?" Stepping behind the coffee shack, he loads and lights. "Might as well be spring," he says. "Can't carry this stuff across the border."

He chokes on greed and passes the pipe, until everyone is ready, except Larraine, who was already ready, who stares at this self-absorbed, self–satisfied and self–centered display. "Are you compulsive? Or addicted? How can you live like that? How can you be surprised that your marriage failed and your kids won't talk to you? You impose on people. You waste their time, and you don't even.... Oh, forget it." Like a squall out of nowhere, she rains down on Stuey. He deserves it, but lightning strikes and sizzles the moment. The others step aside.

Stuey stares, gaining time in which to prep his return volley, but clouds hover, and emotion fades as quick as it came. Yet, alas, Stuey is a man scarred, in whom the damage is done. "Bitch. It's a fucking motorcycle trip."

Larraine won't remind him that his most frequent response to life is childish and petty, because she shouldn't need to. Arms folded and sticking to priciples, she ignores him. He's a mess, oblivious to the cause of his self-inflicted loss. "I could scream," she murmurs.

Stuey sees things differently; he's just a guy who lashes back at she who makes life miserable, whether the misery is his or that of his friend and patron. "You're the one with her nose stuck in fucking catalogues all day. What's that? Bitch."

Stuey's counter confirms Larraine's point, and another interlude must air and sort these feelings gone awry. Larraine profiles harshly, like the witch, which should count for plenty in court. Stuey may seem addictive, but many people do, having fun, on vacation, merely enjoying a bit of hash before hitting the road. Is that any cause for an attack? His forehead bunches. He looks down. He looks hurt.

She turns to him. "I'm sorry. It doesn't have to be this way. Please." She steps toward him. He steps in. They embrace.

"You know I've always wanted you," he says.

Buster laughs. Mo spews latte. Larraine pushes off. "You're a mess. I wish you weren't."

"We can work through this." He lights the pipe.

She straightens the muss. They sip, contemplating character and the day ahead, till Stuey shrugs. "I thought all you had to do was work every day and get to where you made more money than you spent and then have fun." So ends the reflection.

They wait, watching Stuey blow on his mocha, to cool it for more pleasurable sipping. Since it's a wait, Larraine needs to pee.

Stuey tells her to take her time, have a number two, if she wants, no squeezing, because it's only a few hours to Port Coquitlam, twenty miles east of Vancouver, and they have rezzies at a cheap hotel hardly a stumble from the Fuzzy Glo Room, so no rush. He promises a real kick at the Glo Room on a Friday night.

Larraine returns from the restroom relieved but peeved. The paper seat cover dispenser was empty, and no toilet tissue. Not to worry. She made do as she learned to do long ago.

Stuey recalls the shootout that made the Glo Room famous.

Mo chimes in with the weaponry Mama told her was common back then.

Larraine can't help feeling perturbed, heading out to a notorious dive known for gun violence. Nobody asks why she looks worried, so she sighs. Clouds fill in, and Stuey says it'll be cocktails in Canada in no time. Oh, those Canucks and their liquor gene. Is this gonna be a knee-walker or what?

Buster throws a leg over. Larraine begins her mounting ritual. Mo idles, yet they wait. Stuey finishes his latte, ignoring the pressure, because he doesn't need it. "Go ahead. I'll catch up."

Buster agrees. Friends should avoid expectation, because friendship is not marriage. He pulls out. Mo follows. Into third gear and the rearview they see Stuey watching, sipping his double tall 2% fa fa de cafe. Hardly into fourth it's time to turn, except that Buster remembers the money and pulls over to tell Mo to wait for Stuey while he heads back to the bank.

Larraine gets off. She'll wait too. "Is it always like this?"

Buster pulls a U and heads back.

Not too far up the road a huge sign blocks the vista, inviting drivers to friendly banking. Buster imagines three wraps of cordite around each stanchion and wonders if he ever would, or does he only ventilate regrets. He remembers open fields gradually ascending to the trees, before the bank and its sign got planted. He thinks that's the source of his bad feelings. He thinks life is a convergence of things gone bad or good, and the challenge is his, to seek another gradual ascent. Could something so innocuous as bank make him feel explosive? He doubts it, but then it's only a few days since he shot the neighbor. Ah, well…. He greets the teller with a nice-day smile and doesn't ask why a looker would work in a bank. For weekends? For backyard barbecue? She scans his driver's license, as he says through the talk hole, "Ten thousand, please. Big bills. Make that twelve. Twelve thousand."

Sudden insight reveals the world of his making, the world yet to be made. "Make it thirty. Thousand." Motel, food and gas should run what, two hundred a day? That's five days in a grand, times thirty makes a hundred fifty days, but it'll stretch to six months easy. He can run longer with care.

The teller squints over her smile, also fixed. "I'll need my manager."

"I'm in a hurry."

The manager arrives to assess, as Buster checks his messages. First is a missive from Moira. "You should be happy for me and yourself, considering. You never loved me. Henry does, and I'm learning to love him. He's kind. And you're married. We know what you want. But what do I get? Buster, you're no great catch. Okay?"

Is a wonderful, lovely time so little to share? Moira thinks it is, and who can blame her? He glances up and through the sneeze shield at bank personnel, as message two comes up. "Oh, Buster. It's Henry Schurz. Hey, uh, call me. We should review a few things. I think we may be on to something. Later."

Buster hears numbers and soft voices, and the manager says "Hello, I'm Bill Jones."

"Hi, Bill. I'm in a hurry. I need thirty grand in big bills, please. I have an account at the main branch and would like to keep it there." He pulls his driver's license back under the sneeze window. "If you don't mind."

The manager needs one more i.d. and reads Buster's passport slowly. "Okay." The teller counts it out. "Traveling on your motorcycle today?"

"Yes, I am."

"It looks like a good day for it."

"Yes, It does."

"Going far?"

Not too far. Just up to Canada for some hash. "No. Not too far."

"I'd like to get one of those things, some day."

"Yes. You might like it." They smile in agreement.

The teller counts again and says, "Thank you for choosing First Consolidated."

Buster carries the wad outside and stuffs it into a saddle bag and heads back to the coffee place, where Stuey waits, engine running, and yells, "We go north and east to pick up Highway 20."

"I had to get the cash. Mo and Larraine are just up there."

"This is gonna be great. And we'll have the home crew for back up. Not that we'll need it."

"Oh, boy."

"Yeah, it's gonna be a cakewalk."

All systems are go, except for Mo, who needs a double tall piss. Not to worry; she squats behind a backhoe just up the bank. Larraine seems worn, so Stuey suggests another bowl, maybe across the interstate and into the trees, for the discreet cover available there.

Mo tidies up and remounts. They ride.

Stuey leads to the first long sweep at sixty-five then accelerates in a merge to Highway 20, where car traffic races to get ahead, and a motorcycle must go faster to gain the niche, or else lose the exit. Or get creamed. The next stretch is straight and thick with traffic and just as fast. Stuey and Mo burn it. Buster lags to Warwick where 20 becomes 9, and scurvy gets curvy. He doesn't mind lower speed to better ease in his new jugs. Larraine prefers slower, or tolerates it more. The two-lane road is maintained but hardly used, with far fewer gas stations and no franchise foods or strip malls. Life was better when this was the main road, and it feels like old times, until Larraine knuckles his helmet and yells to go faster, to keep up.

Towering conifers frame her difficulty in the rearview mirror. Cloud cover makes her shudder. Warmth is sparse, but sunbeams light the ascent ahead. He slows into it, expecting another knock on the head, but the balm is shared.

Highway 9 meanders above the valley and river below. Hospitable if narrow, the road invites acceleration with its smooth skin and gentle curves. Out of an easy S in the shade they twist to a sunny straightaway. Into another shade, they slow for a drop into a shadow that could be hiding black ice at the bottom. Feeling the way, they punch into sunlight and a bold climb out.

Ascending on another sweep, they bank tastefully into a peg scraper, as Larraine quacks, "I hate it when you do that!"

Yeah, yeah, except that you secretly love it and admire my skill.

These scenes will be up for review in a few hours when they ease into the warmth of a distant bar. For now they rise, in grace, to forgetfulness among the trees. Euphoria in speed and angle mixes with mountain slopes, tall trees and sunbeams. Sugarplums dance in their heads, and memory defers to the moment. God speaks in the hills, but belief is merely another attempt at feeling.

Oh, this mile is good, on the way to redemption, and another mile comes next. Buster wonders what a bank manager is doing now and knows he's checking his 401k, counting down the days. Buster gooses it, straightening into the stretch with love.

Little specks ahead look like scooterists approaching. People in the wilderness were once eager to meet and share their experience of the trail. Human contact was rare and informative and may still be, on a road unblemished by progress.

Like cake waiting for icing, the blacktop curves to the crest where one, two, three riders appear on the far end of the ridge at the top of the world. The imminent meeting only moments away feels old-fashioned and happy, as if nature has not died, not yet, not here.

Three riders coming on are not folks in the traditional sense but fill in as hardcore with cold intention in black steel, not life-stylers but non-stylers. Ponytails flapping could signal a trio of hip waiters, but they're more likely bikers, given their rough machinery and Spartan accessories. Also thick with insulation, gloves and scarves, these riders approach in low-grade thunder, with the unique, metallic clang of chain-drive secondaries through their anvil-banging pistons and clattering valves. And pipes blaring in staccato detonations of chaos.

Their toy helmets are different too, in keeping with their high bars, minimal seats and bare bones up front. Single rear-views on their ape hangers, bobbed fenders, solo head lamps, no instruments and a few dings mark these riders as pure, or at least basic. Seeing front brakes on all three, Buster wonders why they pussied out up front after showing such cajones. But then nobody runs brakeless up front anymore. Do they?

And what's with the lumpy, half-assed backpacks strapped on, two of the three spuming dust like trucks on back roads?

But it's a grand reunion in the stinging, numbing cold and the greater golden joy. Only those who saddle up in early spring attain such moments. Hardly road brothers, they share a difference from the general population that works, breeds and shops, the end. Among these riders coming and going is a spirit fulfilled. Wending nearer, no hands drop below grips in greeting. The motorcycle wave is common to those who may not speak in a supermarket or a bar, but on a wilderness two-lane, the wave is often offered in simple tribute to the sun dancing in the trees and the spine-tingling moment that will survive the last gasp, and two random riders who may never meet again, sharing that gem.

Love is all around. And up ahead, whiskey waits for every man and woman.

Stuey doesn't wave, as some riders don't.

Mo doesn't wave, because nobody is waving.

The hardcore guys with the fake German war helmets and dirt bags on back don't wave, because waving is a friendly thing to do, which could undermine a radical statement.

Buster can go either way, but frankly, once the weather warms and riders come at you all day, waving is a pain in the ass; next thing you know you're waving at full-face helmets on Jap scooters with trailers and teddy bears. Why bother?

Even so, this passing warrants a wave, considering the season opener and the singular nature of any rider long-hauling in these dazzling, frigid conditions. Buster feels better than an hour ago and infinitely risen from recent days. Where bile bubbled, now goodwill comes forth. Tingles shoot the beautiful sweep and fill the hair's breadth between passing scooters, as if with a magical buffer.

First approaching is a shaggy bear whose scooter seems small as the donkey under Friar Tuck. He rides askew, favoring half his ass. A big man riding sidesaddle shouldn't wave. His toy helmet looks like a cereal bowl. He nods anyway with eighteen inches to spare, drifting outside as the outsiders snug to the center.

Buster feels sentimental; piggy wants a wave, so he does.

Larraine quacks, "Don't do that!"

Do what?

He twists for a bite in a bit more lean, narrowing the gap, honing the groove and showing his stuff for the second nitty-gritty boy, coming on close enough to mumble greetings. A quick glance in a rearview frames Larraine etched in fear, and no club colors on the first rider receding. These guys are hardcore but not organized.

The second rider passes, a wiry guy with a dartboard face and straight-ahead gaze, wearing oblivion as a matching accessory in a theme, call it mouth breather in flat black with dirt and dings. His toy Nazi helmet indicates that he gives not a smidgen of a rat's ass for polite society or you or any iota of your brain mush.

Buster waves. He doesn't wave back, so Buster yells, "Pussy!" But the only sound is heavy hammers falling madly on tired steel.

"What?" Larraine calls. Usually a decent passenger who leans in tandem, she now corrects him, leaning opposite to better help him steer. He compensates as the last rider approaches.

Of course riders show off. Buster feels camaraderie in daredevil proximity to the double yellow, or maybe it's only a dare. Either way, this passing is molten: sunshine, speed, nature and angulation flow from the sky. This pass will be accessed from the private reserves next winter, in the cold and wet, when life is harsh and far away. Or maybe next weekend. He will also revisit this third rider for commitment to the show at hand. Reaching high to grasp his ghastly ape hangers, the third rider struggles against the wild fringe whipping from his grips and sleeves like a high-ticket S&M whore at full throttle. Stuey runs apes too and suffers the air scoop. But Stuey's are merely awkward, while this guy's are ridiculous. Stuey is finished in chrome and candy apple red, while this guy is hazed in bugs with a dusty afterburn. Stuey runs straights, but these sawed-off shotguns spit fire on the goose, drifting and hogging, nearly touching the double yellow.

Buster suspects a fine, slick mist in the wake, blow-by past warped rings and scored cylinders now too thin from too many bores. Such a mist settling on asphalt should present nothing more than regular processing by the best tires money can buy. Why would Buster run anything less? But no tires can process wet on yellow—slick as snot on a doorknob, that combo calls for leeway.

But the last rider offers a snaggled grin under a spiked helmet at the wondrous narrowing of margins, in what seems to be a dare of his own. Buster eases into the hub of their little universe, hoping this isn't chicken but an enduring display of something or other.

Larraine expresses herself silently at last, with a death grip.

The moment is made pure in the closing gap between hands outstretched. This is not a wave but a step to the line. Communion is a reach, for Buster a reach under the radical apes, fringe, sissy bar and fire-breathers to a boneshaker shovelhead roaring and clattering like the king of beasts denying decrepitude.

Hey, give a rider his due; it's hard enough to hold a sweep this tight grabbing apes, much less holding it one-handed and clearing the fringe. Buster factors damage control on a lay down as fingertips touch with the pop and recoil of an errant spark.

High as hot shots, Buster and Grimy surge on survival, knowing they'll not likely meet again, and who cares? Lesser riders would take the fall and wake up in the ER with the gouges and breaks that such tricks often come to. Eyes and ears would open on the condescending lectures of doctors and nurses who've never been tempted by sunbeams and speed. Or not open. Or worse yet, paralyzed. But they hold the sweep to within an inch of their life.

That was a stupid move, Buster thinks, taking his left grip again as Larraine drowns out his pipes, yelling in his ear about stupidity, macho bullshit and other redundancies of the male behavior pattern. Who knows what maniac was banking this way on the double yellow? Who knows what was behind those fingers that could have grabbed? Who knows if that silly fringe could have snagged on a finger?

Never mind. They pulled it off like seasoned veterans, viewing the moment of being through dark lenses: laugh lines, squint lines, lines of joy and despair.

Then they're gone.

Who was that guy? You can't help wonder, roaring in unison to the greater joy. Buster gives it full-throttle and a perfect shift to egg the other guy on, and he laughs at the billows in his rearview when the last guy misfires. Buster feels warm and fuzzy, one-up, but he's glad the last guy didn't throw a rod. Hell, you can't throw a rod on eighty pounds of compression, except that you can. Then they'd have to go back to help a road brother who isn't a road brother. The smoke thins and rounds out of sight when Buster says, "You're on your own now."

"What?"

The scenic summit is perfect for another pee and a bowl before the border, because you really can't carry that stuff across.

XII

Okay, We Gotta Plan This Out

Lonny Snodgrass hasn't been called Lon since school days, when Mom asked Lon to help out around the place. "Lon, Hon, take out the trash," or, "Lon, pick that shit up, and I mean now!"

When he dropped out of seventh grade, she advised, "A feller might as well ought to get on with it, Lon."

Some men graduate on their own and they damn well know when it happens. What'd they want him to do, bite down on a nut so tough it'd chip his tooth? Mom understood. She was good for that and ought to be here to see him at the threshmotherfuckinghold of success. Hell, he'd give her a few bucks. Why not?

Grimy Grimes lays out the plan, opening on the old nickname, just like Mom used to do: "Lon, I want you to work point for us."

"Point? What the fuck does that mean?"

"Give it a chance, wouldja?" Hobarth Grimes is a tricky sumbitch. So hold your horses on a brink-of-the-future situation, because the answer is surely cued up. Hobo paces, grasping his wind gussets like one of them TV lawyers going for the conviction. "By that I mean you're first man out. You're the scout. Point man. That keeps me in reserve for bringing up the rear when the shit hits the fan. That's my specialty. It's like a...like a fucking army, sending the infantry in first, the tough motherfuckers to wear 'um down. Then comes the heavy artillery in case of back sass. That would be Buck, the heaviest artillery we got. They do it like that at the car places too, you'll notice, when you try to back out of the deal."

The car lot example, of keeping firepower in reserve, is lost on Lonny and Buck. Neither one knows any more about car lots than seeing all them fucking plastic flags and all that white paint fucking up the windshields with years and dollars down and more dollars out the ass, none of it worth the glass it's written on because all they want to do is get you in there and hold you down while they fuck you black and blue, up the ass no less.

Buck reaches back for an absentminded scratch, till Lonny preempts, "Don't stir up that stink in here. We're trying to conduct a fucking meeting for chrissakes, if you don't mind. Buck stops, but he'll need some ointment soon. Hobo's thinking on a strategy, looking confident. Lonny rises to the feel of it and tries a few phrases on for size. "Point man. First in. Scout. I like it."

Buck Dibble keeps his mouth shut, though he's known for a long time that he's the heaviest artillery around without Hobo saying so. He could squash Hobo Grimes like a cockroach but won't because Hobo might shoot him. Still, he thinks squashing Hobo might feel better than any cockroach. Now why is that? For starters, you'd have to be dumber 'n a flatlander to think he's got your best interest at heart. Still and all, Grimy is the first man yet to take a peep at the future, so it won't hurt to give a listen.

Grimy rambles that he wants Buck on clean up, because they need a big, strong motherfucker on guard at the back door, covering the hind side and making sure nobody fucks around on them.

Buck hears with one ear while the other still stings worse than a badly scratched asshole. *Go on. Get out. I'm busy. Grow up. You guys are plain damn too much.* How could she....

Well, there's no fool like a big fat fool, who may still be a fool, expecting a woman to come around and love him once he gets his money. It's not like you never know, because you do know. A woman won't use that tone of voice if she has one iota of love in her heart for a man. Unless she got treated poorly and now takes it out on all the guys, especially one who, well, really does love her.

"Buck! Come in, Buck!" Lonny pushes his shoulder. "Where the fuck you at? Still dreaming of what's-her-name's pussy? Wake up, pencil dick. You're guarding the back door, covering our ass, which seems poetical when you think about it."

"Yeah, yeah, whatever that means."

Hobo stops and glares. "That means you're the motherfucker we're counting on to pull this off."

"Pull what off? Hobo, you talk like a politician. We don't have any money. You want to steal the hash?"

"I never said that. We need to get it is all. We might have to pay for it later, but we can't do that until we sell it, and we have to get it first, or be the same sorry fucks next week as we are this week."

"I'm listening," Buck says, wondering why he's a sorry fuck this week or any week, but then suspecting what the reason might be, which isn't too complicated. It's the inability to put one foot in front of the other, even with the path marked plain as day.

"We'll take a look at the hash, because that's how you do it. That old fucker; he'll want to see the money, and that's when we tell him we have to get it, but we need the hash to get it. Then we get it. It's simple, and it'll work, even if that old fart can't see it. He will."

"What if he doesn't?"

"Don't worry. That's where I come in. We might need to leave him some collateral, you know. That's where you come in."

Buck laughs, "What's he want me for?"

"Not you. Your scooter."

The big head jerks on this note, as does the medium head nearby, much as the shaggy head must have jerked when God said, "Abraham, kill me a son."

The big head shakes. "Nobody fucks with my scooter. It's all I got. Besides, it ain't worth ten grand."

"Yeah? What would you sell it for?"

Buck looks off and slowly nods. "Ten grand, if you want it."

"That's what I mean. Would you put that rattle trap on the table for a while if it could turn into a brand new scoot with a bitch on back who'll mind her manners?"

"What's a while?"

"That's your call. You stay back. You let me and Lonny get down the road, and then you go. You say it's a emergency call or some shit. Your mama fell down. Your asshole itches and you need some cream. You'll be right back."

Buck looks puzzled. "How do I know you guys...you guys will...." He can't put certain variables into words without insulting the principals, so Hobo helps him out.

"You'll know everything you need to know in the person of your close friend here. He'll represent your interests just like you're representing ours."

Buck sees Lonny practically tasting the action, highballing for the future with Hobo Grimes. "But what happens if...." Buck gets stuck again on downside potential that can take so many forms.

Hobo stands firm. "If what? You tell me what in hell is gonna happen. The old fucker'll call the cops? Or he'll get in your way? Shit, Buck, we'll pay him once we get the money. We proved it today. This'll work. We coulda hauled four hundred pounds over the border. What makes you go chickenshit at the heart of the matter?"

Buck shrugs. Hauling three bags of dirt over the line proved nothing, but he won't say so, because if Grimy Grimes thinks Buck

Dibble is that easily fooled, well okay. But he takes this opportunity to present mutual indemnity as another cog in the gears. That is, they'll share the downside. "How about we have this agreement, Grimy, in front of Lonny. He'll be our witness. If anything goes wrong, and I lose my scooter, then I get yours."

Now Grimy squares off. "I ain't saying there ain't no risk. Man, who'd a thought you'd pussy out. We all might lose our scooters. We all might die. Shit. No wonder that bitch cut you loose. She could smell it on you."

Buck Dibble has a mind to press his thumb down on Hobo Grimes' head, but Hobo'd pull his gun and do his little dance, if Buck didn't kill him, which could be riskier than stealing some hash. So Buck presents a compromise. "Okay, how about all of us lose the same, if any of us loses anything. One of us loses, then all three pay it back."

Lonny turns to Hobo.

"Suits me," Hobo says. "No sweat off my balls."

They agree to break before supper. Buck hankers for private time after a long ride and a tough planning session. But he doesn't have a cat to feed or an answering machine to check, and it's not likely anybody pinned a note to his door, even if she knows where it is, which she doesn't. Still, a little time out seems in order.

Buck pulls his shorts back up and then his pants. He hesitates but zips his chaps back up too, what the hell, and finally pulls his boots back on. He'll swing around to the Drug Rite for some asshole ointment then maybe hit the prime rib special at the Quittin' Time Inn, because he'd be plain damn impractical to start a serious diet on the same day as the Huge Double-Down Dinner, a twenty-four ounce slab o' prime rib with mashed potatoes and another slab for free if you can finish it. He can, and he can trim the fat, some of it. What can they say, 'Oh, you gotta eat the fat too?'

Lonny sees the hunger on his extra large friend and knows what night this is. He'll hang with Buck and says on his way to the pisser that it's Special night, only eight ninety-five.

Grimy finishes his beer and belches. "Sounds like a winner. I forgot about the Special. Come on. I'm buying."

"Hey!" Lonny calls.

"I'll meet you there," Buck says. "I gotta make a stop."

The other two smirk but stay mum because of sensitivities rising over romance and itchy buttholes. Buck wants to exit the awkward silence, broken only by a whiz and a beer can crushing.

Private time and dining alone on oatmeal and hippy sprouts might sound better in theory and feel better in a few hours. But the Quittin' Time Huge Double Down is a rare light in hard times, and the place has one of those gimp crappers with the grab rails that come in handy when you're applying the ointment with your boots and chaps and shit on, and you have to squat and find the bullseye with that little nozzle that can stab the soft part and like as not make you fall on your big, fat hairy ass in the meantime. The Double Down is only practical, and anywhere else would present it's own set of risks with hardly the reward. Besides that, the whole day has been tough and feels like progress, maybe. At any rate, Buck Dibble is done for now. He shuffles out the door without another word, except for the unspoken *fuck you, assholes*.

Up the road feels like distance gained. Buck backs to the curb of the Drug Rite across from the Fuzzy Glo Room and sits for a minute to ponder what progress he could make on nine more clicks back to the Quittin' Time and the Double Down hugeness. He'd pack more poundage and mount up again for a nipple twister back to this same spot for the drinking segment of the evening. What does he need that circle jerk for, some grab rails? Let the dipshits wait. Let 'em wonder why the backdoor man isn't wagging his tail over big money and bitches with manners. And three more pounds o' beef down the gullet.

He winces on a sting and moves gently to get inside and up next to whatever consolation a squeeze tube might provide. Maybe now's the time for New Blue Cold Gel they advertise on that show where the County Coroner plays it dumb like a motherfucking fox, and on that billboard over by the old folks home. He's been thinking about that *Blue Cold Gel* stuff. He burns. They say it has twice the cooling relief. So? Why not?

But he can't find it in asshole ointments or on down the aisle to toothpastes. He winces again, imagining a squeeze of new blue gel toothpaste up his rough red dukey chute. And he laughs. What the hell. He can't make heads or tails of the lineup, what with the toothpastes and butthole greases looking alike. *Why don't they just put Asshole Ointment on the label, oh, no; that would be too easy.* Or he could wake up feeling like last week's trash and brush his teeth with…. Shit, that's disgusting.

It's not in toothpaste, so he drifts back up to assholes, where he scans more slowly. What the hell: Anusoothe, Analink, Arctic Dream, Asssonice, Buttrexe, Tain'tsobad, ChuteKooler, DingleDown, Dead Out, IceHole, Flamebegone, Freedom Cream, Brown Round Pads, Polar Soft, Torch Song…. There it is! No wonder he couldn't find it. New Blue Cool Gel could be toothpaste. The tricky part is: New Blue Cool Gel ain't even the name of it. That's what's in it. The name is Asssonice, with New Blue Cool Gel.

Buck feels better on relief potential. He realizes that it's not ass on ice, though that image is soothing. It's ass so nice, on account of the extra s, which also serves to sizzle the hot sumbitch in cooling relief. That brings another smile, but it slams shut on a dime. *Aw, shit, I hate that….*

Buck Dibble hates it when a woman, especially one in his viability range, sees him grasping a family size tube of Asssonice, with New Blue Cool Gel, in the moment of eye contact. He hates it when she's wearing a dress and probably teaches third grade and will tell her kids on Monday what'll happen if they don't do their homework and eat a bunch of greasy beef instead of their spinach. They'll grow up big and fat and have to wear ratty leathers and be a slave to their rhoids is what.

He hates it more when she's in blue jeans and flannel and clearly thinks, *Man, I'd hate to have that big dumb fuck's itchy ass.*

He hates it most of all when she's similarly built, not bloated like him but well rounded in body and face with bright green eyes and peer group accessories, including leathers and road shadow under her eyes from a day in the saddle like himself. He could have met her across the street at the Glo Room, but no!

He casually steps sideways to study the toothpastes as Mo scans the asshole rack and the toothpastes and moves to the next aisle over for some tampons, putting them eye to eye yet again, though the metal shelving between them. He peers through.

She peers too, and as he blushes, she says, "You'll be sorry, you get it wrong."

"Huh?"

"Don't put toothpaste on your asshole. It burns."

"How do you know?"

"I did it once. This jerk switched the tubes as a joke. I wasn't laughing. I'd like to see him try that on you. Fuck!"

Buck laughs too, wondering how life can change on you just that quick; one minute it's day in, day out, no friends, gray skies, desperate schemes, and the next thing you know it's a bright golden meadow with all those...all those fucking birds and shit just singing their little asses off right there on the fence.

"I'm Buck," he says.

"Mo," she says.

He shrugs. "Dibble. Buck Dibble."

"Mo Dowd. Suppose I'll see you over there." She nods across the street.

"Yeah. You will."

"Well." She picks a box of Supers without looking. "Good."

He grabs a tube of toothpaste. "Yeah." And she leaves, so he can get his Asssonice in private. Who could be hungry on a night like this? Then again, she'll be over at the Glo Room for a while, until it gets good anyway. Besides, he's done playing puppy dog for every one of them comes along with a tease, not that so many do, but this is two in two days, even though Missy doesn't count. But this one sure is friendly. Hell, he does not need another sit-down meal, but he'll get so damn hungry along about eight....

XIII

Rendezvous

A four-hour ride becomes six with pit stops. Arriving east of Vancouver in rush hour, they suffer the bumper-to-bumper crawl off an exit, where they pull over to let engines cool and check the map. Another hour of traffic ends at the hotel. It's dark when Larraine slides off and Buster backs in at the Fuzzy Glo Room.

Mo crosses the road to the Drug Rite next to the hotel for tampons and that aspirin with codeine sold over the counter because Canucks don't take no shit from no headaches. She laughs at the rat bike out front, but the dings and crust show more miles than your average dog 'n pony, so she gives the rat biker his due.

Back at the spray 'n wash a block up, Stuey is getting presentable, buffing chrome and digging bugs from the headlight housings, turn signals, levers and front-facing Philips heads. Why the fuck they'd put a Philips head facing front he'll never know. He'll buff his chin spoiler while he's at it. Why not? Pipes and wheels take the polish in minutes. They cost six hundred each.

Buster waits out front for Mo to finish shopping while Larraine fixes her face in a rearview, murmuring that only a road whore could work in such a small mirror and no light to tell if the spots are on the mirror or her face. If she had a flashlight, but…what's the use?

Buster wishes she could be a road whore for once, however briefly. He shows the same stoic smile, because she won't, because she can't, because it didn't turn out that way. But it's happy hour at the Glo Room after a great ride, and Stuey can catch up. They feel better already, off the beasts and easing into the ass and elbow crowd for half-price drinks. Buster and his double date drift to an open spot at a narrow drinking counter. The waitress waves three little napkins and yells that it's happy hour and her name is Missy. Pressing Mo unavoidably, she bends in and turns an ear up to hear what Mo said. Mo backs up, having said nothing.

Buster ogles Missy and her rack, displayed to advantage for optimal return, which he admires on several levels. He yells, "Your tits are perfect!"

Mo yells back, "Thanks!" She yells that she wants a beer.

"What?" Larraine yells from his other side.

"Your tits are okay."

"What?"

Missy yells, "It really gets good later!"

"How good can it get? I also want a beer!"

Larraine shrugs to make it three; this place would never have Organic Mango Rush.

Joe Boggs taps her on the shoulder and yells that it really gets good later, sliding three shots to the newcomers. Joe gets the picture; she's Buster's wife. The other gal knocking her shot is catching up to high time. Buster sips and cringes, as the crowd squirms like an organism in cell division, as reveler density thickens.

Stuey approaches in leathers and headscarf, feeling better with his scooter out front, buffed and gleaming. Fresh off the road, ruddy with residue, he beams. His friends laugh at his compulsion to maximum buff and polish; it's dark outside, and he hasn't washed his face. He's missed the first two rounds and raises doubts among the crowd, many of whom squint at his boutique leathers and no scars, no tats, no stink and too many teeth. Is he a rider or urban scum, yet to break a sweat for an honest dollar or skip a payment or shine the rent? His jacket and chaps are The Montana Collection, a thirteen-hundred-dollar (U.S.) ensemble establishing discretionary income. He's a rich fucker. At least he has no fringe.

Missy unloads three beers and nineteen more shots of tequila. Like an executive with a secretarial need, Stuey bends as if to offer an ear and sniffs her cleavage, as she presses Mo again and turns to take his order. He yells that later, if she wants to....

She yells, "Whaddaya want?"

So he yells into the din, or into a mystical gap in the din, because the din goes silent, as if his voice parts the noise like Moses at the Red Sea. Between periods and capitols, words and phrases, into the pall at twenty past the hour, he wails. "I'll have a Chardonnay!"

Heads turn again to the dude in matching leathers, headscarf and gloves, and a chorus rejoins: "Chardonnay?"

"What?"

"Oh, man!"

"Chardonnay?"

"Fuuuck."

Stuey's smile warps under the load. Cruel judgment sets quick as Crazy Glue, sticking him on puffery and pussery, where he can only squirm, raising a shot and toasting: "With a tequila back!" He slams it like a man of confidence, but the lull holds with no mercy, banging the gavel on conviction.

"What's your costume?" Missy yells, twisting the blade like a gladiator before a bloodthirsty crowd, perhaps sacrificing this tip for the greater potential. "I mean, what are you supposed to be?"

The lull lingers insufferably as this would-be rider remains hobbled beyond redemption. His status is obvious. A real man can't say he's a real man, because saying it establishes doubt, which prevails here. He doesn't know what to say, and another shot will show only alcoholism, which may be better than pussyism but is hardly a face-saver. Stuey appears to be guilty of the pose, a man wild in his mind but not in his heart and certainly not in his throttle.

His friends are also helpless, until Mo accelerates as necessary in this difficult turn, and she yells at Missy the waitress: "What's your costume!" Clearing herself from the incredible rack pressed upon her, she barrels through cruel aspersion, squaring to Missy and wailing anew, "What the hell are you supposed to be? Mae West waiting tables? Can I shake one of those things and listen to it? Whaddaya think? Real or Memorex? Christ on a crutch! Can a guy get a jar o' wine in here without a pussy whipping? Fuckinay, sister, you put those jugs on me one more time...."

Objection sustained. Rising ripples concur that a man shouldn't be pussy whipped or thirsty, and tits should be real or at least shown, and come on over here, Missy, and press 'em on me. With decibels restored to howling good cheer, a wayfarer could wonder if a lull ever was or could be.

Stuey reaches for two more shots for himself and his new road brother or sister or whatever. They clink and slosh to affirm the bond, as another swatch of road slag tumbles behind.

Perfection draws nigh when Wade Donaldson asks if anybody wants some hash.

"Yeah!"

"You got hash?"

"Donny can ask around. It oughta be here." Donny is Wade's son, a lanky boy of twenty-eight who grins often as not, who serves with filial duty as game procurer for old Dad's old friends.

"We want to take some home," Stuey yells.

"Stay calm, Chardonnay. He has to play it cool, you know."

Yes, yes. Coolness is key, and so is a decent buzz to get this sphere of being from the cocktail phase into the dinner phase. So the troupe drinks and drinks, to harmonize pressure and flow with great good cheer.

Missy serves Stuey a jelly jar of wine, presumably Chardonnay, then turns to Mo to humbly suggest, "You know, you didn't have to jump down my throat. I was only having fun with him."

"You left me no choice, Missy. That kind of fun sets a man up to take a fall. He's a friend of mine."

In a blink, it's love. Mo remembered her name, and that's proof enough for Missy Malone. That Mo has the spinal fortitude to stand in defense of her road brother makes her rare. How many seasoned women can handle a crowd like that?

Mo reads the signals and throws an arm over Missy's shoulder like John Wayne did with that young gal in the one about gumption.... No, it was about grit, and she says, "Hey, no hard feelings, little lady."

Missy bats her baby blues. "You can hold one to your ear and shake it and listen any time."

"What?"

"Nothing. I'll tell you later. Okay?"

"Yeah, sure. Whatever."

Missy loves the reconciliation and a seasoned woman to look forward to, or, at any rate, to look at.

Larraine cannot relate or curb her recoil on such odious stimuli.

Stuey is laughing at two jokes from different directions, both scatological, so she sips from his jelly jar. It's not bad, so she has another, till Stuey clinks with another shot glass, and they drink up. He aims to get to where he needs to be. She stares, so he asks, "What? Am I doing it wrong again?"

She laughs like a doyenne at a droll notion, like, say, serving coffee on saucer doilies, and she allows, "No-ho-ho. You did beautifully."

"I did?"

She sips. "How many men here would have the integrity to order what they really want?"

"Integrity? Is that like balls? I think most of them do have it, but quick sex isn't on the menu. I don't think Missy puts out too often. She's showing off for tips."

"Can you give yourself a chance? I'm paying you a compliment here."

"Sorry."

"Thank you. That's what I mean. You do have a sense of…what? *Esprit de corps? Joi de vivre? J'ne sais quoie?*"

"I try to run a *laissez-faire* government."

"I'm serious. How often do I get to love your panache instead of hating your vulgarity? Scratch that. I don't hate you, Stuart. I hate your uncouth compulsion. A little bit goes a long way, but my God, you can't stop on a bit, can you? You know I don't admire you often. You ordered what you want. You showed strength. Combine that with an apology when you're wrong, and you could be a real man. I think, Mr. Stewart, you could be intriguing, if you could only but allow it."

In another rare interlude, Stuey is speechless, imagining himself as the silent type. No, not silent but controlled, like a suave guy in the movies with pithy quips on perfect timing. She makes conversation but sounds chronic: "All this cigarette smoking, and nobody looks happy. I don't get it."

He reaches for a crumpled pack on the narrow counter, draws a breather and lights up. "Cigarettes don't make you happy. They make time more manageable." He thinks she appreciates the tasteful rejoinder. She moves nearer. Hell, they're practically divorced. And she does take his meaning, drawing a cigarette of her own.

"I used to smoke, you know," she says, fitting in.

"I can imagine…." But there he goes again, compulsively uncouth, so he shifts gears way before redline. "Intriguing. Women like that, don't they?"

"Yes, we love it. That is, when we can find it. Which is very rare. You must know that."

"I never thought about it. I have so many needs of my own. Maybe I'll change."

"That sounds like potential. And it is intriguing."

"I keep bad company. These guys don't think about that shit."

She ignores him to make her point and have another quaff to help her mood. "I assumed this wine would be young and cheap. What kind of list could this place have? Still, it's buttery along with the oak and…what? Is that pepper I taste? It's not bad, really, considering the ambience."

Stuey takes a sip. "*Peu peu.* I think the ambience helps. I think the pepper is why I drink this shit and didn't even know it."

She rolls her eyes, and so ends the renewal phase, because it's time for dinner. Or would that be chow? The gang all here retreats to a dining room for a banquet befitting a convergence of road brothers on the night of a day of riding from all points to the center. It's the eve of untold glory and many miles ahead. Larraine sits next to Stuey, a first.

But Stuey knows what dinner repast will entail, or would that be the inevitable melee that comes with chow? None of it will intrigue, except on pathological analysis of man behavior and bonding ritual, on tearing away the years, to reveal the wild boys they still want to be, they need to be and now, before it's too late.

Derek Donaldson only rode fifty clicks but dances on his chair at the head of the table, far from home. Derek is Wade's brother,

Donny's uncle and a business associate of Stuey and Joe's. The troops drift in, slosh and hug in hail-fellow reunion. How's it been and how's it hang?

A small voice rises in the din. "But it's aww right now. In fact it's a gas. Yeah it's aww right…. Jumpin' Jack Flash is a gas gas gas." The tiny tune from Derek's headset bubbles up to signal fermentation. Derek's spastic dance suits the anarchy to which the boys aspire, for which they grasp, in which they revel.

They laugh and take their seats. Many more drinks are served, shots and more shots with a few vodka tonics and a tequila grapefruit for the vitamin C, because we're nothing without our health. And here come the courses in waves of goodness, to enhance the tumultuous inebriation, exultation and jubilation. Among these brethren of the wide sweep is communion with God and each other, as ingrained with gratitude and a wish for more as any prayer on breaking bread. This is life. This is fun. *We are here.*

The spirit within breaks free, and it's time to eat.

Feeding and playing together unify hearts as one. With singular psychiatric revelation, Stuey pulls a doll from his pack, a plastic statue hand-painted in bold lacquers. It's Dominatrix Barbie, with tiny huge breasts in a scant halter, long legs and a g-string. Her plastic bandana unfurls to a stiff breeze three inches to one side. More movement is molded into her little plastic machete in mid-swing. Holding her up by one leg, he feeds her from a fingertip dripping with mashed potatoes and gravy. "Girl's gotta eat." He doesn't laugh. Nobody laughs. She's perfect, signed and numbered. He admits paying three fifty for her at the little model shop near the stadium in China town, picked her up on the way to a game, because she's a work of art, and he's wanted her for a long time. He calls her Billie, after his ex-wife. Then he plants her, feet first, in the bowl of mashed potatoes. Nobody asks why he brought her along.

The boys eat, willing to cut Stuey the slack a man needs, after neutering by a woman he once loved.

Buster sits on the other side of his wife, whose constraint is no surprise. Her ability to show no pulse in the highest times is still impressive. Lifting her nose to the scents of three meats, four fishes and two fouls, she gazes at the Billie doll, knee deep in the mashed potatoes and gravy bowl. She mutters something about needs and fucking lovely.

Many hands reach. The pack feeds headlong into frenzy.

Randy Hague raises a toast to friendship till their dying day, to breaking bread and drinking wine or tequila or vodka or schnapps or...or motherfucking chardonnay and rat piss, if that's what they want to drink, to more fun and more.... He knocks a shot and one more to bolster a new round of ballyhoo. Buster keeps up, because he can. It's what he came for, though he wonders if this is it, loud and liquored up with table service. Randy chokes—wrong pipe— but clears quickly with a belch over a bilious bassline. "Wiping his chin he said with a grin, if my ear was a pussy, I'd fuck it!"

The boys laugh, mid-woof, and settle in to cruising speed.

Joe Boggs is still in the main room telling six tequilas that they've not been poured in vain but will meet their destiny soon, because down the hatch times six is no different than one or a baker's dozen, if a man brings method to the challenge. Joe has theorized for years that peristalsis should be a one-way street, even in high times, even on the verge of anarchy. Joe is an alcoholic who tries to ease his burden with fundamental theories. Like this one, comparing his esophagus to a street and drunkenness to anarchy. Joe downs two and waits for traffic to thin. Watching Joe is amusing, and when a young woman smirks in passing, he pulls her near.

She is also flirtatious. Joe isn't even forty, so the hard miles have not dimmed his easy good looks and wavy blond hair too badly. "Hold still!" he says. "Still." She freezes as he swoops to lick her neck, which could be an assault, but she giggles. So he salts the wet spot and wedges a quarter lime into her smile, peeling first. He knocks the next shot, tongues her neck for the salt and moves up to the wedge, engorging her grimace with quivering romance, which primes her for a shot of her own, which happens to be right here. Everyone but the young female has seen this routine, and she seems quite taken with the flourish and flamboyance....

But with hardly a sleeve wipe, her head pops back by a grab of hair in the fist of him what brung her. Pain racks her face like lightning in a summer sky. Turning with a yelp, she turns to her disgruntled date and spits in his eye.

Joe laughs, "Man. Looks like the Flintstones in a love spat!" He wobbles into dinner and explains, "I would have laid her out on the bar, but.... Fred would never allow a navel shot."

The boys eat. Somebody asks what.

Joe slumps on a chair like he's not sure what comes next.

Derek's headset slides onto his neck, so he can explain liberation from the practical world. "It's important to understand the two lives we lead. One is at home, and one is on the road."

"You don't behave like this at home?" Buster asks.

"If I'm not drinking, I'm home. If I'm not in trouble, I'm home. If I'm not having fun, I'm home."

The boys nod, grinding for distance from home.

Derek's nephew, Donny, is gnawing a bone when a muffin hits his head. He returns the volley, but banking off a wall and a hanging light fixture, the muffin splashes into a woman's soup. She and her companion flinch, wondering what and why. They share a booth on the periphery.

"Hey! Hey! Hey!" Dave DeBanque calls. "That's it! Waitress! Bring them another bottle of wine! No. Bring them a better bottle of wine! That's on me. No. Bring everyone in this room a bottle of wine. And I'm paying for everyone's dinner. Anything you want."

"Dave, no! Don't do that," Derek implores.

"Yes!"

"No, man."

Dave glares, so Derek relents. "All right. Dinner on Dave!"

Primitive good times with overbearing friends are amusing, but a squirming wife must be reconciled. Larraine won't eat, not here, not like this. She looks to Mo for support.

But Mo is fielding a spud on the fly—*left-handed*—catching a line shot like it was a creampuff, which it resembles when all that yellow and white stuff oozes between her fingers. Her sidearm return is one svelte move that scores a direct hit to Randy Hague's head, casting potato and cream to all sides. Is she left-handed?

Randy takes the hit with stunning composure, not wiping his brow. Nobody yells food fight, because they don't need to.

Larraine shrinks like a lost virtue.

Buster takes her hand.

Smiling bravely at this rough juncture, she remains faithful to the graces.

Randy Hague leans her way from two seats over to commiserate. "Must be tough, being Buster's wife." Randy is six-three by three-six and bulldogs his handlebars into curves at thirty mph over the posted limit, scraping pavement. He can't compete anymore or lay it down in the dirt, because he's too old, and he wobbles when he walks and when he doesn't, because skeletal alignment is like first love. You don't get it back. He lights his hash pipe, like it doesn't matter.

Stuey eats mashed potatoes from Burt Billips's hand and appears to thrive on Larraine's cringe. "Yeah," he garbles. "We're assholes all right. Fucking animals. Disgusting. But Buster is so cold. He never loved you right."

As if looks could freeze, Stuey is suddenly stuck in Larraine's icy glare. She is not the cause of Buster's loveless disposition, and this carnage is no excuse for a personal debasement. She wants an apology, a retraction, a sign from someone that this is wrong.

"Hey, sweetie pie. I was kidding." Stuey says, licking his fingers and sticking his tongue in the crotch between index and forefinger to clear the residue. He winks at Larraine, because a roadman takes nothing for granted and never knows when the gates may open.

She turns away.

Burt Billips' cherubic smile is chronic and oppressive, aimed here and there to assure good, clean fun. He chats the waitress after feeding Stuey. He's a rosy-cheek, sincere fellow, though the boys think he's working sincerely on a hard close on the waitress, who slouches beside him with an empty serving tray. She's telling him of her children. He says he loves kids, stretching his smile to deepen his dimples, as his father tells Randy that Burt is a loving boy.

What?

Father?

What's his name, Mr. Billips? Does he bungee his walker on the back of his ride? Mr. Billips passes Randy's pipe without smoking it, smiling like a Rotarian, promising to try it one day soon.

Try what? And who cares?

Stuey knocks a shot and reaches for Buster with a handful of mashed potatoes, but Buster won't feed.

This is disgusting.

Larraine is repulsed, a lady among trolls.

Derek Donaldson grips a slab of meat and stuffs the hopper, ripping and chewing. Flecks speckle his teeth and cheeks like bug splat on a Florida windshield. Usually a pristine fellow with a starched logo T, he perks, as the waitress says her children are one and one and a half, and she's twenty-two already and still single.

Derek compliments her natural build for breast-feeding, and with a loathsome grin, he says, "You did something with your hair."

Feeling her hair with her free hand, she smiles shyly. "Do you know me?"

"I'd like to. Is ten o'clock too late?"

"I don't get off till ten-thirty."

"Perfect," he grins. "We'll take a moonlight ride."

"Oh, God!" She clears debris and blushes under Derek's winsome gaze. He aims the greasy grin at Burt Billips. Some call foul, bird dog, cock block, but the rest whoop for the take-away and three-pointer.

Stuey gobs a lamb chop and garbles, "Show him a bird, and he wantsh the wishbone."

Laughter prevails, even from Burt, because he is a loving boy after all.

In a more serious moment, Derek says his new scooter came on a cold, wet day, so he sent it directly to Armageddon Motor Works for new jugs that displace a hundred thirty cubic inches with Mastodon heads and a ram charger for a hundred forty horsepower. He giggles at the outrageous power-to-weight ratio.

But wait!

Two nitrous cans mounted above his highway pegs with sequential feed give him another sixty horses on short spurts. Short spurts are his specialty. That's two hundred horsepower on a six-hundred-pound motorcycle. Each nitrous jug carries ten hits at four seconds each. Oh, Derek Donaldson will take no shit from the semis or Japs—or guinea crotch rockets up the double yellow. And he does *not* worry about keeping his front wheel down. He likes high-speed wheelies. Wait till you see his exhaust in the dark.

"But Derek," Buster says, "with only twenty hits of nitrous, you'll run out. Then you'll be depressed."

"No! I got maps of the nitrous refill stations across BC and nine states." Tonight Derek will prove the wisdom of nitrous by making his date hang on tight. He will then accept her grateful offering.

The boys eat and fantasize in a rare lull, in which nothing is heard but gnashing, grinding and slurpage.

Randy Hague asks, "Larraine, did Buster get some this morning?"

"No," she says.

"Yeah," he consoles. "Me neither. Home." He chows.

Larraine shows the half smile of disgust. In a look, she's done. She tolerates Stuey from time to time but not this time. Even seeing him in a new light, she watches it fade to black. She can't take Derek, who eats green beans with his hands. She excuses herself.

Buster follows.

The boys murmur *wives* and resume play, flinging beans, hurling spuds.

Randy glistens, shaking a bone at Wade. "You woke me up from my nap, and you didn't use ice like we agreed."

Wade blushes. "I didn't want to be a bother, but the ice machine was broke. I thought a little bearing grease would do the trick."

The boys guffaw, licking fingers, gnawing bones and drinking.

A man and girl pass Larraine and Buster at the alcove near the dining room.

Larraine can't take it and can't fathom the homosexual aspect of the group. She has no problem with that sort of thing but hardly anticipated such a demonstration of latent desires.

It's not that, Buster says. The boys joke about ass fucking, but it's a spoof. Really.

She asks if heterosexual men suck each other's fingers.

In the dining room, the man with the girl says he knows a good time when he hears it. His Goldwing is out front. He wants to join in.

Wade says no, but your daughter can.

The boys whoop and holler.

The man leaves.

Larraine says it isn't Buster but rather the group she can't stomach or tolerate for that matter, much less understand. She can't go on. She'll go home in the morning on a bus. For now, if he wouldn't mind, she'll return to the hotel for some personal time.

"Not at all," he says. "Thanks for understanding."

She looks puzzled. "I just told you that I don't understand. Do you understand it? Do you see who you've chosen to spend your time with? You were there. Didn't you see what I saw?"

Buster shrugs, because he might understand but has made a different choice. He goes along for the difference between this and the home regimen, like Derek said. This isn't necessarily good and may be bad, but it's removed from the norm, removed from what could be called acceptable, or, in some circles, appropriate. That's what he understands, and he feels confident that she can also comprehend a natural process in him.

Yet they stand in silent failure to understand each other.

He returns to dinner, where Mr. Billips is saying, "I don't drink, and I don't smoke. That leaves me with some early evenings."

"You must have a vice," Buster says, taking his seat. "One vice minimum. It's required."

"Well. I was lying about the drinking. And I love pussy." This gags the boys and makes them feel young again, hearing someone's dad talk about pussy, but nobody mentions Burt's mom.

Mr. Billips goes beet red, as Buster wonders how many times the pussy line will play, and if Larraine is right, that liberation is an illusion. He wishes she could see his dilemma. He shares her disappointment. The charade replays like TV. "Woo hoo" and "Eeyihaa" score the chow down. Bone throwing and gristle gnawing signal the end of hunger, so the crowd meanders back to the bar for drinks and more drinks. In a short while, on second wind, the boys glance about to see how the evening might liven up.

Their playful energy rouses the locals on hand, who grumble at the uppity fuckin' goofballs commandeering the place, their place. Local culture could be known and respected, if someone would open their fuckin' eyes and take a fuckin' look. But no.

A poster on a far wall shows a mashed owl in a skillet and says *Spotted Owl Helper—with Fleas and Macaroni.* Frazzled patrons huddle nearby along the trophy wall, under mounted heads. Deer, moose, bear, bighorn sheep, mountain goats, lynx, lions and bobcats, look down on those who killed them. Stuffed and past their prime, the local crowd and animal heads stare, glassy-eyed, at the struggle going on here. Sallow, bent and low-slung with wide foreheads and baggy jeans snugged under huge bellies, the local boys drink and sniffle, watching the outlanders think and snivel. Heavy boots shuffle for some shit to kick. A few dull offspring look resigned to the forlorn future, when they'll get their hats and bellies and a two-pack habit as the work disappears, thanks to this highbrow crowd. The world closes in. With no more trees to chop, a man can see who's at the business end of his troubles.

But Dave DeBanque is here. At the top of the clear-cut food chain, Dave reads these workingmen. Reads them? Hell, he was one of them, akin to the common grit, so he twirls a finger for a house round. Make that doubles for the local boys. The doubles go down on a grunt and a grumble with another double on the way.

But drinks and more drinks hardly soothe the rabble, rousing for a rumble. Sure enough, the reverie cracks on a tremor, when a yuppie running straight pipes, like he invented that racket, rides his motorcycle into the bar. They've seen it before. The barkeep may be looking at the mother of all tips but can't help muttering, "Oh, fuck. Another original asshole."

Harry Woo eases his scoot through the door, revving for radical good cheer, until the indelicate balance tips. The locals step up.

Harry parks it and strides to the uppity end of the bar, sensing trouble, taking inventory. "We've never been in a fight, but we might be in one now. Are you in?" Harry Woo is big and doesn't look like a stockbroker in a suit, white shirt, daring tie and brogues. But denim and leather can't hide his elocution, enunciation and private schooling, even as he wobbles: "Fight? Are you in? Are you ready?"

Striding over to the hometown crowd, he yells, "You want me to pull your fuckin' hat over your eyes? Do you?" He leans away from a lazy hook and turns back to the unsalted end of the bar. "Should I pull his fuckin' hat over his eyes?"

Dave shakes his head. "Not yet. We'll buy 'um another drink first." So the drinks overflow like a storm drain, till Farley Dunn steps in from the counting room.

Farley Dunn is local too and savoring his best week ever, and it happened in the last three hours, and someone just called for three more rounds of doubles and the credit card cleared. Farley Dunn owns the Fuzzy Glo Room. He's also called Deputy Dunn for his second job, which is nearly as vital to the community as his first job. He yells: "I want a truce! These fellas here are our guests, goddamnit! They spent four thousand dollars on dinner! They spent another seven thousand dollars on cocktails! You look around you now! Nothing but folks enjoying theirself. We run a good, clean bar here under the rule of law, so.... Uh.... Shut up and drink!" The law demands peaceful drinking among factions. So they do.

Young Donny huddles with two other men, hard-ridden grits, reviewing price, weight and supply. Farley Dunn stoops behind the bar and rises, pinning on his badge, mumbling that he coulda been RCMP instead of babysitting the riff raff night after night.

Donny calls for a pitcher to lubricate the wheels of commerce in the rare efficiency of the moment, in which Dave pays. Dave wants it that way or needs it that way. Dave drifts on a barstool.

Buster feels the old doubts ganging up. Where do this dog and pony go from here? Another rough landing seems unavoidable. But what can he do, walk out on a historical evening? He can, because tedious repetition of rote behaviors stifle a personal molting worse than suburbia.

Burt and Mr. Billips drift out, planning to call Mom in the morning.

Randy Hague leans on the bar, mumbling that he might fall down. He might....

Joe Boggs sleeps in the grass near the parking lot.

Harry Woo yells at the locals, the one about the Pope going to Memphis, where everyone thinks he's Elvis, what with the cape and the limo and the entourage.

Stuey pores forth in Dave's ear on money, pussy, empire and where we must take this thing to maximize potential.

Randy rises to waylay the female with the rough boyfriend, as she passes by. She's back, alone, looking for Joe, but Randy'll do.

Stuey says the world is theirs by rights and circumstance, until he pauses to stare at one more Bombay Sapphire martini in another perfect moment, twelve bucks a pop and covered.

Distant thunder signals a moonlight ride, Derek and his waitress. The boys nod, knowing the sweets go to him what musters the energy for lust at light speed on a dark and blustery night.

Buster weighs the pros and cons of riding with this circus or going it alone.

Missy serves Mo another beer on the house or on Dave or on Missy. Anyway you slice it, it's a token of appreciation for...for just being you. "I needed that," Missy says. "I needed you to keep me from ruining that guy's reputation. You know? I'd a hated that."

Mo drinks. "Yeah, well. He needed it too. He's an asshole most of the time. Mostly harmless, but what kind of pussy orders Chardonnay after a ride?"

Mo's assessment bolster's Missy's crush. Mo talks like a man, no macho posturing but plain and simple. She rides like a man and shows honest values. Does it get any clearer? They get to know each other. Missy says she loves chatting like this, you know, without a thumping dick banging her on the head.

Near midnight Donny takes the lead. He found some hash, smelled and smoked it and even ate some. "It's good. How much do you want?" He addresses Stuey, the decision maker.

Stuey asks, "Four hundred a pound?"

"Four hundred an ounce."

"Oh, yeah. Four an ounce. We want ten grand. Buster has the dough. Right? Okay. Wait a minute. That's Canadian. We want U.S. Make it, what, fourteen grand. Where's the hash?"

Donny looks at Stuey like some things should be obvious. "He has to go get it. The guy."

"Who has to go?"

"The guy. The guy has to go."

"What guy?"

"The guy with the hash, duh. Whaddaya think, he carries it around with him? He needs the dough to get the hash."

"Donny boy. If he has to go get it, then he ain't the guy with the hash. Fuck. These kids today."

"Okay, but he can't get it without the dough. I'll go with him."

Buster cuts in with the hard line, like it's his money. "Is that supposed to make me comfortable?"

"Donny won't fuck up," Stuey says. "He lives here."

"Then what, you'll cover if anything goes wrong?"

"Yeah. Or maybe you should go."

"I don't need to go. I don't care if the deal goes away."

"Look," Donny says with youthful authority and strained finality. "I'll go. No fuck ups. We'll leave a motorcycle here. That's how we do it, and that's the motherfucking bottom line."

"You'll leave a motorcycle here?"

"Yeah, you know. For the collectible whaddayacallit."

"Collateral."

"Yeah, for the collateral." Donny says that he and two other guys will go for the hash. The two other guys look familiar, but all those rat bike guys with beards and road tans look alike.

These two guys gawk when Buster counts the cash into Donny's palm, sixty-eight C-notes, U.S. That's for ten grand Canadian in hash, because price quotes should convert to local currency, like arrivals and departures, and ten grand Canadian is plenty—plenty o' money and a shitload o' hash.

One guy huffs up.

Buster smiles, "Take it or leave it. If it works out, we'll spend more. If you're not satisfied, we understand. That's how we do it. My way or the highway. And I promise you: I don't give a flat flying fuck if you and your so-called deal go away. How's that?"

Hobo grumbles, itching to grease this dude, but he'll take it. What the fuck?

Lonny glares, itching to tell these urban scumbags just how hard they're gonna get fucked up the asshole, but that would spook them, because they're pussies. So he shows a tough grimace.

Donny says, "Come on." He leads the way, happy to head out on Dad's scooter for the hash. He opens on a smoke out and goes to a double lot brody and gets scratch in second for the dramatic departure, yelling, "Fuuuck!" That's for the piece o' shit between his legs failing to rise for a wheelie, but he compensates, winding it to redline through fourth.

Wade laughs, "Donny's a bigger fuckup than any three idiots put together."

A third guy in XXXL mopes by the door, eyeing his cold scooter, the collateral, though conversion to local value on this one might top out at twelve cents on the dollar, U.S.

The boys sit and glo. Yeah, right, we'll pay the money first. Jesus; what kind of fool is Wade raising? But that's what they did.

Mo leans in to tell Missy that she knows the big burly guy. She doesn't know him really, but he seems reasonable.

"He's a pain in the ass. A real lug. But he's harmless. Wouldn't hurt a fly. Not like the mean streaks he hangs out with. Man, you shoulda seen him a few nights ago. I had him on the hot plate. You know how they twitch, thinking this is it, the big score, pussyrama, all you can eat?" She holds that note, but Mo stays focused on her beer, because she knows the note and the hold. "Then he comes out to the house next morning, maybe thinking I really did want him to ream out my asshole…."

Still nothing.

"That was the best. He's hemming and hawing. Couldn't even get it up to ask for it. I was tempted to give him a lube and oil change just to see him cry with gratitude. Dude probably ain't been laid in a few years. I didn't. Guys that big have little dicks anyway."

Mo drinks half her beer, pondering romance, no love for a few years, big guys and what they may have. "He's not bad looking. A little bit of a simp, maybe."

"Little bit? He's softer than Charmin."

"I had a boyfriend like that. I liked it. He was big, too. He wasn't so little."

"I could be wrong," Missy concedes. "I been wrong before. But not too often. Man."

"What?"

"We oughta tell him we want to do him together. You know, just for fun. Man, he'd keel over."

Mo drinks the other half, wondering why every person she meets presents a challenge sooner or later. Men are deficient, and so are women. Here's a lesbian willing to have sex with a huge biker just to get into another gal's pants. Maybe life gets most efficient when it's spent all alone. "I'm gonna go talk to him. See if he might know Jimmy."

"Who's Jimmy?"

"My father."

"How do you know Buck? The big boy yonder."

"I saw him in the drugstore. I can tell he's okay. I can fairly tell he lives around here. He's shy is all. Most guys would be, meeting a gal at the hemorrhoid rack. But I suspect he's shy all the time."

"I'll go with you. Between the two of us we can draw him out."

They shuffle toward the big galoot, when through the front door strolls Jimmy Hatrick in a turquoise shirt, yellow pants and an odd stink, call it skunk 'n hash ambrosia. He ambles to the bar, looks both ways and sees Buck. "Where's your friends at?"

"Went to find you?" he says.

Jimmy looks around. "Where'd they think to look?"

Buck shrugs, hoping Lonny went along blindly, knowing Hobo went looking to separate Donny from the money, so he might head up the road by his lonesome.

"They have any money?" Jimmy asks.

Buck nods and ticks his chin at the money crowd, all in a stupor.

"Those boys gave your boys the money?"

Buck nods again.

"Why'nt you go with them?"

"I'm the collectible."

"You mean the collateral?"

Buck nods.

"What the fuck they want you for?"

"My scooter."

Jimmy nods, eyeing sideways out the door at Buck's claptrap ride. Eyeing the other way, he sees matching leathers and pressed collars, and he asks the painful question: "They got the ten thousand, didn't they?" He nods, because he knows they did. So he walks to the money crowd table and pulls a chair, reaches into his vest for a slab of hash. He smells it and lays it out. "This what you looking for?"

Stuey grabs it, smells it, scratches it with his finger and says, "How much?"

"Like the man says, ten grand."

The sorry, sad stare encircles the table, every man knowing the money is gone, and Donny won't bring it back. One of the lingering local guys drops a loonie in the jukebox. It clangs down the gear ladder to *Stardust Memories*.

The clock ticks to the wee hours, where talk is *blotto voce*, and a solution seems as unlikely as an Irish jig at sunrise. Mutterings call for one last toddy, for the road. Nobody says no, with a tab still open after all. Peace seems marinated, if not formally sealed.

Mo gets up to sit next to Jimmy. She leans his way and says, "Tell me about Tina."

Buck thinks the friendly gal in the drugstore likes old guys, and he double takes on Missy, who looks him over. He can't imagine why, except to remind him of remote prospects for getting next to her or anyone.

But there she is, smiling. "Hi, Buck." He laughs short at this scene from a dream. He knows what Lonny would say, but Lonny's wrong. She wants to be friends. That would be tough, what with her inner beauty and suggestive body, but he'll give it a try. Until she says, "I got a personal question, Buck. Are you horny? I mean, for a woman? I assume you like women."

Jimmy tells Mo what she mostly knows, that Tina is a mean drunk, has been for years and can't even bounce checks closer than two hundred kilometers because everybody knows her one way or another, including some ways that's plain ugly. He pulls no punches, profiling a woman who passed away but still hangs around. "I could go over there and get some anytime I want it, till she got so damn mean I didn't want any part of her. She changed bad."

The wee hours pass slowly for those who don't sleep. In the forced march to sunrise, the money crowd turns in. Buck Dibble's lays his big, shaggy head on the table and soon snores like a chain saw, twitching on adenoidal fibrillation as sugarplum fairies dance a topless jig. He gulps air, bolting up to scan for what and where. Missy Malone snores daintily beside him. Not quite awake but surging in the heart, Buck realizes that he's slept with Missy Malone. The sweet reward remains unbagged, but the bag feels less empty. She slept through his snoring, so this could work out. He would caress her but settles on the easy stare before rejoining the sugarplum fairies.

A few tables over, Jimmy talks through the years and regrets, till Mo interrupts. "You do know who I am?"

"I do," Jimmy says.

She smiles with difficulty. "Are you glad to see me?"

"I am. You can believe me or not, but I love you."

Strong words from a derelict father, but she looks again and sees a tear welling up and breaking loose.

XIV

Off Again, On Again

A dirty window separates the hot tub from the dining room of the Mad Drab Hotel across from the Fuzzy Glo Room. The road crew seems present, more or less. A few scoots sit at the Glo Room curb, but that's only a step and stumble across the road.

Scents include chlorine, eggs, coffee and hash. Randy Hague smokes his little pipe in the tub, chest deep.

Some of the boys watch their coffee. Some have steak and eggs. Some defer to practical needs, with oatmeal and prunes. Somebody asks if it's still on Dave's tab. Another trumpets rude reveille. One chokes and sputters. Some laugh, but none seem amused.

Randy examines his pipe in disbelief; he only just filled it. Looking up at the hung-over crowd he calls out, "Fuck. You oughta see you guys." He reloads and fires again, recommending the pipe for reentry. Sinking into the foam he calls, "This is great. It's like camp but with motorcycles instead of a lake. And no counselors. And no fucking camp." He slips under.

Joe asks, "Is that the hash?"

"No. He brought that along."

"Across the border? Where's the hash? Did we get the hash?"

"Buster got the hash. Didn't you?"

"No, he didn't. Buster got fucked for ten grand. Unless Donny got the hash. But he couldn't have, because the hash was sitting across the table, and Donny never came back."

"What's Donny got to do with it? Why'd Buster get fucked?"

Larraine clomps down the steps in travel heels with her bags.

Did she pack her travel heels anticipating a bus ride home? Ah, well, why question a woman soon to be a friend? Buster hopes she hasn't heard of the lost money.

"Being with the men is good for you," she says.

"Do you know something I don't?"

"You love this."

"It'll be great when it's over."

"You boys will have a wonderful time," she says.

"I'll call you."

"Okay."

She hesitates at the door as Derek shuffles in, dazed as a big cat after a feed. "Nice girl," he says, on his way to personal hygiene and a nap. Larraine walks out to the waiting bus.

Buster follows to wish her a safe journey. She returns a smile and half hug. She boards, and so ends, it seems, that phase of life that's taken up most of life. Will long miles be easier without her? Without the boys? He feels needy and complex by himself, without company. This too is amusing, so he laughs.

Wade steps up with a wave to Larraine and commiserates. "I can't imagine my wife here."

"No. It was a mistake."

"No mistakes," Wade says. "These rides are like life. That's why we come. You mostly like it. But you die some every day. You got to look at the bright side, Buster. Better to spend your time raising hell than sitting home moping."

"You mostly mope at home, Wade?"

"Probably about the same as you. I suspect it's the winter weather that brings it on, but it's the other stuff too."

"You mean like reefer and alcohol abuse? And no excitement? And no riding?"

"That's what I said, didn't I?"

"You thought it through. Didn't you, Wade?"

"I got time to think at home." He nods up to the second floor. "Looks like a late start today."

"You mean a false start?"

"Give it a chance. We'll get there."

"Yeah, right. Making progress all the time."

"I called Donny. He's not home."

"It's Stuey's deal now."

"That's brave of you."

"It could always be worse. He wanted to give those guys three grand more. U.S."

Wade shakes his head and fishes in his shirt pocket. "I got a sample. You oughta get high for ten grand."

So they light a ball of hash and smoke Wade's road pipe as the bus headlights blind them. "God, I hate those things."

Wade nods.

Buster says. "Makes you wish for a gun, just...blow the fuckers away."

Wade exhales as the bus pulls out. "We can't have guns."

Larraine waves out a window, glum, proving a point.

Buster waves, affirming the end.

Breakfast at nine runs to eleven, so survivors can brush off the cobwebs, dull the pain and compare notes. Joe Boggs didn't count his shots, but it was six or twelve when that girl came along, before he went for a lie down in the grass near the parking lot for a few heaves and a nap. He's fairly certain he missed dinner, because he can't remember what he had, except for some incredible peach cobbler.

Wade gives him the news: "You fell out before dinner, after she came back. You didn't have dinner. We didn't have peach cobbler."

"She came back without the boyfriend?"

Wade nods.

"Did anybody...."

"Yeah." Wade sips his coffee and pokes his pancakes.

Joe nods, "Maybe for the best. She was so young. She had bad breath. Even with a lemon wedge, she tasted foul. That's not a good sign. I prefer a clean woman, knows how to take care of herself.... I can't remember how I met her. It must have been...." Joe drifts in faint recollection, his brainpan grating on cinders and slag.

Harry Woo dared two local boys to throw him over the bar. They accepted, landing Harry on his head. Up from the blood puddle, Harry went to the Emergency Room for stitches at sunrise. He got a bandage, a lecture and some take-home literature on problem drinking. Back in his room, he got cleaned up and came down for caffeine a few hours later with his hair brushed over his wound. His lips quiver on assurance that he's good to go. He calls last night an opportunity, an ash pile to rise from and ride out of...in a minute. He needs a minute to sit and....

The day might be good for the scenic route, north through the mountains, where it might be cold and wet. Or they could head east, into the hills, to stay warm and dry, or warmer and not so wet.

Buster suggests that the route might intercept his money.

Wade calls Donny again and waits for twelve rings.

Everyone looks surprised when the collateral approaches, belching on a backfire out front. The scene gets curious with the waitress on back, the one with the rack and bad manners. She dismounts. Buck releases the leather loop holding his kickstand in place. Leaning the beast onto the stand, he checks stability and hefts himself clear. Hanging his spiked helmet on his handlebar, he pulls his vest down and pushes his hair back. It springs again, but fuck it. Turning to Missy, he shifts one foot to the other, like he doesn't know what to say.

They woke early to an empty Glo Room, and she needed a ride home. Could he take her? Of course, he could, home or anywhere in the world.

"Just get me home. We got time for anywhere in the world."

Missy was late in feeding her caterpillars, and the poor babies can get traumatized. Pupation could come any time, and morning care is critical to life transition.

"You really love them."

"Yes. They're so fuzzy. Like you but more manageable."

The ride to Missy's was tough for Buck, imagining himself as cute and sensitive, which is not like being a pussy, except that it is.

Back in the greenhouse for the second time in short order, he watched her pluck woolies from the box and set them on her chest and shoulders, unbuttoning her blouse for more room for more woolies. She said it warmed them up. He imagined her peeling her shirt and turning to him with a come-and-get-it.

She didn't turn but asked where he learned about poetry.

"I don't know. Books, I guess."

Then she turned, her bosom flecked with caterpillars. "You read poetry books?"

"Not that many."

"Not that many? Buck! What else are you hiding from me?"

"I'm not hiding anything, Missy."

"But…why do you hang out with those bums?"

"Lonny's my friend. I don't hang out with Hobo."

"But you could have…. I don't know. You're a great guy, Buck. You could get a girl, easy."

"What girl, Missy?"

"Look, Buck. I'm not trying to tease you or anything. Okay?"

"Okay. I'm looking."

"It's like this. I don't like men. I might like men, or a man, if I could ever meet one. A real man. You're about as close as I can imagine around here. You got manners. You know how to keep your mouth shut. You know love sonnets."

'Thine eyes I love, and they, as pitying me, Knowing thy heart torment me with disdain....'

Her jaw drops....

'Have put on black and loving mourners be, Looking with pretty truth upon my pain....'

"That's all I got, and I only got that yesterday. It's Shakespeare. But you know that."

"Oh, Buck!"

"I can get more. I think I can...." She closed the space between them, as he knew she could, unless she was pulling his chain again. A chance would not come twice and maybe hadn't come once, but burning a few lines had eased his heart...Until lo, the morning shone brighter still. They embraced slowly and held it there, her lead, arriving at a place unimaginable to him, even in the tangible flesh. She could feel it. Plucking her squirmy pets from harm's way, she cleared the field.

"Bet you'd like to be one of these fuzzy little guys."

Buck could only stare like a statue.

Closing the curtains on the matinee, she said, "I'm sorry. I don't mean no, and I don't mean never. Maybe sometime we can, as a favor. It means so much to you. But I told you: I don't like men, but it's been a very long time, and who knows? I might be wrong. We may be surprised. Wouldn't that be something? Ha! Big Buck Dibble is the man for me! Buck. I didn't say that, okay? I only said.... Forget it...."

But she'd gone and made it perfect. Buck didn't give a hoot if Missy wanted to munch some carpet now and then. Who doesn't? And if she's been lesbo for such a long time, that means he'd get first dibs on the hootchie cootch, or good as. First Dibbles?

"Okay? Not now. I need time to think. Okay?"

"You want to think about me?"

"Please don't say anything. You'll ruin it."

"Ruin what?"

"Buck." She moved in again. He feared a sisterly hug, because of the obtrusion between them. "I don't blame you," she said.

"Did I do something wrong?"

"No, Buck. You didn't do anything wrong. You're so right. You're not, really. But you could be so right."

"You mean that you and...me could, uh...."

She stepped back, grasping his arms. eyeing him up and down, taking in the hulk. "Boy, you'd be a handful."

"Missy."

"Buck. You know Mo, who rode in with those guys?"

"Yeah. She yelled at you for mashing your boobies on her."

"Yes. She's magnificent. Isn't she? She thinks you're cute."

Cute? So the big man cringed red again, getting it wrong on every step. "She said that?"

"In so many words."

"What words?"

"She said she thought it was cute, that you pretended to look for toothpaste, right there in the hemorrhoid ointments."

Buck purpled. "What's cute about hemorrhoids?"

"Obviously nothing. Come on, Buck. Don't drop back into the moronic mindset you share with those assholes. She didn't think you were cute for having hemorrhoids. You pretended not to. Get it? It was the pretending. You were trying to save face in a subtle way, so a woman would think well of you. Can't you see that? You showed sensitivity instead of banging everyone on the head with the old billy club. That's what got to her."

Buck doubted his rhoids had moved to the asset column. Just thinking of the pesky little devils made them itch.... But he dare not scratch! But he dare not ignore, or the itch could surge and bring on the lunge. But he dare not scratch.

As if the gods were out to taunt him, she touched his face, her fingers falling to the top of his chest, where they lingered. "It's like this, Buck. A real woman doesn't care if you have hemorrhoids or dandruff or crotch rot…. Well, crotch rot could be a problem. But you get my point. Don't you? Open your heart to possibilities. You'll find a better world. Okay?"

Buck gazed down at her fingers for a possibility to emerge. "What are the possibilities, Missy?"

"You want a woman. You hang out with bums. All you need is to lead with your heart. A woman won't resist that."

"Missy?"

"I'm not saying you can have any woman you want. I'm only saying that any woman you love truly will love you back."

"Missy?"

Like a pigeonholed politician, she smiled wryly and patted him on the cheek. "I apologize, Buck."

Apologize? For what? For telling the truth? An itch caught fire and surged. Buck Dibble could take the pain on love unrequited. Bring it on. But the itch got itchier. She turned away.

He reached back, grasped the culprit and held it with omniscient power, briefly, before coming to his senses on a gentle rub with no abrasion. He sighed in marginal relief, knowing his nemesis would spring again.

"I apologize for anything negative. Or unkind. I'm a fool, too. We all are. We hurt, and we hurt each other."

"I don't know much, Missy."

She stepped away and into early sunbeams. Buck fantasized the impossible, that they could proceed with…what? Romance? Courtship? That seemed old fashioned, but so what?

"Let's go find Mo." Missy closed the caterpillar box and said she felt much better with that out of the way. Did she mean feeding her fuzzies or getting to know the real Buck? He assumed the first but weighed the second.

Outside, she told him she was happy to have him as a friend.

Oh, brother.

"I know what you're thinking, Buck. Don't. Friends can help each other out in more ways than you've imagined. For all I know, you're hung like a rhinoceros."

What the....

On the ride back in, he realized that a man of few words sounds about the same when he's speechless. At least she didn't mind when he had nothing to say. Mind, hell. She liked it. You don't need to say much on a scooter anyway, though he wanted to know why they needed to find Mo. And where was Hobo Grimes, that crook, and his old friend Lonny Snodgrass? Rumble. Hey, Rhino 'n Rumble. Not bad. Did Missy mean she might let him you-know-what? He'd rather do it for love and let their guards down and rest up and do it again like people in movies. But a favor now and then wouldn't be so bad. That could turn into love. He saw that in a movie too. Sure it was two guys in prison, but it could work for him and Missy. Why not? When might she want to give it a try? Would it be sooner than later, on account of the rhinoceros potential? He felt game enough and ready. He wondered if the hotel had a breakfast buffet, as they pulled up the drive.

"Don't be coy, okay. Those boneheads'll find out anyway."

"Find out what?"

"Oh, yeah, like you guys don't brag about your conquests. That's okay, Buck. I'm just saying don't do it this time. Okay?"

"Missy. That wasn't a conquest. Nothing happened."

"Nothing happened? You're on deck! I better not see you hanging out with those bums, drinking too much or eating that pizza's been in our freezer a few years, because Farley got a deal on a container load thawed out when a train derailed. I'm gonna try to see you in a different light now. You wanna be a big, fat, hairy tub o' shit who goes gaga stupid if a girl just winks at him your whole life?"

The real truth of the situation fairly bangs him on the head.

"That guy is gone, Bucky. Now I got a close, personal friend who happens to be a big, strong man. He has manners and knows Shakespeare and what a woman might feel. For all I know, he may be sensitive to a woman's needs. You call that nothing?"

Fuckinay. This is getting thick. Maybe Lonny had it right, and I shoulda just asked: *eatcher box, Ma'am?*

"What, Bucky? What are you thinking?"

Bucky?

"I'm thinking I hope they got the breakfast buffet in there."

"Man, you go from Fred Astaire to Haystack Calhoun in a heartbeat. How do you do that?"

"I don't know. Who's Fred Astaire?"

"Oh, man. And I thought you were different."

"I'm not so different, really."

So they stroll up the walk, casually touching, to where the boys wait and speculate.

Buster seems nearly nervous to pursue a wilderness adventure and his money.

Buck says he doesn't know where those boys went, but he'd guess east, warm and dry. He looks east. "That's what we oughta try." The others wonder why he came back around. Who needs that boneshaker cluttering up the ride? Is that an oil drip?

Buster says, "You don't need to go. I don't need your scooter."

Buck looks puzzled. "I got a stake in this too."

"You mean your cut?"

Buck drops his eyes. "No. Lonny's a friend of mine."

What does friendship have to do with a theft among thieves?

Mo and Jimmy shuffle from the dining room. She knows what the boys are thinking. Who cares? But she blurts anyway, "This is my daddy. I mean my father."

Oh, right, the eyes roll, till Missy cuts in: "You pencil dick boneheads. It's her father, for fuck sake. You pea brains ever think about anything but fucking? Fuck!"

The boys ponder their special reality, wondering what burr got stuck in her shorts, and if the big sumbitch got lucky. She's a tad rough and tough, but there can be no doubt: *I'd like to tap that.*

Meanwhile, after assessing likely direction, parental connection and potential infection, Jimmy says he's never rode bitch behind any man nor beast, but saddling up behind a road gal who's his own flesh and blood is a different prospect altogether. "For a ride out to the place, that is. I got the animals to feed and other duties."

Jimmy wouldn't bow out if he had his old scoot, but he don't so he will. But he lives a few clicks east. "Mo here can drop me off on the way out." He admonishes the boys that she'll at least know where he lives, in case they get their money back, which they won't, and he hardly wants to show them where he lives. "Then she can catch up with you." He scans the mountains to the east. "Them other fellers is gone. You got no idea how much ten grand is to them. They'll not likely head south or cross the border. They got a hundred days of riding weather. Then they have to stay put. They'll be broke by then, so you won't want to find them."

Mo says she'll run him home, because this crowd will be Q-tipping and fixing their faces for another hour anyway.

Missy leans in to whisper that she'll wait for Mo to get back.

Mo needs to let this gal down easy. "Yeah. Great. Whatever."

So Missy learns about love and confusion.

Mo and Jimmy head out, taking the first curve at sixty. She's a regular peg-scraper and wants to make her father proud, and so he is. At his place, he says, "You're a damn good rider, daughter." She shrugs it off. "Don't share these whereabouts. But the door is always open for you. I'm surely sorry for the times we missed.

We're a family now. Friends. Father and daughter and anything you need."

Mo laughs short, "Yeah. I know where to find you." She says she'll be back in a week or two and maybe they'll ride together after all. He says his riding days are over, but maybe.... He writes his phone number on a bar receipt and tells her not to lose it. When they hug, he whimpers. She steps back to see if he's faking, but he's crying. So she cries too, mounting up and pulling out before the emotions stack up.

Back at the motor lodge, the boys stand around, waiting for guidance. Missy tells Mo they can get together when Mo comes to see her father.

Mo says yeah. Maybe.

Buck decides to play it natural, as coached, and says nothing.

Engines idle by noon with the boys repeating the destination aloud so everybody knows where to go when they get lost.

Joe Boggs asks if it gets good there.

Buster doubts this punch-drunk bunch and wonders what difference two hundred forty more miles will make and where he'll go next. Wade lights another chunk over a last look at the map. They smoke it out and head up the access road to the highway. Buster thinks a sense of waste may be a good thing to share. Or maybe it's better to waste a sense of share. Or sense a share of waste.

Fuck, here we go again, wastrels wasted, wasting time.

A morning is not wasted but blessed in the living airs of forgetfulness, rolling again into beauty. Goddamn. There's something to riding down the road, with time coming on and flowing by.

Two hours later, the groove is cut on mountain ridges, sweeping flatlands and riders stretched ahead and behind as far as the eye can see. Long sweeps shrink to curves, to fourth gear and third, coiling into switchbacks and climbing to the pass, where it tightens to second gear and hardly a jog over the summit to the far side, to wider radii and opening throttles into the foothills, west of the Selkirk Range.

Lead riders pull off for a valley view that spreads forever, fading to purple haze.

Mr. Billips and son Burt wend a few miles back, because Burt's father takes his time. They drift like specks, coming up the road. Big Buck also takes it easy to improve his mechanical odds.

Randy Hague ambles to the shrubs to drop his chaps and pants for a squat. Stepping clear in no time, he says, "All part of being on the road." He laughs at those who stare. "What? You guys want to look at it? It's big. Not my biggest. Sometimes they're huge." Nobody moves. "I *wish* someone would look at it. I'm gonna tell you about it later, and I'll need some back-up."

"We're probably okay, Randy."

"I'm not talking about who's okay. You'd be proud of me."

"We're proud of you, Randy."

"Yeah, well. You'd be proud of this turd. It'll get bigger in the telling, unless someone comes over for a look."

Stuey strolls over and looks. "Yeah. It's big."

"How big is it?"

"Anyone got a tape measure?"

Some laugh. Some groan. Randy goes back with a bungee cord and stoops to measure. He rises, holding the cord by its measured length and says, "Look at that," stretching it to two feet.

Some start up and ease out. Some hold back, staring off at a grander scheme, as they shrink in significance or gain insignificance. In heat-rippled stillness, sweat rolls on a whispering breeze.

Wade fires another chunk. "I like it here. Derek. Spread my ashes here, will you?"

Derek takes a hit. "You mean when you're dead?"

"Yeah. Wait till then."

"We'll make it a festive occasion," Buster says.

"Yeah, well, don't plan it yet."

They agree that waiting for the others will lead to waiting for the others, so they mount and ride, strung out between point and cleanup like a loose squall line. They ride together but alone, measuring mortality and not giving a fuck and feeling happy. These miles will survive them for as long as it takes.

A few hours more and the day turns to gold. Breaking for pain pills, beer and beef jerky, Randy says, "This stuff and nails, you could build a shelter."

One of Dave's saddlebags is full of ice and beer. The ice melted, but the beer is cooler than the air, and it's time for the hair.

They guzzle, belch, nod, mount and ride.

With the sun behind, they open it up.

Randy takes the lead, passing with a grin, his thumbscrew tight on seventy-five, into and through the curves. He's the best rider out.

Gold turns to orange, then azure blue and twilight. They wish on first stars and ride into moonrise.

Some see God as a thing with no arms or legs or beard, a thing that isn't cast in man's image but is constant and eternal, shifting shape like the high plains.

Buster feels a long lost love in his heart, and he worries that humanity has no sense other than self-interest with specific regard to market demand and price fluctuations. Humanity will cover this place too, turning magic into practical use and economic stimulation. Then the magic will be gone.

The first riders arrive late at The Hob Knob Motor Hotel.

The others are an hour back.

XV

The Road Less Traveled

The Insomniacs ride at night, which is hell on wheels on a new moon in elk season, and those big bastards stand in the road for the warmth, hardly worried about high-speed impact. But the Insomniacs are rough and tumble no matter the odds or weaponry. Hell, elk and moose on the road in the pitch fucking dark will prove you're man enough to take it, or not.

The Jingle Bulls used to gather once a year for the Spirit of Brass Balls ride, a three-day torturefest to Christmas Eve, culminating a man-dose of sleet and snow with a cocktail known as the Reverberation, a mix of eggnog and grain alcohol. The J-Bulls shortened the Brass Balls jaunt to one day when winter got colder, and a man gets measured in one day easy as three. The J-Bulls and Insomniacs enjoy mythical status, they're so rarely seen, and their adventures grow taller in every retelling.

Even the Dreaded Fellows tolerate those two clubs. Who cares about a bunch of guys riding at night or in the freezing cold? J-Bulls and Insomniacs are the only intolerance exemptions of the Dreaded Fellows, which is not to say that these clubs coexist. Understanding is to dominance what ice water is to hell; nobody gets some. The Fellows plain don't give a fuck. Coexistence does not occur. The nocturnals get along with the diurnals on the simple basis of never running into each other, and don't go out of their way to look for shit most of the time.

It's not for lack of smarts that Hobarth Grimes called north instead of east. It was instinct, what separates a seasoned rider from a wannabe. The difference is in knowing, among other things, which way to go. Some men avoid pain. Some men tolerate it. Some men seek it. A few need it. How can something hurt, if it's part of you? It can't. Pussies head east. Pussies follow the first warm weather for more of the same, because they're pussies. A real rider knows the deceit inherent in first warmth. It's a daytime event, a fair weather friend, leading to nights dropping like a flash freezer.

By the slimmest chance, a light twinkles up ahead, in the piercing sleet. Neon red calls out warmth renewed for Hobarth Grimes and Lonny Snodgrass. The flashing sign reads *Johnny's* but might as well say *Home Free, Motherfuckers*. Both men grunt and laugh short, trembling in their saddles, flexing hands and feet to feel something, anything, as their torsos shrivel. Inner warmth lasted a few clicks on financial security, but that was hours ago, and death by freezing could be the next stop. Faces nearly numb, they welcome stinging pain as a symptom of survival, because frostbite is pain free.

The future seems suddenly certain, with shelter just yonder to secure them for the night. Not that either one could retire on seven thousand dollars, much less half of it. But those greenbacks are U.S. and more dollars than either has seen on any sundown or payday.

It's too damn bad about Buck. But fuck, he'll catch up sooner or later. Why would those rich fuckers want his old rat rig anyway?

Maybe Hobo and Lonny don't see the line-up on the far side of the building, in the lee of the sleet. Maybe they do and think the place is a biker bar, or maybe they're too near frozen to wonder who in hell would be out on a night so cold, it slices ears like a razor blade.

They set practical questions aside to pull in slowly and avoid breaking loose in the snow, but they hurry too to get inside to this place of salvation. That would be salvation for some, last call for others. Two Indians lean against the stoop, propped up. One Indian twitches, before feebly raising a bottle. The other takes the bottle from the first in mid-rise and drains it, then lowers his hand to the snow. The two Indians settle again, still, so winterkill can play out, now that the antifreeze is gone.

Lonny pauses, "You think that bathroom was heated?" He turns to Hobo—he means the bathroom he barricaded from outside once Donny handed over the cash so he could take a dump, which wouldn't take long with a double cheese and bacon burger knocking cotton, and he sure as shit didn't want to get the cash dirty. Young Donny'll come out of that crapper a little smarter than he went in. Sooner or later. What the hell, couple skid pallets propped under the doorknob are better than a two by four upside the head. Ain't they?

Hobo also pauses to flip a gob between the Indians. Then he's up the steps to replace this harsh scene with a breath of springtime. And he pauses to savor the brand new filling in his thought bubble. *Call me moneybags—that'll be Mister Motherfucking Moneybags to you, motherfucker.* Fluttering back to Earth, he asks his new partner, "Did you say something?" The bundle in his jacket practically throbs, ready to spread across a table like sunrise on a high plateau.

"No. I was just wondering about that kid...."

"You were just wondering what the fuck difference it makes who's freezing out here in a crapper? Why do you give a flying fuck about Donny or anyone, with a future itching to start two steps through that door?"

Lonny takes his meaning. So they walk into it.

Shaking off the snow, they stop short at the invisible wall two steps in. "Whoa, buddy," Hobo murmurs, gawking down the bar stools at leather jackets from the rear: rockers under skulls with barbed wire, daggers and flames shooting out the ear holes and eye holes, and likewise on up to the neck stumps. Like intruders, they stand stock still to take stock on the minefield before them and break inertia anew, soft as soft-boiled eggs tapping on Gramma's teacup. Step gingerly onward, they toe that fine, thin line, not tiptoeing like pussies but not clomping in like rude fuckers either.

Wait a minute. Clomping might be best. At any rate, it's a left right left. They can't very well just stand there and look afraid. Grimy Grimes and Rumble Snodgrass share an instinct on the survival issue, seeking kinship on what's close to the bone in this crowd. All that fluffy future fuckola can wait. A bunch of snow and ice and freezing fucking wind don't count for shit at this juncture. Because this. Is. The motherfucking McCoy on the survival issue. The situation calls for peak alertness at all moments and movements, gestures, words and glances, you name it, no mistakes.

Those at the bar pay no mind. They're half in the bag.

So this might work out.

Hobo and Lonny belly up and wait longer than it ought to take for a thirsty road dog to get a motherfucking beer, but that's okay.

Lonny won't say boo, because Hobo's the point man in this outfit, and Hobo holds his complaints stoically, like a man who knows how to hold 'em, again of a like mind with present company, going along as a man of few words, like the great ones usually are. Hobo knows Johnny Hatlo, who's run this bar ever since when, but this is not home turf for the grimy one; it's nearly three hundred clicks out, leaving Lonny and Hobo no choice but to wait for Johnny to ask, "You wanna drink? Or am I supposed to read your mind?"

Johnny obviously doesn't recognize his old friend and patron,

Hobarth F. Hobo Grimey Grimes, known for what the name recommends. The iffy atmosphere murks further when six burly heads turn in unison, to see who the fuck wants his fucking mind read.

Hobo regrets his timid grin and tries to fix it but fails to look like anything but a fearful pooch, one who wants to please but can't be certain how exactly to avoid the slap, like he knows he's been bad and vows to make good. "Whiskey. Rye," Hobo murmurs.

Why didn't he order two? Now Lonny has to order and might fuck it all up, which seems hard to do, but you never know when a Dreaded Fellow might ask what in the motherfucking hell is wrong with your....

"Uh.... Yeah. Whiskey."

Johnny nods once, and it's over and out on the drink order. So far, so good. The boys are in there like a dirty shirt and soon to be warm all over. Then again, tension won't take a holiday just yet. Here comes the once-over, the burly boys taking free license to eyeball the new guys up and down. This is trying time, with all present knowing full well that the eyeball scan can turn in a blink to who might be bitch to whom.

Lonny and Hobo dare not return the gaze or utter another fucking syllable. But they can't stand there like statues, so Lonny lets his crooked smile ease on out, balancing things with a headshake and a mean motherfucking grimace for the freezing motherfucking weather. "Fuck! Inay! Fucking cold motherfucker." He speaks lowly, with sincerity and respect.

Thank God the big TV spares the moment from silence, though God in His strange way fills that moment with an ad for a new drug to cure rosacea, whatever the fuck that is, until we know what it is, with that pasty fucker up there looking fresh-fucked up the ass, as the TV voice proclaims, "Twelve million Americans look like they're blushing!"

Trouble is, so do Hobo Grimes and Lonny Snodgrass, their cheeks rosy red from the freezing cold. The TV guy is talking about red cheeks, and nobody knows what fucking dots might get connected here, but it doesn't fucking matter, because the once-over is into twice and three times up and down, leaving Lonny nothing for it but to take his jacket off; what the fuck.

"Warm in here," he offers, avoiding eye contact at all cost.

Well what the fuck'd you do that for? Hobo would like to ask but can only wonder, and that dumb motherfucker Lonny can't read his mind or the writing on the wall, leaving him, Hobo, with his jacket zipped up over the wind gusset to keep the cash from spilling out. He feels like a point man in the clutch, keeping his shit together, or, more precisely like a sitting fucking duck. Fuck. The fucking Dreaded Fellows! *And I got seven fucking thousand dollars under my fucking jacket. And you take your fucking jacket off? Fuck, man!*

So another layer peels away, figuratively speaking, exposing a weak underbelly on one more error or bit of bad luck or failure to see the picture, which Lonny and Hobo have avoided one hundred ten percent so far this evening. Both feel the fickle nature of survival, and Lonny does see his gross error in peeling his jacket, but it's too late. What can he do, change his mind and put his jacket back on after it's halfway off? No, he can't, not without looking like a fucking idiot, doesn't know if he wants his jacket on or off, most likely doesn't know about his fucking pants too, dumb fucker.

So what's Hobo supposed to do, take his jacket off? Let the wad fall out? Fuck. Man. Or wait for a Dreaded fucking Fellow to ask what the fuck; you don't like the weather in here?

Thank God again, a Dreaded one makes the next move, because Rumble Snodgrass just fucked up so bad, he wouldn't take another move even if he knew what it was, and Grimy Grimes knows nothing but that he can't take both hands out of his pockets at once without the wad tucked inside his jacket falling out the bottom.

The move comes from down the bar, from the least burly of the burly heads, the one at the far end that becomes visibly female, as it backs away for a better view, then slides on out and moseys on down to the new arrivals. Or it used to be female, before it got like it is, which is still female in the technical sense, just as a scoot with three million clicks might still roll downhill. This person is to womanhood what STP motor treatment is to water; it'll pour, kind of, but it sure as hell won't trickle or refresh in any way.

The age is hard to tell because of the mileage, the leathery skin, heavy bags under dewy eyes, stooped posture, frizzy, greasy hair and a raspy voice that opens three steps out. "You got any cash?"

Lonny watches the bartender, hoping the drinks will get served and go down the hatch so he and Hobo can head back out and take their chances with death by freezing, over and out of this hell.

Hobo freezes.

She says, "I need some cash if you guys got some. I'll write you a check. I need to write a check for some cash." She smokes the last half-inch of her cigarette like it's as good as the first puff in the morning. "It's good. The check is good. You don't believe me, you can ask these guys." She smokes it down to the nub and then some. "You believe me, don't you?"

Lonny turns to her, since it's evident who's point man now. "No. We don't have no cash for you. Don't have it."

"How you come to drink in a bar, you so broke?"

"Couple whiskies is all," Lonny says. "Plenty men got no cash, step up for a whisky."

"Got a smoke?" the woman asks.

Lonny nods, reaches for his pack and tamps a few out. She takes five.

"Thanks. I'm Tina. Who are you?"

Lonny gives up another smirk, not exactly like a shy dog curling a lip, because things are getting along, and nobody can know where it'll lead to after introductions. The Dreaded Fellows got to get recruits from somewhere. Don't they? "I'm Rumble."

A few burly heads turn again, which could be good or bad.

"This here's Hobo."

She laughs and coughs. "Homo?"

"I said Hobo. His real name is Grimy."

"Whyn't you say his real name in the first place?"

Lonny lights his smoke. "Call him what you want."

She nods to those behind her. "This is Caveman. That's Crash. Snake, Octane, Manhole and Asphalt. Be careful with Manhole and Asphalt. Those two can be a mouthful, and either one could kill you. Or gag you. Huah! Uh huah huah acchhh chhh chhhuhhggg...." Heaving into small crisis, she holds Caveman's shoulder to keep from falling down.

Another burly head leans back, either Snake or Octane. "Rumble? You like to rumble?"

Lonny can't control the smirk at this point; try as he might to get it off his face. He compensates by looking down as he says, "I had my share."

Caveman grunts, works up a loogie and gulps it back. "The fuck you know about rumbles?"

Lonny looks up as if to ask, you talking to me, Sir?

Octane intervenes. "The fuck. I'll kick your fucking ass."

"Yeah? You and who else?" Caveman wants to know. "One of these faggots? Or you and both of 'um?"

"Neither one. Just me and my little friend...."

Lonny and Hobo haven't ridden all that far together, but they share an intuition that the outer layers are falling away faster, that they now verge on a brawl that will end with losers and bigger losers. They've been called faggots and can't accept the label but can't argue against it, and now Octane is about to pull weaponry, most likely a gun, but maybe only a knife.

"Here you go, boys." Johnny Hatlo serves the rotgut neat, which would be good; down the hatch, over and out. But when he says, "Three dollars," Lonny looks over at Hobo and shrugs.

Hobo shrugs back in exaggerated disgust, so anybody can plainly see he's sick and fucking tired of suffering this fool.

So Lonny shakes his head, because Hobo still doesn't get the message. So Lonny says, "I don't have any money. You got all the money."

Aw, fuck. Man.... Hobo's thought bubble is plain to read as the scorpions dancing down his neck. Now they're done for, because no man could pull three singles from this wad o' hundreds. And what else can he do, ask Lonny to reach into his pocket?

But then Octane provides blessed distraction by pulling a vial from his shirt. He removes the plastic top, presses the vial to a nostril and grunts like a rutting boar, trying to snort the contents past his septum to ram charge a different state of affairs up into his brain, or to the inner chamber of his skull at any rate.

Tina explains. "What Octane loves most of all is when he turns into High Octane. All rightie now, boys. Now where were we?" She stumbles on a turn into the far wall and turns halfway back, sliding into a chair.

Hobo turns away to fish inside his jacket for three dollars, pulling at the cash till it's fluffed up like a drift of leaves but still shows nothing but hundreds. "Well, fuck me in the asshole if I ain't got but...." He catches himself murmuring and speaks clearly for understanding: "This fucked up old newspaper to keep warm with is what. Fuck. Lonny—Rumble. You got three bucks, you cheap fuck. I know you do. Now give it."

Lonny nods, taking the cue, putting a finger tip between his eyes to touch his memory. "Oh, yeah. Fuck, yeah. Out on my rig." Sliding his jacket back on, he turns quick and natural with a nod to

Hobo, who knows Lonny never left money on his rig. He never had money to leave, and besides, what dumb fuck leaves cash on his rig? This is the exit. If Hobo can't get a message this plain in the clutch, well, Lonny R. Snodgrass won't be waiting around too long.

All of which turn of events stokes the coals on a different thought process for Grimy Grimes. *Just who the hell is Lonny Snodgrass?* Well, a man can wonder, wondering as well how fortunes might fare without what's his name. Could this be a campfire at the fork in the road? That is, the loot divvy went from three shares down to two shares, and now it looks like one. Or would that be up to one?

Lonny feels the burly eyeballs on him, as he strides for the door, and in two more steps, he's out.

The breeze is picking up, or he's softened from too much time indoors. A shiver makes him sneeze. But that's good. A solid sneeze is loud, so he fakes another and sneezes on across the front deck and down the steps, where he bumps an Indian with a bottle frozen into his hand. The Indian plops over, passed out or dead. The hand gripping the bottle rises on a stiff arm and stays vertical. The other Indian, also glazed, proves the need for a man to stay on the move.

"Achoo! Achoo!" And so on to his scooter, he mounts, cocks the kicker, rises and achoos again till the tired jugs take over with hardly a spark to go on. A sputter sounds like another sneeze, and in two more kicks and she turns over. A man in survival mode feeds it gently to get it up and get it on or face the grim fiddler. Lonny gooses, but not too much! His old scoot is half froze in the battery but may be willing, because this is the clutch. He determines then and there that he'll never sell or trade. Man and machine are in this together.

Loyalty and devotion are all that's left, if he thinks about it. But he ought not think too much, easing out, numb in the feet and hands again but warming inside at renewed prospects for life, a little bit longer at any rate. Rolling into the darkest, coldest, wettest motherfucker in recorded history, he's headed back south, via the shortcut at Gumption Pass.

What the fuck; might as well get this over with. Those shitballs want to follow; let's see what they got.

He hesitates; maybe he ought to leave Hobo a note, but he's got no motherfucking paper, no motherfucking pencil, and his fucking hands would freeze anyway. So what the fuck? Where else would Hobo head to but south on the most miserable night of the world?

Back inside, Hobo Grimes feels none the worse for wear and figures he might make a go of this thing, because a clutch motherfucker ought to know how to play it. What the fuck? Wouldn't be the first comeback to victory in the fourth inning.

"You got a woman?" Tina asks.

Hobo opts to fit in on this response. He ignores her.

"You got a woman you beat and don't pay attention to what she needs?" Hobo wants to drink his damn whiskey but hasn't yet paid, and time is running short on that no-count Lonny coming back, especially since everyone heard him leave.

"Is that what you did?" Tina asks, her voice rising to shrill accusation. "You got her wore out with your demands?"

Hobo turns and looks down, stepping past her and murmuring, "I gotta piss. 'Scuse me." He feels the bar settling in, like he's not there, not really, not like a nuisance or a problem. Hell, if he aimed to split, he'd head out for a piss off the deck, but here he is heading back to the men's room, which ought to show anybody who gives a rat's ass that he aims to stay around and socialize. Now that you mention it, a piss ain't a bad idea; you get so cold, you forget how full up you are. In the men's room he fists wads of bills into his back pockets, his boots, his pants, just any old where, till he looks a little lumpy but not so different from the crowd out front. Settling into relief, he realizes that few things let a man relax like a two-minute piss, and you can't really ease on into long-term perspective till half way through the second minute. He glows with prospects, because the future is a bright motherfucker. You got to love that urban biker scum, dealing in hundred dollar bills. Hell, it'd be tens and twenties if those rich fuckers ever worked for a living. Then he'd be good and fucked. He imagines stuffing all that cash into his boots and pants instead of just seventy C-notes.

Fuck.

But nature takes care of her own now and then. Hobo Grimy Grimes shakes off and tweaks his hog for a last dribble, which attention to detail spares a man from the piss residue ganging up like it does. Repacked and ready, he walks out like a man at home in the world, jacket open, warmed up. To prove his place, he pulls a hundred from his shirt pocket, lays it on the bar and says to Johnny Hatlo, "Here you go, brother. Got my emergency stash." With a riding man's largesse he ads, "Might as well blow the wad. It's a shame to get halfway there on the good stuff, when you...."

"I knew it! Mister, you got the cash. You had it all the time. Now gimme here..." So the old snatch snatches the cash and holds it up to the light. "U. S. Why you lyin' sack o' snake shit." Stashing the hundred into her shirts, she pulls out a rumpled, soaked down, dried out, moth-eaten check. "Wait a minute." Pressing one end of the check to the bar she smoothes it flat with her other hand. "I'm just gonna make it better. Wait." She plucks a chewed pen from her hair and scratches through fifty dollars and scrawls a hundred dollars over the top. She writes slowly, muttering syllable by syllable, "One hun-nerd mo-ther fuck-in dollars. You. Owe. Me. Good. It's already made out to cash, see, so you can cash it anywheres."

Hobo doesn't need to sneak a peek down the bar to sense a dozen bloodshot, sunken eyeballs putting him in the crosshairs. So he slides the check across the bar and shrugs, till Johnny Hatlo says, "We don't take checks."

"That's okay. He's got more." She snuggles in to Hobo. "Buy a lady a drink? Johnny, pour me a Crown Royal, wouldja? Why the fuck not? I wrote you a good goddamn check, didn't I?"

From down the bar comes grumbling like a failing structure, till a Fellow says, "I'll have one of those too, this broke fucker's buying." A wave of half nods fills the gap.

"Make 'um triples," another Fellow grumbles. "Hey, Johnny. You ever pour quadruples? What comes after quadruples? Fiveruples?"

Johnny looks at Hobo for approval, and Hobo nods, because somehow or other, this feels like progress, like a night looked back on before too long, recalling how he came by his Dreaded rocker and fire-breathing skull holes.

"That's what you did. I know it is," Tina sputters.

"Looks like your friend took up with them Indians out there." This is from Octane—make that High Octane, who squints to dim the light in his severely dilated eyes.

Hobo turns toward the door and also squints, as if for meaning or resolution or a decent answer. He turns away and says, "He ain't my friend."

"Said he was your riding partner," Octane grunts another snort from his vial.

Hobo shrugs. "He ain't. Just some…. I don't know. He hangs around, tags along. That's how he is."

Caveman sits closest to where Hobo stands. Without looking up, he says, "He said he'd go out for more money. Why'd he say that when you're standing right here with a hundred dollars? What the fuck is that, man?"

Hobo grunts and snorts into a headshake. "I don't know where he gets that shit. Little pussy's always broke, always going for money he ain't got. Most likely left here thinking he…you know…fooled everybody again and got free drinks. Little fucker."

Caveman looks up, displeased, "You know he's a little fucker and a cheap-shit cheating cocksucker, and you ride with him?"

Hobo grunts into another headshake, aware that a new pattern will form up against him if he doesn't steer the puzzle pieces into a picture of his own making. "No. I don't. We's both headed up this way. I rode out. He followed. That's all."

"Headed up this way? It's a fuckin' blizzard out there. Where the fuck you headed? Where the fuck's he going?"

It's plain obvious that nowhere on God's icy earth would warrant a ride tonight, unless it was a ride to the bright future. And no matter how well a man has developed his instinct for lying with integrity, this question poses problems of credibility, leaving Hobo no alternative but the lame ass answer: "Just out for a ride."

Now that's some bullshit, and the big heads down the line all turn south. Hobo feels thirsty for something with a jolt to sharpen his wits. So he knocks back half the triple sitting in front of him and nearly laughs at its smooth slide down the hatch. "Fuck, man. You can't even feel that shit. Hardly get your money's worth. Then again, you can drink more of it. Johnny?"

Johnny pours another triple into Hobo's glass.

Nobody says nothing for the next half-minute, giving Hobo time to knock back half of it and reassess removal from this place to, say, a few clicks up the road. Or however far the next shelter might be, which could be fifty clicks, or sixty-five. He can do that.

Tina wedges back in. "I want one too. One of them triplets." She turns to Hobo. "I know that's what you did."

Caveman elbows her back, out of the way. He grumbles at his drink and says, "I think if we hang him upside down by his boots, we could shake a few more hundreds out of him."

Hobo turns to make room for Tina, in case she wants back in. She doesn't.

So Caveman says, "Tina, you was tired from the get-go. Didn't have no spunk for any fun at all. Not like this fella."

She reaches past Hobo to take his drink and finish it. "I hope you got some spunk," she says pointedly to Hobo. "These boys are gonna fuck you up. They gonna beat the holy motherfucking snot outa you."

Hobo reaches for an inside pocket, like he's going for a smoke. But as he grasps the butt of his piece and sees no reaction from the boys at the bar, he shifts and comes out with a smoke plucked neatly from the pack. He lights it with matches from the bar.

"That's 'cause they like you. If they didn't like you, they'd fuckin' kill you."

Hobo smokes deeply, in reflective repose.

Caveman leans over, as if to share a confidence, and rips a fart.

Allowing a moment for afterthought, Hobo knows that Dreaded affiliation will require a beating and survival of said beating. But taking things in a different direction may divert the beating and still pave the way to Dreaded brotherhood. "I'm looking for some hash."

Caveman sits up for another assessment.

Hobo lets him take his fill.

Caveman asks, "Who the fuck are you?"

"Hobo."

"You got money?"

"That depends. You got hash?"

"How much you want?"

"What's it cost?"

"What it's always cost? Fifteen a gram. Three hundred a ounce. Four thousand for a pound."

Ch ching ch ching. Hobo Grimes may not be the quickest wit on the numbers, but he senses survival and prosperity as straight away alternatives to a beating he may not endure. "I'd take a pound."

So Caveman reaches to the inside like Hobo did, but instead of plucking a cigarette, he comes out with a slab of chocolate. Not really. It just looks like a jumbo Hershey bar. "You seen the goods. Now you pay up, one way or t'other."

Hobo wishes like hell he'd sorted out the four grand so he wouldn't have to show his whole wad, but then he has it stashed in four places and can stop when he gets to four, but then they might want to check whatever places he doesn't empty that still look lumpy. But what the fuck? "Can we try some?"

"No."

"Okay. That's okay. I'll take it." So he reaches into his left boot and comes up with sixteen bills and pulls another twenty-three from his right boot to keep things symmetrical, kind of. Let's see, sixteen and twenty-three is, uh....

"That's thirty-nine," Caveman says.

"Yeah, yeah." He finds three more in his inside pocket and thrusts a hand down the front of his pants, suddenly realizing he's already over. He stuffs the extras back in and scratches like hell. "Fucking crabs."

"Go wash your fucking hands, ass wipe. With soap!"

"Yeah. Good idea," Hobo says, on his way to the back again, picking up the hash on the way, thanking his lucky stars for knowing how to play a situation by instinct. Once inside the WC, he wonders why he'd need to leave, now that the deal is done, and all parties seem satisfied on a fair trade, more or less.

He washes his hands, thinking this could be the beginning of the beautiful relationship. He can practically feel the Dreaded colors on himself, Hobarth Grimes. Why the fuck not? He takes a moment to practice his all out grin as a substitute for the pained grimace in the mirror. Good whiskey is good all right, but he can't remember so much sauce swilling down the gullet in so few minutes. This is way more sauce than his tired old esophagus has had to process in a long time. But this is the big league, and a man on the verge of greatness wants to show balls, big motherfuckers, with humility and respect but not pain....

But here comes another surge on the hot motherfucking poker in his chest, which is a great opportunity to get this right. So he fixes his face in the mirror and puts mind over matter, turning the grimace to a pleasant grin, as a man of huge fucking gonads can do.

Hey! Motherfucker. It's been good doing business with you.

Back out front the five men at the bar are up and mulling, zipping up and prepping for blizzard conditions. Nobody says boo, making Hobo wonder if they suspect he called in the Mounties on his cell phone from the bathroom, except that he doesn't have a cell phone and wouldn't have one, unless he decided to become a faggot and make a few calls all the time, and any man here can go ahead and frisk him if they have any doubts on that issue.

On second thought, a frisk might not be such a good idea, with those stray lumps of cash here and there. So Hobo zips up too, going along with the program.

Octane asks, "Where the fuck you going on a night like this?"

"Up the road. Can't stay here all night."

Snake sidles up. "Hey. You sell that and need some more, you find us."

"How?"

"Tina."

"You call this number," she says, plucking another check from her rags and pointing to the phone number. "Just say you're the punk from Johnny's, should have been beat to shit but bought some produce instead. I know what you did."

So the Dreaded Fellows stride out as one, mumbling at the cursed bitter cold but saying nothing besides.

"I'm going too!" Tina calls out, like a tree falling in a forest with no ears. "Please take me. You know what I can do."

Asphalt turns at the door. "They'll put you in jail, Tina. Then what the fuck good are you?" He closes the door behind him.

She melts into a chair and mumbles.

Hobo holds back, until he hears the last one pull out. Then he pulls on his gloves, head sock, facemask and the bulky goggles he hates because they're so clunky, but who cares on a night like this?

That's when Johnny Hatlo tells him he's right at a hundred dollars short on his bar tab.

Hobo has a mind to brain this motherfucker, or maybe just shoot him to teach him a lesson, but he thinks not, with things going so well. Then again he might just as well tell this shitferbrains bar monkey to get it from his floozy whore.

Then again, it's a small town, more or less, in a hundred-click radius. Why let a measly motherfucking hundred drive him to commit a messy motherfucking murder, even on a shitbag like this? Or fuck up an old whore the Fellows use as a hash contact? So he pulls off a glove, digs for the bill and flips it over the counter, picking up an unfinished shot and downing that too, for the warmth. Never mind the burn; it'll balance out soon enough.

He pulls the fucking goggles over his eyes, knowing they'll go to zero visibility when the sleet stacks up on the lenses, but he can wipe it off easy enough, unless it freezes, which could make him crash, but then his eyeballs could freeze with no goggles, which would be worse. He wraps his scarf and tucks the ends down into his gusset where the freezing wind wants to flow right down to his nuts and kill him quick. He pulls down his earflaps and loosens the chinstrap on his toy helmet, so it can fit around all the extra wraps.

He turns back at the door to see the bartender wiping down and the old whore slumped in her chair against the wall, looking a little better, actually, through these goggles. He laughs, stepping out and into the blizzard, trying to count how many times he cheated death in the last little while.

Easing past the frozen Indians, he reckons he'll slide by the Reaper with some chin stubble to spare once or twice more before bedtime. He throws a heavy leg over and kicks it to life on the fifth try, then eases back onto to the road in freezing sleet. A real rider has to love a night this cold and dark and wet, idling on a shoulder and not even knowing whether it's left or fucking right, because he's warm and fuzzy as a man in a blizzard can be. And riding conditions this fucked don't get any better for the tall tales that come out the back end or the seasoning that makes a rider real.

Fuck it. He hangs a right for the lake thirty clicks up and those fancy pants motels in there. Or seventy clicks. *That's only an hour at seventy per or two hours at thirty-five, which might sound slow, till it's your motherfucking ass in this sideways bullshit motherfucker. Then see how fast you want to go.*

Motherfucker.

Dark as a black bear's butthole and twisty as a two-dollar pretzel, it's a night of nights. But a man who can't ride seventy clicks in any kind of shit ought not call himself Hobo Grimes.

He rolls the throttle slowly on up to seventy, trying to feel his grip and traction and knowing he won't. He has to sense the vitals, which your average rider can't do in a million years. But he's moving, so the traction must be there.

Hell, seventy ain't so bad, once you get the hang of it.

He heads on up the road easing on down to sixty and then fifty, what the fuck: hour, hour and a half. His grip cats can't flog him under about eighty, and that's not good, since they could keep the fucking blood and shit moving along. They flop, fairly limp. And he enjoys a laugh as only a man with a two-wheeled soul can do, at the idea of getting hung up by the boots to shake the money out. Hell, he'd have took it or anything else they threw at him, though he did sweat the sexual relations prospect there for a long fucking minute.

But that wouldna been no problem too, because there weren't no way in hell Paul Bunyon would have swung his ax at such a sorry excuse for a woman. Much less chopped her down. No way.

They might have required her to give him skull service, and that might have done it. *Hell, I heard there ain't no better head than your old lady head. All them years of practice. Or maybe I read it somewhere, on a wall or some shit. Might not have been so bad, if she took her teeth out first. Then they'da made me fuck her.*

Man.

Hobo Grimes trembles with the bitter cold gnawing its way in and icing the flames between his belly and his chest. He shivers for what he avoided, what could have been worse than death and a might colder than this godforsaken night. Goose bumps rise and tighten his skin, and he feels the wadded check rubbing against his chest. Who can ever tell what the future might be?

Hash man for the Dreaded Fellows? Why the fuck not, if a man is tough and smart enough and got the means to pull it off?

He laughs again at prospects ahead for a room with a hot shower and towels that haven't even been used, not once, and sheets and pillows and shit at what, sixty bucks a night?

Fuck, man. I got another three grand in my pocket. Well, twenty-seven hundred anyway. Too bad those rooms ain't two or three hundred a night. Might run into those rich fuckers, see if they want to buy some hash.

XVI

The Last Hurrah

Joe Boggs nurses a drink, his first since last night, two hundred forty miles ago. The hours and miles bunch up in singular pain and joy. Joe's head throbs on shrinking intervals, demanding resolution. Another bit o' the hair should restoreth the soul.

Joe's been thinking about luck, its random nature and cyclical pattern. You get a little luck, good luck, and then it's gone, surely to return, unless bad luck wants to hang out for a while. Joe is a man of the world but can't fathom how he fell into this bit o' luck. Maybe she just happened along, a Good Samaritan in the night. That seems odd, so few people stop to help strangers these days, much less to help a puked-out drunk.

But that's where an open mind comes in. He remembers lying down in the grass but can't remember how he got to bed. He woke up with sunlight in his eyes, cheek pressed to flesh. In a moment or two, he thought he was awake and this was no dream. He could tell it was a thigh next to his cheek, hairless and likely female. So he eased on up to the scent of it and felt stumped. Baked peaches with a…crust? But not like a pie. It was more blended, more of a….

"You mean like peach cobbler?"

"Yeah. Peach cobbler. I thought it was strange; because perfume smells like flowers, not peach cobbler. But, let me tell you, it didn't smell like dick."

The boys nod. Best to wake up smelling no dick. Meanwhile, it whimpered up top, so he inched up and came to a vagina, where he sniffed again and sure enough smelled peach cobbler.

"Her pussy smelled like peach cobbler? That would scare a normal man."

"Listen," Joe says, "It was fresh."

"You mean like Mom used to make?"

"No. It was like pussy. I mean, fuck, you know? I have faith that God takes care of me. I can't see the use, otherwise." On the theological note, Joe downs half his drink. The boys reflect on God and baked goods, till Randy asks if he wasn't afraid that she was one of those weirdoes who likes to stuff a bunch of peach cobbler or some shit up her pussy, and there he is expecting a mouthful of pussy and getting a load of peach cobbler instead, which wouldn't be bad if you knew it was peach cobbler. But who wouldn't have a few doubts?

"I take your point, ye of little faith. Let's just say I had faith. Let's just say it was unbelievable. The beauty of it was, I didn't know what she looked like. Didn't matter. It was like a mirror universe where left is right and vice versa and a kiss isn't just a kiss. Pussy. Peach cobbler. You know how they used to say that everything is everything. I always thought that stupid, so obvious, it made no sense. But there it was, merged or converged or whatever you want to call it. Don't get me wrong, but I felt all cinched up to modern times. It felt…what they say now, appropriate. It felt appropriate. You know? It was…sweet."

"Sweet might be good."

"Listen. Insight comes when you don't expect it. I didn't know how I got there. So I'm eating this pussy, and she starts moaning, so I come on up to the belly and the breasts, and they're great too, and guess what?"

"It's a guy."

"No. I said she had a pussy, didn't I? Guys don't have pussies. Or tits."

"Coulda used to been a guy."

"She didn't used to be a guy. She used to be a class-A, four-star, bona fide hunk o' beauty. Still looks good. About sixty-five."

"Sixty-five?"

"That means seventy."

"No. She's sixty-five. Her husband made a billion in brewing, but they travel separate. I'm telling you, it was a blessing. I got fucked with the gift of insight, and that's a winning combo. She was smart, good mood, rich. Paid for the room. Rubbed my back. Returned the favor. I got her card. Look at you guys. Stuck on shrinking inventory."

Joe finishes his drink. "She was a gift. I got a new outlook."

"Yeah, and a bunch of new inventory."

"Why didn't you bring her down to breakfast and introduce her? You know we like to meet your new friends." Joe Boggs lets that one go on a short laugh, and the weary group sighs and waits for another story to top that one. "You plan to go in sober next time?"

Joe's wry smile and upward glance suggest hope, that going in sober might be a good thing to try, and maybe he will, some day.

Buster says he saw the Dalai Lama that morning from the bathroom, because the TV is set up to watch from the crapper. He had to lean over but not much, and it was also a nice combo, broadening horizons while ditching a load. The Dalai Lama said that Buddha was a prophet, not a deity. Buddhists have no deity but follow a prophet. "He said they have no personal God, and that's a good thing. They have God-like forces. It makes sense. If people could recognize God-like forces in that light, the world would be a better place. But they can't or won't, because they need God to help out with personal favors. They need God to beg to for what they really want."

"They need someone to talk to when they're getting a blowjob," Harry Woo says.

"It's like us, on the road in a Godless world, connecting with God-like forces. You can't be part of brutal beauty and rugged expanse without feeling it. You're coming off a ridge, into a valley that stretches ten miles to the next mountain. You see riders ahead, little dots on the road. That's us from a distance. Things gain perspective out here. Love, compassion, violence. Need."

Joe Boggs ponders God-like forces. He sips another drink as if problem drinking is one of them, and he shrugs. "A man of bourgeois constraint might worry about the long-term potential of a beautiful woman, who happens to be sixty-five and married." Joe lets the image and a bit more drink sink in, and then elaborates, that he, on the other hand, fancies prospects for Vancouver's finer hotels, with pornography on demand or a club sandwich at three fucking a.m., if he wants one.

"Hmm," Buster intones. "Free of bourgeois constraint but still requiring personal favors and room service." Buster says that Joe's needs sound like certain constraint to certain rebirth, when he'll try once more to transcend desire, instead of licking his chops over some senior pussy because she has money and appreciates his *savoir-faire*. "That's failure, Joe, in this world of desire. Repeat as necessary."

Joe nods and grins. "Yes, I think you're right. But I'll take it. It's so beautiful up next to my failure tally, before she came along."

Harry and Randy stay mum, wondering if Joe's onto something.

The second group lagged an hour back, because they slowed to tolerate the cold, because they had Burt's father in tow.

"I knew that was a bad idea."

"Hey, we're all bad ideas. He's out here doing it."

"Doing what?"

"You know. Whatever it is we're out here doing."

The slow and the old arrive late and eat quickly, before the dining room closes. Then they retire, agreeing that it was a good day, and tomorrow will be great too, and the bed is going to feel better yet.

"Pussies!" Stuey calls across the lobby, as the practical faction trundles off to beddy by, as if the slow and old are out here doing something else. Stuey is not drinking chardonnay. He swills martinis, doubles, "Bombay Sapphire!" He calls the brand, because he's on, feeling chipper, and so staff and guests at this dusty plateau pit stop can know that Stuart Stewart is a top-drawer drinker.

Buster wants a beer alone, to align the golden afternoon and mountain passes with life, its sweeps and ridges, hairpins and slag granting meaning to the greater context. He wants to savor the aftermath, to revive the tingles. Passages and wide-open space reflect what's left of a feeling that might survive the final forgetting.

But a tired scene shapes up with Bombay Sapphire pouring like lemonade to dollars in double-digits and triple, as if a gin drunk and a three-bill bar tab might define the nature of mobility and manhood, but it doesn't. The scene feels tedious, not classic; alcoholic, not stimulating; compulsory, not relaxing.

The end.

So Buster hits a milestone on clarity: This convergence of kindred souls seeking anarchy had its moments, and it's over. Time has come tonight. He's gone, or good as. He'll veer casually tomorrow with no drama and minimal farewell. *Adios, boys. You know I love you, and maybe we'll ride again.* Tonight shouldn't get any worse, with everybody hung over and weary.

Mo says she's too young to turn in with the seniors and takes a seat. She orders a beer.

Stuey guzzles his seventh or ninth martini to make way for his eighth or eleventh, grinning for yet another glory for all time.

One of the Canucks offers a stogie. "It's Cuban!" Nobody believes him, because his cigars smell like a paper bag—Cuba, Illinois, maybe—and he's cheap. But that's okay, because Cuban cigars match Sapphire gin for the best of everything, one more time.

Stuey lights up and inhales, and on a quart of gin swilled like soda pop, he shuffles into his next yarn: "Sho ish muhfuck.... Fucker shaysh...." Until the busboy informs him of no smoking here, and this section of the bar is closed, so no drinking is allowed here too.

"Yeah, yeah, yeah. Sho ish fucker shaysh, how mush money will it take?"

"Sir."

The busboy is a hundred pounds at five four with spinal scoliosis and a pencil neck. He listens to Stuey's story, till Stuey tells the motherfucker to shove this motherfucking deal up his motherfucking ass. Stuey illustrates by gripping the motherfucking busboy's neck. Stuey's other hand is shaking; more gin is spilling than swilling. Men are watching, so Stuey tightens his grip.

The busboy doesn't actually rise off the floor but does get his neck stretched. The wispy larynx bulges, and a scrawny protest sounds like a rodent's last plea.

Stuey tells him to relax, because this bunch rode four hundred fucking kilometers today and deserve a little respect. Three bouncers arrive, looking inflated for the Macy's Parade. They spread their feet and fold their arms. They demand an exit, or they'll call the cops.

Toe to toe with a bouncer, Randy Hague folds his arms to match and to ask, "So? What the fuck you standing here for?"

So the bouncers call the cops, who show up in two minutes to arrest Stuey for aggravated assault and haul him outside and shove him into the squad car. On the way down to the back seat, cuffed and roughed, Stuey resists long enough to wheeze over his shoulder, "Make bail for me, boys. You know I'm good for it."

Then he's gone, looking good for a ride downtown or to the outskirts. Well, he won't likely get the chair before sunrise. So ends another day, and it did get worse than it had to or would have with the first hint of common sense. Buster and Mo watch the scene unfold and fold over. Mo sighs, "Am I missing something?"

"No. I won't miss it either. I'm heading out tomorrow."

She nods. "If you leave, I'm leaving. These are your friends, not mine. They ride okay and aren't much worse than the usual fuckups, but they can't drink too well and throw money around till it's embarrassing."

"That they do. You headed home?"

"Yeah. I could swing by and see the old man but I just told him goodbye. Besides, I think that Missy gal has it bad for me. I can't relate. Maybe I'll ride a few miles with you, till you know where you're going. I love this area when it's not too crowded."

"Sounds good."

Talk and hangovers in the morning are casual, with more moaning over coffee and high times. Randy Hague cleans the long fingernail on his right hand with a penknife. "My nose dries up on this side of the mountains. I get those crusty goobers up in there. I pry 'em loose with my scooper here. Little snuk and a breeze carries 'em off."

Buster nods. The waitress pours.

"It's amazing. I can be riding along and ditch a cruster. Underway and all, getting clear and breathing easier. Feels better. You ever do that?"

"Yeah. It's amazing."

Harry Woo walks in, refreshed. Downtown with Dave, to make bail for Stuey, he saw an adult novelty store and gave love a chance on Karen. "Isn't she sweet?" Karen is inflated, like last night's bouncers but with big red nipples showing through her T-shirt. "She's the deluxe: three holes with collapsible teeth *and* a cervical drain plug." He shrugs. "I like to mix it up." The t-shirt is his, for more appropriate presentation. The inflatable doll routine is also a retread, another grand drollery in the road-dog cavalcade. Harry buys a blow-up doll every year as a joke, kind of.

"What about a drain plug down below?" Buster asks.

"Nah. You gotta hose her out down there. But nobody uses those anyway." And up they go to dress and get better acquainted. Karen flops. She will be a loving object of disrespect and chronic need. The morning moves, as the gates of recovery squeak open.

Buck Dibble tells Mo that he doubts the money went this way, and if it's okay, he'll ride along with her and Buster toward home. She says they're headed long way around, but he can tag along for a while, if it's okay with Buster. Buck blushes. She wishes he wouldn't do that. Buster shrugs and says they'll ride with the bunch to the five-way and part company there. Buck heads out to the lot, wondering where Lonny and Hobo Grimes are now. His old scoot poured smoke in the stretch yesterday, so he adds oil. Any oil will do. It all burns the same. The boys laugh, either at a private joke or at Buck, adding oil. The sun peaks through, so it might be a decent ride.

Mo tells Buster it was worth the trip, finding Jimmy. "He's a strange old man who won't shut up, but he loves me. I guess I needed that. That Buck is okay, but he won't stop staring or squirming his itchy ass. Fucker's in the bathroom longer 'n me."

"You didn't have to room with him."

"I know. I wanted to see him in his shorts."

They stroll out for Stuey's triumphant return, freshly sprung on Dave's credit card. "Can you believe that shit? They don't take American Express! Fuck."

Harry asks how much, and Dave shrugs, a measly three grand.

Stuey says, "I'm paying him back! Fuckinay, man!"

Buster doesn't ask if Dave is in first position or second but tells Stuey he owes seven grand U.S. prior to the three grand Canadian. "Not bad for a ride with the boys. Better not let the bitch find out. She could use this in her case for addictive personality."

"She already did. And she won't find out. She does, I'll kill the fucker who tells her."

He fires his threat into thin air, but Buster wants clarification. "Will the debts be paid before or after the murder?" Stuey will not distinguish such a snide remark.

Finally, they move out of the lot to an empty two-lane going somewhere or the other way. The road spirit blurs, wending and fading, heading south and round about, more or less. Buck brings up the rear, behind Buster and Mo.

The point riders slow for small towns or gatherings of shacks and shanties, abandoned trucks and silos, and the laggers catch up. Blaring through more populous places, like Pikeville or Gray, Boyington or La Salle, they rev, so the bumpkins can gawk in envy and resentment. It's plain to see these riders are bound for glory, destination unknown. Local folk feel the power and shield their eyes from such splendor in chrome. Or maybe the bumpkins only wonder at the strange ways of city dwellers.

The staggered line stretches again at the outskirts, into the foothills and far plains. Distance is long and fast with a rest stop at eighty miles. The wilderness within stretches too, with passages of numbing efficiency.

Karen rides in stoic joy, arms flapping, lips puckered, a country girl at heart in a cowboy shirt and blue jeans. At rest stops, Harry feeds her jerky or offers a cigar. The boys laugh on cue and begin to love her willing good looks and no moods.

Stuey is up to two packs a day, out in the wilderness with more freedom to process among true friends. He seems deep in thought, idling on a pull over, relaxing, lighting a fresh smoke from the nasty nub, telling Buster how his girlfriend Sue begged for it the night before the trip.

Buster waits for a punch line or a point, but the story is over. So he asks, "Is that good?"

"Yeah. Great," Stuey says. "But her appetite gets demanding."

"Feast or famine. She could be in love."

"She gets clingy. You want to fuck her?"

"Yeah, well, they get clingy. The good ones. No, I don't want to fuck her. I mean I'd rather wait. Let her freshen up."

Stuey's cigarette dangles from a loose clench, like the Wild Bunch did, and he says, "If you don't want to, it could be perfect. Women smell indifference. They're weak for it, like bankers want to lend to rich people." He exhales and watches. "It's a fucking trick of nature." He hopes for comprehension.

"A paradox of life." Buster says.

"A guy can cash in, if he times it right." He chomps the butt, twists the throttle and pops the clutch to throw shoulder slag and calls, "She washes it off, you know!" He scrapes through a curve and roars to the lead. No wonder he loves the scene; it makes such sense out of what he came to be. Buster murmurs farewell to himself and his friends. His erstwhile compatriot is living the dream, but he'll wake up Monday, back at his desk. He doesn't punch a clock, because it's not a job but a position, and he wants to be there. Are you kidding, for that kind of jack? It's enough to keep a man going, and Stuey believes he'll be out of his slump in no time.

Cigarette sparks burn tiny craters on a rider's face, but Stuey accelerates into it. Manning up isn't always easy. Stuey wants to feel the burn, hardly twitching when the embers go deep. What a goose. Buster regrets his offer to share Sue, the girlfriend, and regret turns to sadness; Stuey is so removed from what Buster wants to gain. Then come golden light and rolling hills.

Sitting at the five-way crossroads, the boys idle, ready to

follow, given a lead. Nobody rolls forth, till Mo Dowd pulls up and reads the scene. She dismounts, rubs her ass and advises, "You could blindfold me and turn me in circles. I'd give you the same answer. How the fuck do I know?"

The boys laugh at the hub of the Trans Canada Highway, Routes 29, 56, 14 and 132, then shut down, lean them over, slide off, shuffle, spit, piss, light a joint, drink a beer, scan horizons, scratch nuts, rub asses and savor the ride.

Someone mumbles, "Too bad about Buster's money."

Someone laughs, "What money?"

Someone remembers Bill Knudsen, who couldn't make it this year. Bill was a great rider and a great guy and is sorely missed. Bill could hold his liquor and go with no sleep and draw the women, till his wife found out that he and Derek were cruising the better hotel bars of Vancouver, scoring with women who often paid for the drinks and went wild.

Oh, man.

Harry Woo says chasing women is like playing the stock market or fishing. Everyone wants in when a guy brings in a boatload, but they look the other way when a guy gets skunked. It's the same deal on the circuit; you put in the hours to make your average. Bill's scoring wasn't at will. Billy K put in his hours.

"What's she like?" a lone voice ventures.

"Who? What's who like?"

"The wife. What's Bill's wife like?"

"Not bad," Derek says. "Unbelievable tits."

"And a nice ass," Stuey adds.

"Yeah," Buster says. "We all wanted to fuck her." The boys laugh short. She's a wife after all, Bill's wife. What a great guy.

And so it ends, just like that, on a great guy who got caught, on a wife with unbelievable tits and a nice ass, on laughter and constraint, for decency. On a joint declined and a leg eased back over, an engine started and a clutch eased out, as a throttle rolls on, a hand waves in the air and a voice calls out, "Adios, motherfuckers! See you on the corner!"

Voices rise under Buster's exit. "Where's he going?"

"How the fuck...."

"He'll be back."

"What makes you so sure?"

"No, he won't. We're done." Mo fires it up and heads out.

Buck is not far behind, throwing less smoke on a bit better cruising speed, indicating that a piece of sludge got lodged in a leak, improving combustion and overall efficiency.

"The fuck?"

"What's up with that?"

"Guess he had enough?"

"Where we headed, anyway?"

"I don't know. What do you think?

"I don't know. Got a map?"

"Stuey does."

Stuey digs for his map, complaining that the motherfucker is never where he needs it, complaining that Buster just fucking bailed out on his friends, and that's some bullshit.

The rest sit and wait for guidance, their road brother and his two friends shrinking in the distance.

Just so: Buster Fetteroff breaks away. This road heads west-northwest, and he hopes Mo told those crackerjacks not to follow. He tries to remember when he last rode a wilderness stretch with no idea where he was headed and thinks this may be it. He cruises easy, because it's more comfortable, and speed seems foolish with no destination. In twenty miles, he's adjusted to only two riders in tow, so he pulls over to see what's up.

Buck knows the road. It's sweet and easy with a great place to stop on the other side of the mountains. "It's sweet and pretty, and they have these special ribs." The pass is easy, about two hundred clicks to the far side from where they sit. From there it's another hundred sixty around south to home. "So if we want a rest, they got some bunk cabins in back. They ain't too bad."

Home is relative these days, and Buster wonders why Buck would get a bunk cabin only a hundred miles out. Then again, nobody wants to break down in the dark, and as Stuey always asks, what's the rush? The place sounds vague but good. Mo shrugs. "I might as well ride along with you guys and head south from there. Otherwise, it's a couple hun across the plateau. That's miles. I hate that fucking wind."

And just that quick, three riders instead of nine take a whiz, smoke some dope, drink some water, stretch out and head out in ten minutes with a plan.

XVII

Treasure of the Monashee Mountains

Would you look at this shit? Giant motherfucking snowflakes coming on like them steroids in that one with the shaggy motherfucker gruntin' and whimperin' and them homo robots and that biker dude with the rat ship, when they went to mach fucking nine or some shit and all the little white dots turned into lines. Whoosh, into the future faster than the speed of time. No, wait: faster than light. That was it. It was bullshit. Nobody goes that fast.

Besides, where the hell can you go but the future? I've known some sorry ass ditch grunts spent their whole fucking life going backwards. But this is real. Trouble is, I can't go fucking whoosh into the future even with the dots going into lines, and I sure as shit can't stop. I could stop, but who's to say I wouldn't put my motherfucking foot down right over the edge of the motherfucking cliff?

My left foot would work. But why the fuck would I want to stop? To warm up? Have a cold beer?

Fuck.

I oughta get some motherfucking snowflakes tattooed in there with my scorpions. Who the fuck ever figured on snowflakes for badass motherfuckers?

I can't speed up and can't go much slower. For that matter I could drive right off the goddamn road and not know it. Wherever off the goddamn road is. I mean tall tales and rough stuff is one thing, but this is gonna kill me. I'd bet on that. I think I'd win too. It's about fuckin' time. What'd be a real kick in the ass is a motherfucking hotel right the fuck here, twenty-seven hundred clams a night. 'Course, now, that'd be for the fucking presidential....

I'll take it, motherfuckers!

And he would, too....

Except that Hobo Grimes checked into the abyss at a special rate of zero.

Motherfuckerrr.... Or so he thought on first feeling no sense of place, otherwise known as free fall. The second feeling was more concise, less serene, also known as impact. By the third bounce, he knew he'd begun the peaceful rendering, knew he was headed home, or to where a road dog might take a break, or a few breaks. Oh, they wouldn't have Hobo Grimes to kick around anymore.

Hardly a handful of clicks to the west, Lonny Snodgrass doubted the wisdom of running Gumption Pass on any night, much less a godforsaken motherfucker sure to chew him up and spit him like a wad. Where could he stop? Under a tree? In a cave? With no options to speak of, the blizzard was aimed to thrash a man on a motorcycle and bury him. Oh, he stopped, but not by choice. His old scoot just caromed into the oblique angle of a railroad track and lay down in the snow, hitting zero from thirty-five on two bounces, tweaking forks and bars, dinging fenders and the tank. He lay in the snow, numb and ready for a nap. Freezing to death is painless, but Lonny Rumble could set any motherfucker straight on that issue, feeling alive in every part of his body, on enough hurt to make three men wince.

After what felt like a long time, up from deader than a doornail, he woke with a start, sunshine melting the snow on his face. Things didn't hurt so much, cold and numb, but he didn't think he was dead, but wait a minute…. What was that?

It was the rumble that woke him. Small world. He rolled clear of the track, and the train was slow, not all that slow, but a half-froze man on hands and knees could stand up and grab on and pull himself on board, which is what he'd done all his life, if he took a half sec to reflect on difficulty and life in general. Hell, this lunge was easy, what with the friendly fellows on board eager to lend a hand, likely seeing the value of his company.

Lonnard Paulson Snodgrass first learned his legal name at age nine, when his mother said, "Leonard Lenny. Lonnard Lonny." She wanted a Lonny but she couldn't put Lonny as the official name. "I din't see no fuckin' problem. But they left out the postrophe in Paul's son on account of nobody'd pay no heed to me or my Viking bullshit. I was big on our Viking roots back then, but if you want to know the truth of it, leavin' out the postrophe was fine by me. Yer daddy weren't a bad man but for when he was. Lanky galoot, used to ride through here 'n fuck up a storm. We was young. At's where you got yourn."

Lonny recalled his father briefly, as the boxcar boys held him down for another frisking. He would have laughed at what they got out of him but didn't. They pulled his pockets out and his his pants down. No loss there, till somebody packed some cold slicky stuff smack into his butt crack and wanted to know, "Who's yer daddy now?"

That was nobody's business, and he, Lonnard Snodgrass, could take it. It could happen to anyone. At least the grease eased things up, and them steel wheels clacking made for a distraction. And he put his mind on east as the direction of the future. He thought about east and what opportunity might wait there.

He wondered who'd want to cornhole such a bony ass, but the strange ways of men would remain a mystery. Fuck me, he thought, just pulling his pants back up and falling asleep.

He woke up to another fella holding a cup of coffee under his nose. He took it, wondering if he'd had a bad dream, knowing he was a fur stretch from a good time. Wait a minute. He was headed west again. Musta got turned back around. He nodded and mumbled something about appreciation and feeling a whole bunch better.

XVIII

4-Day Weekend

Buster says the ribs are good, but a half slab is too much, like most things these days. Regretting the bulge in his gut, congealing and gaining mass, he wonders if giving up pig meat might be best, after all. "They are tender," he allows, packing one more, shooing thoughts of a cute little pig, slaughtered and butchered for the sake of the sauce. "And the sauce. Do they make it here?"

Buck never thinks about where they make things, or how but says, "If you're not gonna finish your ribs, I'll damn sure keep 'em from going to waste."

Mo got the chicken because she won't eat pigs. She's been thinking of not eating chickens too, because the whole world is going to hell, and she wants no part of it. She's met a few cute pigs, and the damn chickens get tortured too, along with the hormones and antibiotics drilled into their necks. No sauce in the world can mask that bitter reality.

"They don't torture the chickens," Buck says. "Why would they want to torture the chickens? Wouldn't make the chickens worth any more money."

"Yes it does. They torture the chickens to save money in the process and make more on the back end. Those people are mean, like Mo says. Hormones make the chickens fat on cheap feed...

Newspaper, sawdust. Antibiotics cut mortality, so more chickens get to market, and there's your money."

"It's worse than that. You want to spend your life eating confetti, living in a tiny cage? You'd feel some torture. And why the fuck you wanna eat your ribs and his too? Christ on a crutch, man. You could be a good-looking dude; you weren't so fat. Why don't you give peace a chance?"

"I didn't want it to go to waste is all."

Mo pulls back on the heavy download, telling her beer, "Sometimes you're better off wasting something rather than letting it waste you."

So a pall settles, reflective and refreshing as a change of pace. It's been a good day, better than most. Nobody compares this soulful stop to the rolling rodeo and drinkfest they rode out of, though Mo laughs, "The credit card crowd ought to be commandeering a Red Lion about now."

Buster smiles wryly.

Buck ponders credit cards.

They feel a better presence, like the sorting at the end of the day, as it was allowed to happen, as a natural process. "What a bunch o' rubes," she says.

"Yeah, well. You take the good with the bad. I rode some great miles with those guys. But it gets no better than this. I hear water."

"That's the river," Buck says. "It runs to the Columbia, but it's not really a river, except for now, with the lake up. Arrow Lake, but I don't know the name of the river. Whoever makes the barbecue sauce might know."

Buster is up. "Let's take a look."

The river runs on snowmelt from nearby peaks, its rowdy current bucking into whirlpool eddies, venting pent-up pressure and consequence. The jumble assumes a pattern in chaos, repeating its action and response. Buster sees and says, "About thirty years ago, Larraine and I rented a cabin on a Salmon River tributary south of here. Twenty-five bucks a night for a ten-by-ten with a sink and a hot plate and a frying pan. We walked the bank a long way. I felt bad, fooling a rainbow trout into taking kernel corn on a tiny brass hook. He shimmered in the sun, green and pink. Larraine got him off and put him back, didn't even talk about it. That little fish just faded on out, couldn't have gone too far...." Buster's friends watch him gain perspective on one riverbank and another and transition at twilight. "She brought dried beans and brown rice, like she'd known. We were young."

"Yes, we were," Mo says.

In a minute, Buster asks, "Can I use your cell phone? I need to check in and don't want to use mine." Even in low light, he senses rolling eyes and feels like a man on the run but not yet seasoned to it, "My battery is low. Might be dead."

"Sure, if you can get a signal."

The signal is good, but the news is bad. Larraine made it home all right. But Mumphry came around with the status report. "Tad's in a coma, and it'll be a homicide, if he croaks. It's up to the D.A. to say first degree or second. Or they might go for manslaughter to nail you for sure. He said you shot Tad in the ear, bullseye. He said taking aim is premeditation, but murder is harder to get a conviction on."

"Coulda been a lucky shot."

"Don't tell me."

"Anything else?"

"Yeah. Your pal Henry Shurz called about six times. He wants you to call right away. And a guy called from the INS."

"Immigration Naturalization Service? What do they want?"

"No. That wasn't it. It was the IRS. R. Not N."

"How's Louise?"

"She misses you. She mopes around, looking for you."

"And you?"

"Yeah. I think she missed me too."

"That's not what I meant."

"I know what you meant."

"I guess that's it."

"Your cell is off. What if I need to call you?"

"I'll check back in with you. Or call this number."

"Whatever."

So ends another exchange. Buster's homecoming would be dull as a cul-de-sac or worse. What could they do, take another month politely, divvying assets? Shimmering trout and young love were long ago. The future comes on like manslaughter, at best.

Selling out to Henry Schurz for seven point three feels like bourgeois excess all over again. But liquidation feels like freedom's ring, and the legal defense fund might need shoring up. He could bankroll a simple country life with cash on hand, and he looks up with a laugh, thanking his lucky stars, seeing Moira tease the buttons on her blouse while Henry eats potato chips. He dials Henry, feeling strong as a current rolling through the woods.

"Buster. You're back."

"Not exactly. What's up?"

"You're joking, of course."

"Henry?"

"Yes. Well, you must know why I called."

"Does the buyer want to buy?"

"Maybe."

"I'll sell."

"Good. We only need a price."

"We have a price. Seven point three."

The parties of the first and second parts hold their breaths, till Henry exhales, "You're dreaming."

"I feel like I'm dreaming."

"I'll get back to you. Oh, your cell is off."

"Leave a message with Larraine."

"You want me to leave a counter offer with your ex, with a divorce and settlement coming on?"

"No, I don't. Good catch. Leave a yes or no. Okay?"

"We'll be in touch, Buster. Are the police looking for you?"

"No. Good night, Henry."

"By the way, Buster. Another reason we can't be partners is that I'd be buying into a corporation with terminal liabilities. If you step aside, I can just buy the assets. You know? Good night."

Dark already, the night cools. Mo and Buck have moved inside for sipping-grade tequila. Buster follows.

Tad remains an unsympathetic entity but swells like a boil. Henry tried to use police pressure as a bargaining chip, with value accruing to him by way of circumstance. Then again, Henry is a practicing M.D.... Buster wonders if Tactical Business Bullshit 404 is a med school course.

"Buster. Earth calling Buster."

"Sorry." He nods to an incoming tequila, neat.

Mo says it's a hundred miles back to town. She doesn't need to mention dark and cold or deer and elk on the roads. "The cabins out back run forty bucks."

"How much for a week?"

Buck says, "Same, but you get your seventh night for free."

Buster says. "Why not? I like this place. I couldn't find better digs up the road. I need to hang out."

"It's beautiful," Mo says. "But what'll you do all day? Won't you get a little dingy?"

"They got a bookstore up the road," Buck says. "Used books, some good ones."

"There you go," Buster says. "Maybe I need to get a little dingy." Sipping whiskey and the river flow, and soon they turn in.

Morning comes early with a challenge. The rib shack serves dinner only. That's okay; with only a hundred miles to go, they can hike up for coffee at the used book place on the river trail. Halfway up, Buck says, "It's like motorcycle camp with a river instead of a lake, and no motorcycles. Get it?"

Mo says a river sounds better than a lake, but it's still not funny.

The coffee is fresh, hot and strong. The bookstore woman is cheerful on sunshine, caffeine and a thirty-dollar sale. Buster asks, "Are you in a good mood all the time?"

"No," she rings him up.

"Must be slow in winter."

"Depends on your idea of slow."

"Say, compared to this."

"It is. It's not for everyone. I think *he* was never happy, till he discovered this kind of remote."

"Who's that?"

"Your boy there. Robinson Crusoe."

"Oh, yeah. I never read it. I'll let you know what I think."

On a double take, she doesn't ask if he'll be around.

With coffee and muffins under their belts and a vintage book in hand, the hike back is slow and warm. Farewells are brief.

Mo offers her cell phone.

Buster says she might need it, but she insists. "I got Grizzly Adams here, if things get rough, and you need it more." He gives her his cell and says he fixed the battery. With a headshake and a hug they agree to stay in touch.

She's back in twenty minutes. Buck picked up a rock in his secondary and popped his chain. He's pushing the beast back. The closest shop is in town, only a hundred miles, but she will not ride that guy bitch. "I don't think I can."

Buster could, but he won't.

"I could ride in for a master link, but the primary cover has to come off, and we have no tools."

"Might as well sit in the sun." So they sit in rocking chairs on the front deck. "Like old timers, at peace with the world," Buster says.

"Or any timers," Mo says, as Buck comes in huffing and parks in the shade.

Buster calls, "Buck. What gives with your two friends?"

"Nothing gives. That's the trouble."

"Why you hang out with those guys?"

"I don't hang out with Hobo. Nobody does. Lonny's my friend. Since third grade when I moved here from Northern Alberta."

"So you're not in the same gene pool," Mo says. "Sorry. That's a good thing. I don't mean anything. Forget it."

"Why'd you get involved on a hash scam?"

Buck thinks it over. "I don't know. I didn't like it. I mean, I didn't mind it, but Hobo wants to steal everything from everybody. Lonny went along. I didn't. It might look like I did. It was your money, and that other fella drinking all the fancy gin was making the play. You let it happen. So? What gives on that one? You think he'll pay you back? I don't even know that guy, and I doubt it."

The rockers and decking creak.

"Lonny's my friend. He'll go along with anyone, if there's money or pussy in it. Sorry. I didn't mean to say that."

"Say what?"

"You know your motorcycle is mine."

The creaking stops.

"What the hell you want with my motorcycle?"

"I don't. But I'll keep it here as collateral."

Buck looks sideways. Mo's eyebrows bunch.

"You wouldn't," she says.

"What else you got?"

They could call for a flatbed. Or Buster could ride in for parts and tools. But all the options are chapter and verse out of the *Broke Down Motorcycle Motherfucking Pain in the Ass Repair Manual.*

Or Buck can take Buster's rig, get the parts and head back by afternoon.

"It's Sunday," Buster says. "Might as well take your time."

"They're closed Monday," Buck says.

"I guess I'm here," Buster says.

Mo stands up. "Does this mean I got to hang out there now, keep an eye on your scoot?"

"Not if you don't want to," Buster says.

She walks to her motorcycle. "Let's get this over with."

Buck shakes his head. "I can't…."

"Sure you can. One's just like the other."

"No it's not. You got…."

"Forty thousand dollars."

"Yeah. Where am I gonna park that thing?"

"Park it right. Put a tarp on it. With bungies. Don't fuck it up."

Buck nods and offers a hand for the second shake in a short while. "I owe you one."

"You owe me more than one. Anything happens…."

"I won't let it happen."

"Maybe. You got a bad record on shit happening."

Buck and Mo head out again, this time with Buck in the lead.

Buster Fetteroff sits on a chair by a river, its rumble recalling a geology professor who said the Universe, pre-bang, was so dense, that a pinhead spec would weigh tons in earth weight. The Universe compressed at that time was called ylam, even though time was not yet a thing, and yet had no more meaning than past, which was infinite and also compressed, as was all meaning and dimension. The bang set things free, stellar debris flying out, dust particles to planets, and though clocks were a long way in the future, they could have started ticking just then.

Buster can't find ylam in the three-volume science dictionary he bought for only eight bucks at the used bookstore. The copyright is 1948, so where is it? He could look for it on his laptop, if he had his laptop and a hot spot. He feels better with neither and wonders if he's done—make that arrived at the destination of his making. Who could know in such a short time? But he thinks he sees something....

Mika has a computer, and a third visit in three days seems to prove the theory, that a woman gains beauty, if she's the only woman. Around. For miles. He laughs; maybe an asshole only needs more time to see beauty in anything. Both assessments are cruel, relics of former time. Pre-time? He saw a light on their first meeting and only needed a few days to see the glow inside, an intermittent mix of anxiety, hope or sheer luminescence on spotty wattage. She ditched her sweater with warmer weather. Less bulky, she looks younger, luminescent on her skin as well as in her eyes.

Sure, he can use her computer, though she's had it on only once since moving up from Missoula ten years ago, when she quit teaching at the University. No cable, no satellite and no Wi-Fi make the place pure as the driven snow. "It gets no purer. Just you wait."

"Sounds like a monastery."

"You gotta wear itchy shirts for that. I like flannel."

"You stay here all winter?"

"I do. It's only miserable for about seven months."

"How do you heat this place?"

"Wood stove. Maybe you'll help."

What?

Buster wouldn't mind lending a hand but senses a deeper need which may be a harsh assessment. At least he feels reasonably certain of windfall lying about. Talk flows free on caffeine, from the Btu output of ash, alder or Duraflame to ylam and seasonal particulate density fluctuation in a conifer forest. It's more than he's shared in years. She has no moods yet, and he knows the sad fact of human nature is a tendency to hide bad habits in the courting process. He may be presumptuous in sensing that process, but: man, woman, solitude, need. She also seems tentative, as if hiding a surprise or avoiding his sad facts. He picks up a manila envelope from the coffee table to read the addressee: "Mika Baishan. I think that's...Filipina?" She looks Filipina, smallish, no fat, gentle curves, smooth skin and pretty.

"Chiricahua Apache," she says, looking out the window at her heritage. He thinks she's forty, give or take. As if sensing his thoughts, she turns from the waist to profile, to better see something out there. Or maybe she's on cue, coy as a woman who knows the play. "Forty-six," she says.

Is he that transparent? Or base?

"No way."

"You're sixty."

"I don't look sixty."

"Sorry. You do. I don't look forty-six. We'll say you're fifty-nine. Feel better? You're in decent shape, I think. What are you running from?"

"Are you wearing a bra?"

"No. Why do you ask?"

"No reason. I think you're fifty-two."

"No, you don't."

"Yes, I do."

"I'd rather be hot at fifty than a tired old cock at sixty."

"So crude. I'm trying to get away from that."

"You mean that talk?"

"Yeah."

"Sorry. I've been out here a long time. I agree. About the talk. When's the last time you got laid? I mean, made love."

"A while."

"Me too. I'm not attracted to many men around here. Sorry. I cut to the chase sometimes."

"It's okay. I'm a tired old cock."

"I know. I know it's okay. I don't think you're tired, not too tired. Or old. Every man thinks about it. I guess I'm cocky too, thinking you want me. But I look good naked. I mean my ass hasn't dropped yet. Most men like a firm ass. You know?"

"Did you talk this way to your students?"

"I did to one of them."

Who'd a thunk? But he fears what scratching the itch might cost. He needs a friend, and Mika is fresh and lively. And smart in a worldly way that factors the whole wide of it. She's not so much coy as focused, like when she says, "I could shave my legs. What do you think?" She shows him her legs, practically hairless, except for the light peach fuzz, well shaped and smooth.

"You should be comfortable," he says.

"Well, no, it's not that simple. I want to be comfortable and attractive. Don't you?" Maybe she never fished on light tackle. Thoughts and smoke swirl over the pipe between them on Mika's porch. She offered that too.

"How did you know?" he asked.

"What's to know? Everybody gets high. Don't they?"

"Not everybody."

"Everybody around here. Hey. You're from Washington. Did you hear? They made it legal."

Buster laughs short, relieved as a fool resolved. He thinks a romp could be casual and friendly with no further needs, unless he's still a fool, unresolved in the world of his further making. Could they romp and be friends, easy and sociable like this? Why not?

"What?" she asks.

"What?" he asks back.

"You're thinking. What?"

"In for a minute, in for a mile."

"Yeah. What the hell? Could be fun."

"Are you psychic?"

"You're an open book, man. Most guys are."

"It's just that easy?"

"Your part is." So they loll away the morning on caffeine and BC bud, sunshine and beauty with no further need, or rather no need to rush. Because mutual recognition and attraction can lead to stripping and hitting the mat for a bumpity squish, if they want to squander a great, rich savoring. The feast is theirs to prolong.

"You're young to retire to used books in a forest. Let me guess. You headed up here with a lumberjack. No, you said he was a student, a dipshit highbrow, I think. Sorry, an English major looking for Walden Pond. You bought the bookstore. He tagged along. No, you dragged him along for company, but he froze out in a season, and you stayed."

"That word, dipshit, indicates jealousy. So soon? And how do you know it was a he?"

"Just a hunch. And it's not jealousy. It's resentment of a type, call it ineffectual intellect."

"Very good. And he was a dipshit, which does reflect his helplessness. But he wasn't helpless at first."

"Until real life set in?"

"We bought it together. He lasted a season, a long one. That's not bad for a guy."

"Need a warmer?" He stands for more coffee.

"Sure."

He fetches and pours. "What did you teach?"

"Advanced human sexuality."

"Advanced, huh? Beyond remedial?"

"Very good."

"What's the difference?"

"The advanced course went to hormonal and pheromonal receptivity, motivation, estrus, testosterone in men and women, social mores and their influence on behaviors. That sort of thing."

"What's remedial?"

"You ever been married?"

"Yes."

"Then you know. Which isn't to say marriage has to be bad. You know?"

Back on the grassy spot between his cabin and the river, Buster ponders Mika as the opposite of Larraine. He doesn't hate Larraine or dislike her. If they'd never married, he'd likely try to engage her. Or not. At any rate, it was the time between them, its repetitions and revelations of their dreary, tedious wants, the time they took to grow apart, until nothing remained but courtesy.

And here's Mika, with no sense of fashion, no chic compulsion, only active thought in connection with the world around her. Would they be an old, divorced couple, if they'd met thirty years ago?

Mika says no; they would not be undeniably happy if they'd met thirty years ago. Or maybe they would be. "Synchronous convergence seems likely as often as not and usually has no schedule. We'll know each other briefly or for a while or a long time. Here we are."

She advises that nature and logic are most often convenient, and most people default to convenience. She seems available and receptive, unlike Moira Kunzler, who grabbed him by the lust but then fled but then grabbed again in what Mika calls the cycle of desire. "Intermittent convergence is inconvenient, like a short circuit."

"And where on the cycle is my desire for you? Sorry. Such a forward question. I'm asking theoretically."

"Understood. No apology required. We know a few things, but few people take time to realize what they know. Lust might last, with imagination and love in the mix. But it's nearly always intermittent, best with foreplay. It's repetition and familiarity that lead to love. Lust is quickly sated. Savvy?" Well, of course, he knew that, but he's only recently single and still acclimating to complexity in personal contact.

She tired of campus life, with the kids getting younger and stupider. She thought she'd kept pace with the world, until it veered off course. The river felt better, and the bookstore better still. She couldn't find a man on campus, not that she was looking, but solitude became a loving familiarity, along with flowing water. The dipshit was amusing and did tag along to run a bookstore in the woods, until severe weather set in.

Did she seek another man to weather blizzards in the boonies? He won't ask, because she smirks like a chess player, eager to pounce. Maybe it's him till next spring. But she's smart and fun and better company than he's kept in a while.

He reflects on her, the woman at the bookstore, up the trail, through the forest, by the river. He drags another chair into the sun to prop his legs for another round of *Robinson Crusoe*. It feels good, a new depth in a wilderness unbound, and a book feels Old World, like the cornerstone of a library. He wants to walk back up to see what Mika will do for dinner but doesn't want to impose or look lustful or stupid, though he's not sure why. She's having similar thoughts, after seven winters. He could stay until October, unless Tad Pollack croaks, or the Feds start looking. But where else would he rather be? In another month, she'll achieve full beauty, and they'll go like bunnies into cold weather. But surely they won't take another month.

He'd rather avoid the calculation and head up for dinner with a friend. But the river flows to the golden hours, when he feels lazy and anxious, trying variable rationale on for size, until he heads up to the rib shack in his sweatshirt but will eat no pig. After two beers and a tequila neat, he decides to eat no chicken too. So a day of little doing ends on vegetable soup and a salad. He feels less, in specific regard to feeling better, and hopes for more of it.

On the way to his cabin, he looks forward to Mika in the morning, with a whole night interval making things sweeter still. He'll check his messages tomorrow too. Tonight, he feels the greatness of the place again, free of urgency, the air sweet, the sound lyrical. It's been two days. Or three. Henry Schurz was eager. What the hell?

He heads back up front for signal strength and dials home. Why wait? Sure enough: *You have. Two. Mess. Ages....*

"Hey, Buster. I reviewed the situation with the partnership and got their approval. I've taken the liberty of depositing three million, six hundred thousand dollars into a trust account and given instructions to Emily at Title Surety Escrow to open an account with Schurz partners as buyers and you as the seller of assets only of your business. Emily needs your approval. A verbal will work for now, until you sign. I already signed. I'm sure she can FedEx the docs, if that's more, uh, convenient, but I think we need a quick turn-around in any event. I hope this makes you happy, Buster. Bye now."

Does Henry think it's a deal at three point six? He's a wanna-be master who's merely overbearing. Doctors. Well, he gets to bang Moira, but that's lust, intermittent at best. And look what I get. In two days, I'll set terms on the balance. He'll ask for a counter. I'll tell him to keep pouring until a little voice says when.

The second message is also brief:

"I heard that, Buster. I took some liberty too and spoke with Steven. He can represent us both, if we agree, and that could save a bunch of money. I want the house and half the three point six. That would be one point eight. Why fool ourselves any longer? I'll always love you. I hope you're well. If you don't agree to sharing Steven, I'll get Rick Baumgartner. You remember him. Rick the prick?"

He hangs up and dials Larraine's cell.

"Hello."

"We need to talk."

"Oh! That's wonderful, Mr. Rogers. I'll be happy to pitch in. I'll have to call you tomorrow, okay? I'm tied up right now."

Tied up? I'll bet.

But a familiar voice in the background asks, "Is that your husband? I want to talk to him." It's Mumphry, so Buster hangs up, hoping that Larraine will say something quaint and press the red button.

Out back again, he watches the river. Turbulence makes sense of a rough situation, rolling thoughts downstream. This is how the world begins, like ylam, compressed infinitum, until one more speck of pressure blows it to Kingdom Come. Heading in from the chill, he wishes Mika could displace his worries. He wishes he hadn't checked messages or called Larraine. He wishes he wasn't waiting by a river for Tad to croak. Starlight twinkles, and the chill turns frosty. He feels foolish as a fool lost in a wilderness and goes to bed. It feels as good as a bed ever felt. At least he hiked two miles today. Should he hike back now? He laughs short, rolling over to sleep.

Sixty.

He can't remember a birthday without a single happy birthday. That's okay. He'll pass the big six oh unchanged, anonymous, alone, in a beautiful wood by a river. Boosters and slag fall away, as he climbs to weightlessness, orbital, and drifts to deep space...until a stellar body comes nigh. He wakes to a stark chill. The blankets and sheet rise, as he rounds from the dark side, into the sun. It's a flashlight, blinding. "Hey!" He doesn't flail but reaches for the covers and covers his eyes.

"Sorry. I thought I ought to come over to tell you that your friend Buck called to tell me to tell you that your friend Mo called to say that your wife called, and you shouldn't use that cell phone anymore."

"What time is it?"

"About two."

"When did they call?"

"About eight or nine."

"Why did you wait?"

"I thought you'd be coming over. Then I fell asleep. Then I woke up." Then she crawls in. "This is just to warm up. Okay? I'm freezing. No sexual intercourse. Okay? I mean, not tonight. Okay?"

"Perfect." He hugs her. To warm her up. What does she expect from a sixty-year-old man on a cold call? She rolls his way to return the hug.

"I shaved my legs. Want to feel?" He slips a hand down to feel a thigh and down to the calf. It's different, smooth and wanting the rub. "Is this really what you want?" She asks.

"What is it you're talking about?"

"Us. Sleeping together."

"Sure. Why not? I mean, yes, I think I do. How about you?"

"Yeah. Fuck it. Whatever," she says, rolling away.

"Hey." He grasps her hips to turn her back.

She resists. "You're uncertain. You asked why not. That's opening on a negative."

"No. I meant that...."

"You sense negative potential," she says. "Or you're afraid."

"Apprehensive, maybe, but we're not negative. We're tentative. Aren't we friends? Isn't tentative better than cocky?" She won't turn around, so he lets go with a sigh and says, "I can't do that...university shit. You shaved your legs and came down here naked."

She sighs back. "I wasn't naked. And I wasn't always like this."

"You mean I got lucky?"

"Depends on your definition of lucky." She turns to him, easing the puzzle parts into place, like the whacky woman he thinks she is.

"That was sweet," Mika says at first light.

"Mm...." He goes along with sweetness, what women love to feel in the aftermath. Maybe it was sweet, with more sweetness in the offing. *Why not? No. I mean.... Fuckinay, baby.*

"You're thinking," she says

"No. I'm dreaming...."

"I like that." She eases back to a comfort that seemed distant only yesterday. She murmurs on the prod.

"Familiarity," he moans. "Shouldn't take much longer." And just that easily, they're on.

She murmurs again, later that same morning, "We did wait a long time. It's best...."

"We need more lust. We've earned it, after all we've been through."

"Just you wait," she says. "Plenty of time."

"But you said...."

But further analysis must wait for coffee up the path. She'll have it brewed by the time he gets there. The muffins in the freezer are hard as rock. Not to worry; in the toaster oven they'll turn out perfect.

Like me? He won't say it. "I can only imagine."

"You'll see. You'll love them. They're so good." She moans, "blackberry jelly." Slipping out of bed and into her jumper, she steps to the door.

"Wait."

"What?" She turns back.

"I want to look. I want more."

"Psh," she scoffs, on her way out and up the path.

It feels more like repartee than romance, but it's better than doubt and worry. It's not dramatic but softly edgy and variable. It's easy, but first parts usually are. The love affair with his wife lasted years. Will he and Mika get years? Who's counting?

A cock crows, and off the deck he hoses off in cold water to start a new day on bracing reality.

He walks out front to a big truck with Ontario plates and snugs Mo's cell between the rear bumper and the chassis. The path to Mika's is solitary, like the walk from his house to the garage not so long ago, but different in a forest by a river, in a season of change.

She said a year isn't bad for a guy. Imagining severe weather, he arrives to muffins, jelly and strong coffee. This may not be *it*, but it airs out. The stellar debris is them, gaining distance on the epicenter, post bang.

"What?"

"I was thinking. The big bang."

"Me too."

"You checked me out with the flashlight, didn't you?"

"So? I didn't want to go in blind. So what?"

"Go in?"

"We don't know each other, really," she reminds him.

"We don't know much more now. You wanted to make sure I'm not fat."

"I know you're not fat. But I jumped in with this guy once... years ago...." She blushes, having begun the wrong story. "It was decades really. He was a fisherman, and he had this rubber squid they use for bait, about a foot long, and he tucked it in his shorts with the tentacles hanging out. It was a joke. But I'd never seen a rubber squid. I thought...."

"You were disappointed."

"I was scared, and I ran; joke on him."

"No romance?

"No. He was a funny guy but not for me."

"You thought I might have a rubber squid down there?"

She sits beside him. "I wanted to see if you were disgusting.

Some guys are disgusting. Especially guys your age. They let themselves go. It's a choice, some of the time. Or weakness, a compulsion to eat badly and stay lazy. It reflects decision-making skills and strength. I don't want disgusting."

"What do you want?"

She shrugs. "You'll do."

"Do for what?"

"Whatever."

"Can we whatever again?"

"Yes. After muffins. Okay?"

He shrugs. "Muffins and jelly taste better slowly, after morning exercise."

"They'll be cold. If you feel urgency in anything, slow down. It's better that way."

"Might be better yet, if we wait till dark."

"You're catching on," she says, serving the sweets. "Unless you want the daylight."

XIX

Out of Sight of Land

Hanging out with Mika is mostly easy. She tells time by the feel of it: sundown, sunset, gloaming, twilight, nightfall, first light, sunrise, mid-morning, nooner, spring and summer. She took a while to dispense with numbered calibration, but once she got the feel of it, things loosened up. Buster wears a watch but feels the numbered moorings slipping away. Cabin life drifts across days in rhythmic undulation. Uncounted, unaccountable and unnamed, time takes reference to events, or slides by on a feeling.

Summer warms like a new dream. Foliage rustles with awakening. Cool nights call for embrace.

In week two, she suggests moving his gear and rat bike to her place, to save a few bucks toward groceries. He'll still be free to leave, anytime. She overstates the easy exit, to be sure, to avoid man trauma and maybe woman trauma too. Not to worry; he can stay around indefinitely, because she likes him, because he seems to be as represented, so far.

"I didn't represent anything."

"Yes, you did."

"But I have to leave, if you stop liking me?"

"You'll want to leave, if I stop liking you. You'll want to leave, if you stop loving me."

"How could anyone stop loving you?"

"You're quick, but they do."

Forewarned, he moves in, and she still likes him. She's most often fun and always practical. Physical communion adapts as well to familiarity and rhythm, which is not to say the rhythm method but patterns of stimuli and response. The path continues upriver, beyond Mika's place, to the lake and a boat shed that sits along the shore. The birchbark canoe is hers. "You ride bitch," she says. "That's up front in a canoe." Buster doesn't mind. He hasn't paddled in ages. He asks who in her right mind would spend for birch bark, when fiberglass is cheaper, stronger, lighter and easier to maintain. "It was a gift," she says. "From sentimental old friends. I learned to love this canoe in a way that wouldn't hold up on fiberglass. You'll see. It's harder to get started and harder to stop and feels so much better."

They hug the shoreline for a while, past huge log cabins and cedar homes with Hollywood decks and fabulous layouts, massive timbers and big bay windows to capture the view, view, view. "All empty," she says. "They could be here, sighing at the beauty. That's what they had in mind. But they're home, working for more. That's okay. It's what they do. And they're not here."

Buster's house seems far away and long ago. He sees Larraine in a picture window, and he smiles sadly back.

Each lake house has a dock, some with motorboats on davits, hanging high and dry, covered. "They run in July and August and a few holidays, but they mostly sit there for image and assurance. You'll see. These people must feel something. I think it's mostly relief, knowing this stuff is here. They come out for a week and go home. They love big SUVs and boats with big engines and big fishing rods and guns. It's a control and dominance mentality. They have satellite dishes, because they need TV, so they won't miss anything. They come out on the lake for an hour or two then go back in to clean up and warm up and eat meat."

She sounds nearly bitter, like him. She steers toward the center on fewer words, as the frigid blue water becomes unfathomably clear. "We'll catch salmon with traps, when you're ready. We'll cook them over a fire on green sticks. You'll love it. You never ate salmon like that before. We'll smoke some too. And dry some."

"When will I be ready?"

"When you're hungry."

"What about salad?"

"We buy it."

They hike, chop wood, catch and eat. "Where did you learn these things?"

"From my father." She can start a fire with a rig, two sticks and string, and a base with a bowl for straw.

He uses his disposable lighter.

She wants naked play at odd intervals to mess up the routine and avoid predictability, for now. But, he says, he likes routine, and predictability is something to look forward to. She peels, rolling her eyes and telling him to look forward to this. He goes along, asking why she'd resisted showing her body. She blushes and says a woman never knows.

He tells her of his marriage, more or less. She shares a few failures too, avoiding detail, stepping back from the edge. Confessions lead to more questions. "Where might this path go, once we're caught up and the path is worn?"

She smiles patiently. "You do what you do best. Then you die."

So he drifts to peaceful slumber, wondering if it's what he does best, knowing it's up there on the short list.

In a few days, she asks about the rat bike.

He has no plans; it's not his. He's waiting on his motorcycle.

"You think you'll see it again?"

"I do. But I'll call." He can't call Mo, because her cell is up in the Arctic Circle. So he calls Mo's shop to see if someone will get

Mo to call Mika's phone.

Not to worry; Mo is back at work. She's swamped and doesn't know why anyone in her right mind would come back to a hellhole to deal with of idiots and buffoons for minimum wage. She had so much fun, and now she has none.

She stayed at Jimmy's for a day, and it was swell, old home week and all that, and she hung out with Buck for two days after that. He's not a bad guy but needy. "And he's got no fucking sheets. The fuck is that? Some romance."

"Another disappointment?"

"No. He's different. I like him. What's-her-name comes waddling right in, like she was watching through the window, and piles on for the threesome. I wouldn't have minded, if she wasn't so pushy. Talk about needs. Good thing Buck was there."

"He protected you?"

"You could call it that. He covered. The boy's got stamina, like a starving dog wants to eat. He's going gaga down at the Y, and Missy's giving me the bug eyes. Coulda been on the Internet. But old Buck made good. I gotta hand it to him, but he's got a problem."

"Yeah? What's that?"

"I'm not sure. I'm going back up in a couple weeks."

"What about my motorcycle?"

"He's gonna bring it back. He's trying to line up a truck to carry his scooter back up."

"Great. Hey. Can you check my messages at the house?"

"Wait. Listen to this." She holds the phone in the air to share her life of hours, slowly tolling:

Rider up for real and wear your identity with pride! A few dollars down puts you in charge at Road Warriors. Come on in for real selection on genuine accessories, genuine leather, and triple billet chrome! Goodbye Dullsville. This dude is gonna ride!

She comes back on the line, yelling over the Steppenwolf

medley, swearing she'd like to shoot that fucker. "Get the picture? I got a crowd. I'll check your messages in about six hours. Okay?"

"Okay, but don't call this number from your home phone."

"I got to go. I'll call you later. Okay? This number?"

"No. I'll call you!" He drowns out under Steppenwolf and customers clamoring for imagery development.

Mika watches, so he explains Mo's dilemma. "She's surrounded by urban males seeking identity in leather and noise, while she misses the real deal up north."

"You did that too."

He admits that he did stylize for a new season. But that was different; bigger jugs and flowed heads over a hop-up tranny with true overdrive and decent pipes, fairing lowers and four speakers for a grand entrance isn't show. It's a pulse of life, if you run the miles.

"You need to call home?"

He nods.

"We can hike up to the store toward the ferry dock. They got a payphone. It's about three miles each way. That's not bad. We need beer anyway."

Her observation that *we need beer* is endearing. She doesn't drink beer. She drinks water. He questions the wisdom of calling from any phone in the vicinity. But what can the cops do, tromp around the lake? Through the woods?

She assures him they can and will, if it comes to that. "If it'll make you more comfortable, we can use the phone at the ferry dock. They'll think you were just passing through. But that's more like six miles. Each way. You can do twelve miles. Can't you?"

"I could. Might hurt for a few days. Let's hit the store."

Three miles isn't bad on a trail. Out front, she says, "You'll need quarters. I'll get them."

"Wait." He pulls his wallet from his back pocket and opens on a wad, hundreds.

"Are you a drug smuggler?"

"No. I was kind of an accessory, but that was small potatoes next to the other."

She plucks one and goes for quarters. "The other?"

At the phone booth, she deposits quarters. He calls. At three rings a voice bellows, "Hey, Bud!"

"Stuey?"

"Where are you? Don't answer! Fuck, man, did you stick your dick in the pickle slicer or what? You didn't tell me you *shot* a guy. You're on the lam from the feds! Hey. I told them they got it wrong. You didn't steel nine million dollars. That's crazy. Man, you missed some unbelievable stuff. God, it was great. Hey, great news! I quit drinking! Talk about unbelievable. I just woke up and quit."

"Yeah? How long ago?"

"I don't know. A few days after I got back. I can't believe the difference. That shit was killing me. You must have seen it. I don't blame you for splitting. I'm really sorry, man."

"What are you sorry about?"

"I'm apologizing to everyone. I must have said something stupid to you."

"Did you quit smoking?"

"Nah. I got to get used to no drinking first. But maybe. But man, the energy. The fucking! And that's just for starters. It's like I'm nineteen again or something. I haven't fucked this hard or this long in decades, man. I guess being in love has something to do with it. I got to tell you, man. I think this could be it."

"Who is she? What are you doing there?"

"Who is she? Oh, man. Now I'm really sorry. I thought you.... We hit it off the night before she left. She fell in love when I ordered a chardonnay. Can you believe it? Man, how many years did you have her? You were one lucky fucker, I can tell you that. Hey, we can talk about this, can't we?"

"You're...moved in?"

"You could call it that. What do I have to move? Hey, seriously, this is great news for you. I mean, now she's taken care of, you know what I mean? I know that's what you want for her. Talk about a win win situation, now I don't need to buy a house, and I can pay you back, too. I mean, not right now, but as soon as you settle. Believe me, you'll want to get that train wreck cleared up ASAP. Otherwise the fucking attorneys bleed you for years on the interest and more demands. Hey, Your business sale is terrific. Three million bucks. I had no idea. I knew you were flush, but three mil. Me paying you back won't get much of it back to you, but it's something, and you got it coming if anyone ever did."

"Stuey. Is Larraine there?"

"Sure! Hang on. Hey, hon. It's for you."

"Yes?"

"Can you elaborate the news I just got from a man you love to hate?"

"What part of it didn't you get? Rick the prick says we can get the house and ninety percent of the business sale a few different ways, but I told him we won't be greedy, as long as you cooperate."

"I thought you weren't going to call Rick the prick. I thought we already agreed to cooperate."

"I would have waited, and we are cooperating, but once the business deal came in, I thought a hundred grand here or there in legal fees to get it right wouldn't count for much with millions on the table. So? We can still live in peace with a nuclear deterrent."

"Did they figure out why Tad fell down with a bloody ear?"

"They didn't have to figure it out. He told them."

"He woke up?"

"Yes. He told them you shot him in the ear."

"They can't prove it."

"You don't want to find out. They got the pellet out of his

head and the apparent trajectory route. That finger points to you. But the charge is now assault with intent to do bodily harm, and that's not nearly as bad as murder one or manslaughter. That's what Mumphry said. What a fucker, coming around here, coming on to me."

"Seems like a pattern. Didn't Stuey protect you?"

"He wasn't here then."

Stuey grabs the phone. "Hey, man. I saw that Tad fucker out in the yard yesterday morning. If you hadn't shot him, I would. I went out, you know, to get the paper and take a whiz, and he's staring at me through the hedge. Like it's any of his fucking business, you know what I mean? Anyway—you'll love this—he's got his head wrapped like a kid with a toothache. I said, 'Gee, Mr. Wilson. You're a bit on the elderly side for wisdom teeth.' Get it? He didn't look too good, and I think he can't talk with his jaw wired up. Hey, fuck that asshole. He's showing a pulse, so don't you worry, Bud. Me and Larraine give him something to look at."

Larraine pre-empts with annoyance. "Do you mind?" She takes the phone back and asks, "Where are you?"

In an instant his whereabouts don't matter, as he murmurs, "Just up the road."

A voice warns of time running out. He nods.

Mika deposits quarters.

They clang to four dollars for another minute.

"Hello?"

"I'm here. Where are you?"

"In a forest."

"That's it?"

He could say he's with a woman but would sound vindictive, like tit for tat. "I'm with a friend."

"A woman?"

"What difference does it make?"

"I guess it doesn't, but I'd like to think it's a woman so I can stop thinking you're homosexual."

"Would you be so disappointed?"

"You're right. You always played around. So what's the diff?"

"Not always and not around."

"Speak of the devil, guess who's preggers? You won't believe it. Your pussycat who works for Henry Schurz. Everyone thinks she got knocked up about a month ago. Vicki Smelling swears Miss Moira was banging that limp noodle Duayne Dudney for the last two years, but she cut him off when Henry came around. Can you believe it? Now she's going to marry Henry."

"I think she's not pregnant."

"So did Henry. Wrong again. But don't worry, Buster. Everyone thinks the kid'll be a greedy slob, not cynical and anti-social."

"What a relief. Moira pregnant is much more fun than you banging Stuey."

"You know I hate that talk. We're not banging. We're in a relationship."

"Oh, yeah. Have you 'splained that to Stuey yet?"

"Some men are natural, dearest. Anyway, Moira's up about sixty pounds, so you can count your lucky stars she didn't pick you." How did Larraine know? She didn't know. She's grasping.

"You don't know she gained sixty pounds."

"I'll get a shot with my cell and send it to you. You tell me how many pounds. They make a lovely couple, her and Henry."

"You're still cruel."

"Yeah. I need to stay that way till we get our money."

"I'll call when I can. Okay?"

"When? We need to talk. We have a ton of details."

"Soon. You know I trust your judgment and good taste."

"By-ee."

"Yeah. Flipside."

Just that quick, it's back to the breeze, the rustling foliage and sunbeams, one of which falls onto the face of the woman with the quarters. "Your wife is with your friend?" He nods and steps to a bench for a breather. She sits beside him and rests a hand on his leg. "You know regret has practical limits."

"Thank you, doctor."

"You're welcome. We can ease your pain."

They relax, briefly, until she wants to start back before cooling off. He admires her focus and thinks he's catching on. "Did you learn practical urgency from your father too?"

"No. Practical urgency comes from experience. He taught me what he could, until he died." She'd begun adolescence when her mother married Greg Riley, and she figured things out on her own for the next thirty years, including regret as impractical.

"You mean you didn't like your mother's new husband, but it didn't matter?"

"Very good, grasshopper. It doesn't matter." She smiles, not with warmth but satisfaction. "He's dead too. Come." They head back to the path. He won't press for details, deferring to discretion.

"Where now?"

"Home. I have something I want to show you."

She only just showed him this morning, and he fears a pace and frequency he cannot maintain. But she demonstrates another practicality and life lesson at home, in bed. "Did you know that sleeping together is a bonding behavior?"

"I did. Along with eating and playing."

"Yes. But not sex. We mate outside the clan, to stay alive."

"I'm not following."

"Close your eyes. Now breathe slowly. Let go."

He's an easy lead after twelve miles and an emotional pillow fight. Letting go feels best. Sleep rises like a lake in spring, deep and clear with sunbeams shimmering in deep blue. He wakens to her soft narration on the scent of tea and smoke.

Sitting on the edge of the bed, she recalls a regular outing in youth, when she bought tobacco for her father. A lightly smoldering sage stick near the window helps to recall old Dad. She smiles serenely to ask, "We won't propagate. Will we?"

"I wouldn't think it likely. I suppose we could. Could we?"

She rises when the teapot whistles and pours two cups. She adds honey and says they should ride the rat bike to Prince Harry in Horseshoe Bay. She'll ride bitch on that one. They'll catch the ferry to Nanaimo and make an outing of it, their first trip, for fun.

"It's not mine," he says

"What's not yours?"

"The rat bike."

"It could be."

"Why would I want it? I'd never trust it."

"It's old and beat up. It has seasoning."

"It's a paint mixer on two wheels. Wait till you see my ride. You'll love it, maybe more than muffins and jelly and salmon."

"Maybe. But I think your wife is beautiful, and it's pointless to compare one love to another. I love that old motorcycle. It speaks a more soulful past."

"It groans and howls. It leaks and rattles, if that's what you mean."

"Let's fix it."

"Let's not. Let's set clay pots around it for green beans. Creeping vines will speak of a soulful future, good with olive oil and herbs."

"I like that. But what about the guy who owns it?"

"I'll deal with him. I have an idea."

The next morning, he rolls the rat bike to the grassy area beside the bookstore. She sets pots around it with green beans tied to sticks with string. She plants radishes and squash for color and form. They prep more beds in a bigger surround, which feels like overkill, but she says surplus is great for trade. She adjusts the clay pots around Buck's bike, as a flatbed pulls up with Buster's motorcycle.

Buck gets out of the cab, clean-shaven with short hair and regular clothing, looking like a 99%er, a suburbanite fitting in, keen on security. He looks like a guy who might one day get permission from the wife to drop a few bucks on a lifestyle down payment.

"You lost weight," Buster says.

"Yeah. Ten pounds in two weeks. Losing it too fast can set you up to put it right back on."

Missy slides out the other side. "Two of it was hair. Oh, he'll drop the eighty pounds. Or we'll cut it off."

Buck blushes, unstrapping the ramp and setting it up.

"What did you do?" Mika asks. "Weight won't go away because you want it to."

"Diet," Missy says. "Whole oats in the morning with Fibrocell and fruit. Green salad for dinner and more Fibrocell at bedtime. He'll lose it. Beans, tofu, brown rice."

"I exercise too," Buck says.

"Yeah. We try to keep his mind off food. Big guy was eating meat three times a day. We need some raised beds like these." Missy admires the layout and Mika.

"Shave and a haircut," Buster says. "You went from wooly mammoth to Eagle Scout."

Buck blushes again. "I got a new job. Missy knows the Fibrocell distributor. I went over and talked to him. I'm a promotional speaker now. They say my results do the talking, and all I have to do is show up and tell people I believe in Fibrocell."

"Yeah, and keep losing weight," Missy adds.

"I worked two supermarkets this week and signed up thirty-two people. Didn't have to sell much. They need help when they can't help themselves. Life gets better."

"Good for you, Buck. You're in the chips and got another seventy pounds to go on, but you're not exactly thin."

"Nobody believes thin," Missy says. "They want him a little chunky, so people can relate and have hope. He can go as long as he wants to. We're saving up for one of those life-size photos on cardboard. I got the shot right off, big old fat, hairy Buck. If he can turn thirty-two subscriptions a week, he'll be off the hook in two months. This load o' baloney is not a cheap rebuild. We believe in Fibrocell, because it works."

"Skinny and rich. How wonderful," Mika says.

They laugh, easing Buster's motorcycle down the ramp. Buster checks the odometer to see a hundred miles more. He won't look to see if the speedo cable is connected but asks, "You didn't ride? Not even a little bit."

"No, and I covered it like you said. I think it might have ruined me for my ride."

"That can happen. Thirty-two fat people a week, you'll want a new ride before too long."

"I got to pay Missy first. That's the first hook."

Missy affirms. "He suffered too long. Whining and whimpering, always too lazy to see a doctor. And scared. Now he's pain free. Got him a rubber-band job on the big floppy hummers outside, and what they call laser legation on the high-pressure nodules inside. Zapped them into scar tissue."

Buster's brow bunches in amazement. "Socialized health care," he says, realizing he'd still be hustling for chump change, if he'd started out in Canada.

"It's something," Missy says. "But they wanted a hundred ninety dollars to bleach his asshole. We passed."

Buck blushes again, this time verging on apoplectic, having his anus in review, outside and in.

"I take care of him. We stay in shape. Mo's coming up soon."

XX

A Grown Man Cried

Charles settled with Henry Schurz for three point four, plus fees, to save a hundred grand for him who built this business from scratch. He feels good, remembering when a hundred grand took a while to make, back in the day.

Terms included all cash to the seller for transfer of assets and corporate dissolution, the buyer assuming unresolved liabilities. Doctor Schurz poo-pooed the liabilities. What? The government would give him a hard time? Giddy with a new baby on the way and a new vein to mine, he ogled his full-figured wife in one eye and a dilated bunghole on the United States Treasury in the other. Who better to claim rightful returns than a man with the God-given skill to save people from dying?

Charles? That would be Charles Severance, who is not a.k.a. Buster Fetteroff but a new and separate being, risen from the fumes of rapid decomposition into nothing, nada, poof! And gone.

Charles Severance pondered Chuck but decided against; diminutives are so often diminutive. He shared the new identity idea with his new girlfriend on the way to the boathouse, to set salmon traps. She said okay, but not Chuck.

He smiled at her assessment.

She said smaller salmon would have minimal mercury and parasites.

Then came drying racks, brining and smoking. She said they'd give up salmon before too long, to evolve, to allow those salmon their rightful cycles in the spawning process. She'd thought on it for a while and felt the change would ease them to lasting strength.

He pondered strength while paddling and in the garden, through harvest, drying and canning.

In a sweat, dirt clinging, she warned of winter, when they would long for warm weather work.

Mo quit her job with two minutes notice on a day that felt dismal and near deathly but went bright and sunny at the far end of those minutes. She'd wanted a place up near Jimmy's. Meanwhile, she'd camp at Missy's, like Buck. She might get on at Armageddon or some place. At least those macho assholes are the real deal, and Missy had room. Mo said she weighed the pros and cons and thought she could manage.

Louise the dog had a few good years left and came north on a flight in a kennel. Stuey set it up without asking, recognizing another debt or a friend in need. She seemed forlorn, until stepping out of the kennel to see the alpha male and lunging for a tongue-lashing. Barking in pain and joy, they whined and romped again.

She took to the trail and didn't jump out of the canoe. She buried stuff in the garden. She snored but woke early. "Lie down," he tried. But she wouldn't. So he got up to let her out and put the coffee on.

Larraine paid legal fees on the divorce and paid her new beau's hash debt for a clean slate, as she preferred her slates to be.

Charles turned the rat bike into a garden statue, proposing to Buck a straight-across trade plus twenty-two hundred. That meant a savings of thirty-six grand to Buck. Charles further agreed to carry the debt for a year, with faith in Fibrocell and new directions.

He found a 1963 Cadillac Deville ragtop and called it a barn find though it was more of a living-room find, a creampuff driver, beige on black. It felt karmic, floating and bobbing, mushy at speed and straining in the curves, just like its two-wheeled cousin but better for all seasons, with windshield wipers, a top, a heater and four wheels.

New friends settled into new life in a new world of their making. Mika loved the Caddy, despite the expense to refurbish the suspension and rubber parts, the paint, top and seats, and to add a new sound system. Nanaimo in late October felt brisk and golden, and when the clouds rolled in, they put the top up. Mika wanted to camp in the Caddy; he could sleep in back, and she'd take the front, plenty of room. She tittered for the old spirit. He said hotels have even more room, and lobbies. She asked if he wanted to be a pussy his whole life.

He said yes.

They compromised on a tent with sleeping cushions and roasted salmon on sticks over flames. Sitting by the fire, watching, Mika said she loved it when he did that.

"Yeah. I'm a natural. What'd I do?"

"What do you think?"

He thought and looked at her, until she smiled and nodded.

He shook his head. "I can't…."

"You don't need to. I will."

"Alone?"

"No. We'll hire some help."

"Like a nanny?"

"No. Just a maid. We'll skip the baby shits and no sleep." She leaned into him, clearing the air on simple words. "I didn't mean…. I meant that I love it when you're easy and lovable. It won't be bad. I want to adopt a kid I know. She needs it."

"She needs it like I needed it?"

"I didn't adopt you. We found each other. We're the same kind of outcaste. I want to help her. I love her, too. That's all."

"You thought it through."

"I know her. She's nine. Her Gramma died last week."

"Mm...."

They turned in, thinking of need and a death in the family. He'd got out of his business jam for way under value and got halved again in the settlement. But he was free, with enough money to go broke in a hundred years, if he got careless. The new kid would arrive in Nanaimo in the morning for the meet and greet. He dreamed of Elm Street without the street or the picket fence, without the neighbors or shrubs, except for the one out front shaped like a rat bike. Would she call him Buster, for old times sake? Or Charles? Or Dad? Images and questions swirled down stream, until little waves licked his face, and he opened his eyes on Louise and a new campfire.

Juniper arrived with a friend, quiet and anxious. What if they didn't like her? She knew Mika but not the man. Louise liked her, but Juniper only smiled, uncertain as a little girl.

Buster said he was new too and thought it might be fun, and he cried.

The child stared briefly before stepping up to sit by him at the fire, her arm around his shoulders.

XXI

Touch of the Unknown Rider

Nanaimo in October commemorates the heart of nowhere.

Juniper at thirteen is lively as she was at nine. The world opens to her, and she rises to it like a spark on an updraft. She gathers kindling. He stokes coals. Mika makes coffee.

Mo huddles by Buck, as a stranger strolls over to squat for an ember to light his pipe. Dark-skinned as native oak, he watches the flames. His vest says: *Incognito MC* over a fireball, and the rocker says: Okanagan, B.C. He gets the lump glowing in the bowl and passes to Charles, who says, "It must be Saturday somewhere." Charles pulls and passes to Buck.

Juniper passes cups. Mika pours.

The new guy sips. "Mm. You like it strong."

"Yeah," Charles says.

"Two Trees." He offers his hand.

Charles shakes it. "I'm Snow Eagle. This is Moose. That's Mo. Missy. Mika. Juniper. Louise."

Two Trees nods, "You got a nice ride." He turns to Buck. "Your motorcycle shows our club totem."

Charles says, "Fireball. Comet. Shooting star. It's his totem."

Two Trees says, "We can beat the snot outa you and change it, or see if you want to ride with us."

"Ride with your club?" Charles asks.

Buck watches.

Two Trees nods.

"Just like that? No process?"

"You're too old. Sorry. You look pre-processed. Good for you."

Charles laughs. "Thanks, I think. I ride with the women now. Besides, your club is Salish."

"We're Salish," Two Trees nods. "You have natural names. You ride with Moose."

"He's my friend."

"Friends are good."

"Why do you want us?" Charles asks.

Two Trees smiles. "You have Mika Baishan and Juniper. Your friend runs our totem. You got trunk space. We cross a border for commerce."

It seems like only a few years ago, Stuey pitched a plan to smuggle hash, and here it is again. "You don't know me."

Two Trees raises an eyebrow. "We know you."

Mika says she hasn't seen Two Trees and the Salishan for a long time. Charles wonders what else is old and says he can't cross the border. Or won't. Tad Pollack didn't die, but crossing the border could be careless. The feds lost the scent, but only a fool would be foolish. "Besides, my car is high profile. And I don't want to."

They watch the fire. More coffee calls for more smoke, and after a reflective pause, Two Trees says, "Your car is tasteful enough to notice, nuanced enough to blend in plain site."

"I'll ride with you," Buck tells the fire.

Two Trees responds, "That depends on Snow Eagle. For you, we need process."

Buck looks up.

Charles says, "You guys ride what, ninety days a year?"

"Maybe, Snow Eagle. Or a hundred fifty. Or we snowshoe or snowmobile. But…you'll see."

"What about the Dreaded Fellows?" The question is Buck's.

"What about the Fellows?"

"They don't mind?"

"We don't mind."

Buck nods, catching on. "Why haven't I heard of you guys?"

Two Trees shrugs, "No advertising?" He allows another pall and says, "Big Pharma makes billions. Little Pharma, not so much. But enough. And we have more fun." He summarizes the operation, by which two groups below the border submit drug orders, pharmaceuticals, and the Incognitos Motorcycle Club delivers. Nothing is illegal in the greater law, and nobody needs a bus. But they have talked of a car for a long time.

The fire crackles. The coffee pours. The pipe passes. Thoughts settle, until Two Trees says, "You get a few hundred bucks for your pocket on each run. Give it a shot."

Charles Severance and Buck Dibble become club brothers, though the colors seem a formality in the bonding process. Charles drives the Caddy, its trunk full of pills. He gets stares at the border, at first, when the officer notes the beauty of beige on black and says he loves an understated classic. Charles says, "Thank you."

He rides a mile behind Los Incognitos with a cooler and sometimes with Mika and Juniper and Louise. The boys see value in the family dimension. It makes borders a breeze.

Rx runs become regular, along with rides through the Selkirks, around Arrow Lake, off to Revelstoke and across the Monashee Mountains. They cruise, top down for maximum life, on a mission.

In time, Derek Donaldson faded from former circles to begin again on different footing.

The sky fell on Dave de Banque. How could he go from twenty-five million a year to zero? Extreme spending may have been his death wish, or maybe the fall was politically driven. Dave explained over cocktails down the road, that the Canadian government one day denied his timber rights. Dave's mill was set up for top-drawer MDF, which is not particleboard by any stretch. New powers had debts to pay and political plums to pay with. Dave went under, resurfacing to modest behaviors and realization. "I like my life now."

Stuey got leukemia and couldn't ride, lest a cut or bruise could leave him bleeding out in the boonies. He called it "no biggie, really," and felt he'd be back in no time, once the chemo and bone marrow transplant got done. His last question to Charles: "How did you do it for so long?"

Charles said that Larraine did it for a long time too, and when Stuey died a week after the procedure, he went to the river and cried again.

Larraine became Chair of the Hungry Kids Lunch Campaign and shone like a beacon over the neighborhood and, in spirit, over lesser neighborhoods far away, gaining recognition for selfless giving in good taste.

Harry Woo emigrated to Cebu in the Philippines, where he made friends and money, recruiting computer workers for corporations.

Randy Hague went to Baja to open a motocross tour company.

Neither Lonny Snodgrass nor Hobarth Grimes died on that blizzard night but grunted and groaned up and out, each from his own rubble. They both made it back to town, hitching rides and walking. Each arrived at a hospital for rehydration, inoculation, recuperation and capitulation to the powers that be, the powers requiring adult men to grow up or continue suffering.

They met again by chance at a drab building that looked like a mausoleum but was a rest home. Lonny shuffled up the drive, craving a place indoors to take a leak and sit down. He anticipated the sign: No Public Restroom, but by God he was tired and had to piss, and this driveway led up to the front door. At the portico, an attendant advised of no public restrooms and no solicitors. Lonny laughed short, feeling old and worn enough to begin the rest of his life, as advertised. So he told the attendant, "Fuuck…."

Shuffling inside, he paused for the tingling, eerie silence of the place and proceeded down the airless hall to the only open door and in, thinking it a good place to piss, one way or another.

Sitting inside, alone at a conference table with an unmistakable sneer, Hobo Grimes didn't say shit. Didn't need to.

Lonny stared and sat, had to.

Still and silent, they stared, perhaps at those fateful frames of their last time together. Lonny smiled at what Missy the waitress tried to tell them that one time, about things happening when they're meant to and not until. Hobo may have perceived Lonny's irony as good humor and said, "I got a idea."

Hobo was in sales, what he called his natural talent all along, where he could persuade damn near anyone to sign a motherfucking piece of paper for a chickenshit few grand to own a piece of the rock and start enjoying life instead of wasting it like a cheap shit all the time. Hobo was turning a half-point override as sales manager, and because his big fat fucking heart was open to a lifelong friend, he would get Lonny on, because he could. He'd show Lonny the ropes and knew Lonny could get the hang of it, because the future was theirs again, and this time "There won't be no cash or hash about it, just a bunch o' fucking numbers on some fucking paper with all these…lovely people plunking down to hang out here like they own the place, and we get rich. I shitchu not."

"Yeah. Okay. I really gotta piss."

Not too far down the road in the not too distant future, a family in a creampuff Cadillac stopped at a gas station across from

The Rest of Your Life Home for the Comfortable. The Caddy pulled up behind a modest sedan, where two guys pumped fuel and cleaned the rear glass, sales reps focused on needs, whether they be your need, a car's need, any old fuckin' need.

Charles Severance got out and set to squeeze the handle, telling himself yet again that thirteen miles per gallon didn't mean shit with such a great ride and gas at Canadian prices. The two sales reps eased on back to admire the vintage Caddy. Stay-press shirts, skinny ties, tattoos, whorehouse cologne and faded grime seemed a balanced mix. They looked up as Charles looked up.

The years could not disguise the duo known thereabout as *The Closer Bros.* Gold-nugget rings, bracelets and watches underscored their success, in case it wasn't obvious at first blush.

Recognition came quick, but what could they do? Fight at the gas pumps over long gone money? They could, but age and insight prevailed, and Hobo took the lead on bygones going south. "I'll be dogged," he said.

Charles nodded halfway, read the nametag and said, "You boys selling comfort?

Yes, sir, they were, in case a man might want in on the plushest return on investment money can by. That is, space and time at *The Rest of Your Life* can fit any budget and any need at any age. Charles smiled because Hobo didn't say any motherfucking age. Hobo took that smile as interest in the product, which a gold-nugget closer will do. " I sold two units this morning without trying. That's how good they are."

"Timeshare?"

"Used to call it that but too many people got confused. Now you get more time, and you get more space."

"How do you get more time?"

"What a terrific question. We combine the very best parts of your standard timeshare with your reverse mortgage in an annuity framework. You can see it happening, and in the end, you got your needs met and you live longer. It's that easy. Come on over and take a look. You're gonna love it. Big discount if you're not yet seventy. Bigger still under sixty.... Uh, Buster, ain't it?"

Charles smiled again, finally clunking all full on his aircraft carrier with the little lady watching up front and the dog and girl in back. Disengaging and rehanging the pump he said, "I think you're mistaken." In a minute, he's cruising down the road again. The females share health snacks, as the eldest asks, "What are you so smug about?"

He shrugged, "Couple guys back there. Thought they knew me."

In time, Buster walks by a river, taking inventory of things, before and after. He identifies milestones and feels grateful for them. He sees that before and after are the same in many ways but before and after are different because of critical junctures. Roads taken and not taken do not lead to the same place.

The beautiful flow whispers regret for nothing and gratitude for everything. He thinks one day he'll be sorely missed, yet remembering old friends, died or moved on, he feels indifferent. Love comes and goes. Eternal love is rare.

Impressions linger from youth, but he doesn't wonder where or what on anybody. Random people with common thoughts, people grown old and gone away, join the roil in the way of all. He loves his place and people, his muscles and joints and the will to move one foot in front of the other.

He looks up as a breeze shakes the leaves, who rage in color before falling.

He chills with love for the flow out front, blue sky and gamboling clouds up top. He heads in for lunch, a sandwich, he thinks, with tomatoes from the garden, avocado, onion and mustard. And he considers *habanero* sauce, for the feeling.

About the Author

Robert Wintner has authored fifteen novels, three memoirs, three story collections and five reef photo books.

Touch of the Unknown Rider is a sequel to *The Modern Outlaws*, all the boys older, still seeking and riding.

Robert Wintner is the *nom de plume* of Snorkel Bob, Hawaii's biggest reef outfitter. He lives on Maui with his wife Anita, Cookie the dog, Rocky, Yoyo, Inez, Buck, Tootsie, and Coco the cats, and Elizabeth the chicken. *Touch of the Unknown Rider* is a road saga, meant to record and entertain, with insight.

Made in the USA
Monee, IL
15 May 2022

96460940R00164